"If the Shelley exis̶t̶s̶ ̶i̶t̶'̶s̶ ̶s̶o̶m̶e̶where in this pile of junk," Grace said. "And it's all got to go back to Mallow Farm within twenty-four hours."

"Then you've got twenty-four hours to search for it, haven't you?" Peter started up the stairs.

"Are you serious? And are you just going to bed?" she called after him.

He paused. "I'm going to have a nightcap, and then I am indeed going to bed." His smile was exaggeratedly lustful. "You're welcome to join me."

Isn't that my luck, Grace thought. *The night I've been waiting for, the night he finally asks me to stay—and means it—is the night I have to spend prowling through eighteen crates of bric-a-brac, dust, and spiders.*

Peter smiled an oblique smile and said, "Be sure to lock up when you're finished, love."

Also by Diana Killian

Verse of the Vampyre
High Rhymes and Misdemeanors

Available from Pocket Books

Sonnet
OF THE
Sphinx

Diana Killian

POCKET BOOKS
New York   London   Toronto   Sydney

An *Original* Publication of POCKET BOOKS

POCKET BOOKS, a division of Simon & Schuster, Inc.
1230 Avenue of the Americas, New York, NY 10020

This book is a work of fiction. Names, characters, places and incidents are products of the author's imagination or are used fictitiously. Any resemblance to actual events or locales or persons, living or dead, is entirely coincidental

ISBN-13: 978-0-7434-6680-6
ISBN-10:   0-7434-6680-2

This Pocket Books paperback edition April 2006

10   9   8   7   6   5   4   3   2   1

POCKET and colophon are registered trademarks of Simon & Schuster, Inc.

Cover design by Ben Perini

Manufactured in the United States of America

For information regarding special discounts for bulk purchases, please contact Simon & Schuster Special Sales at 1-800-456-6798 or business@simonandschuster.com.

To Pamela and Laura—
for the women that you are.

To Faith and Emily—
for the women that you will one day be.

❧ Acknowledgments ❧

Many thanks to everyone at Pocket Books for your behind-the-scenes efforts, and a special thank you to Micki Nuding for taking such good care of the orphan child.

Thanks to my agent, Jacky Sach.

Thanks always to Kevin.

And, of course, thank you to the Partners-in-Crime writing group, one and all.

❧ prologue ❦

Pray write to tell us how you got home, for they say that you had bad weather after you sailed Monday & we are anxious.
    —Letter from Leigh Hunt to Percy Bysshe Shelley

*A*ll week the priests and *religiosi* wound up and down the baked streets, praying for rain. Unheeding, the Tuscan sun beat down, crops turning to dust in the fields, grapes withering on the vine.

On Monday afternoon, July 8, the *Ariel* left the harbor in a lowering, stifling heat.

For a time, the slim man with tangled fair hair watched the distant witchlight flickering in the leaden sky. The sultry heat seemed to crackle with weird energy. The stillness was oppressive.

The boat's other two occupants, Edward Williams and the boy, Charles Vivian, conversed briefly, their words barely filtering into his consciousness.

The young man raked fingers through the golden hair that was perpetually in his eyes, then turned his attention once more to the book of Keats's poetry.

The boat creaked, the sails whispering to each other.

The storm that whipped up off the black-glass ocean was like an enchanted thing, so sudden, so parlous. The pages in the book flapped like chattering paper teeth.

"Shelley, Gad's sake—!" He came out of his trance to see Williams struggling with the tiller.

Thrusting the book half-folded back into his jacket pocket, he lunged to help with the sails. Rain stung their hands and faces like an angry swarm, soaking them to their skin in seconds.

The many laughing misadventures of the long summer could not prepare them for this tempest. The main sheet had jammed; they could not bring the sails down.

Williams was swearing, his curses carried off in the shrieking gale. The boy crouched in the belly of the boat, eyes black as India ink.

Ariel bucked and plunged like one of Willmouse's toy boats in a bathtub sea. As though a giant hand pushed a wall of water toward them, a wave hit them from the side; the yacht was almost swamped. Shelley was sent sprawling. The provisions they had purchased in Leghorn scattered about him, bottles bobbing in the rapidly pooling water, and he remembered Wales, remembered political pamphlets in dark green bottles and will-o'-the-wisp balloons.

"We'll have to swim for it," Williams shouted. He grabbed for the boy, who fought him off in a blind animal panic. "Shelley—"

Shelley clung to the gunnel with wet white fingers, laughing unsteadily. "Are you mad?"

The wind whipped the words away, as it whipped away any chance of survival. They were miles off the coast of Spezzia. Even if one could swim—and he could not—it was too far.

He righted himself with difficulty, wrapping his arms tightly about his torso. Almost instantly he lost his balance and had to grab for the tangle of rigging.

Williams abandoned fighting the boy and came to him, but Shelley fended him off, shaking his head.

There was nothing for it. Williams began to strip, pulling his shirt over his head. The *Ariel* heeled. In dreadful pantomime, Williams flailed blindly, lost his balance, and plunged off the side. He vanished beneath the sickly-hued waves in an instant.

Shivering in the water and debris, the boy began to keen. Shelley tried to smile at him.

The world dissolved in wind and rain and thunder.

" 'Old King Tut was a wise old nut,' " Grace Hollister read aloud, selecting a sheet of music from the stack beside her. She was sitting Indian-style on the floor of Rogue's Gallery, surrounded by neatly sorted books and papers.

"Possibly a wise young nut. Though not wise enough to keep himself from getting clipped." As Peter Fox's mocking gaze met hers, Grace was reminded of a line by Thomas Moore: "Eyes of unholy blue."

"That's right; some scholars now believe Tutankhamen was murdered, don't they?" She studied the crimson-and-sand-colored illustration of a cigar-smoking pharaoh peeking out from behind a pyramid. This King Tut looked more like a Vegas mob boss than Egyptian royalty. Not that Grace had much experience with Vegas mob bosses—or any mob bosses. Until recently she had led the life of a sheltered academic, teaching Romantic literature to the privileged young ladies of St. Anne's Academy for Girls in Los Angeles.

"They do. A three-thousand-year-old cold case." Peter lifted a wooden writing box out of its wrappings. He opened it, picked out assorted pen nibs, old-fashioned paper clips, and a winged dagger cap badge for the 22nd Special Air Service. Peter studied the badge, set it aside, and made a notation on his clipboard. "Who Dares Wins," he murmured, and his thin mouth curled in an odd smile. "Very nice."

Summer was the height of tourist season in the English Lake District, and so naturally the busiest time at Rogue's Gallery. Between customers, they were still working their way through the boxes and crates that had been delivered two weeks ago from Mallow Farm. The new owner, Mr. Matsukado, was a wealthy Japanese businessman. The Shogun, as he was referred to locally, had decreed all of the seventeenth-century farmhouse's original furnishings unsuitable. Peter had bought the lot, much to the chagrin of his local competition. Much of the haul had turned out to be of the pink china roosters and bronzed baby shoes variety.

Grace adjusted her reading glasses and brushed back her hair, which had deepened to sorrel while away from the California sun.

"Why, Valentino as a sheik, he wouldn't last half a week in old King Tut-Tut-Tut-Tut-Tut-Tut-Tut King Tuttie's day." She checked the date on the music. "Nineteen twenty-three. A year after Carter discovered Tut's tomb. Had they even opened the burial chamber yet?"

"February 1923."

She selected a faded brochure in red, white, and blue. "*The Maid and the Mummy*. A musical farce in three acts. This *is* an oldie—1904."

"Something of a theme, no?" Peter was making more notes in his own personal hieroglyphs.

A thin slip of yellowed paper slid out from the musical brochure Grace held, and she unfolded the paper. It was a letter. The date at the top read October 8, 1943.

"Listen to this," she said.

Dearest Girl,

It's difficult to know what to write. I'm a devil to treat you so. Oh, I know it too well, and to wrap it up in thumping philosophy only cheapens . . .

She broke off. "I can't read the next few lines." She squinted at the lines long ago dissolved by . . . a watermark? Tears? Gin?

There's a kind of high comedy in our breathless obsession with tetchy old Fen's verdict, while half the youth of Europe is churned to powder in the cogs of this mechanical slaughter of modern warfare. And yet if our little discovery should turn out to be one of Shiloh's poesy, then there is a rightness to it, a queer poetic justice. I must let this go. One day, I suppose we will look back on this time and shake our wise gray heads over all this doubt and uncertainty.

Goodnight, Dearest. I'm better for loving you so.

For a moment they were silent. The lazy hum of bees and the sunlit fragrance of the garden drifted to them through the open window.

Grace blinked rapidly behind her specs. "It's signed 'John.'"

"Helpful," said Peter. "There can't be many chaps named John." He reached for the letter, which Grace held in one still hand.

Huskily, she said, "Nineteen forty-three. World War II. I wonder if—"

He directed a quizzical look her way. "Why, Esmerelda, I believe the heart of a romantic beats beneath that leathered academic hide."

Momentarily distracted, Grace spluttered, "*Leathered* hide?"

"Never having had opportunity to fully explore the hide in question—"

"Take my word for it, my hide is perfectly . . ." She stopped, aware that they were digressing rather wildly.

"Soft? Supple? Silken?" He ran light fingers down her bare arm.

It was a touch she felt in every cell. With great difficulty, Grace ignored that casually seductive caress, holding the letter up and out of his reach. Her brows drew together as she reread the elegant faded hand.

"Shiloh," she said slowly. "*Poesy.*" She turned to Peter, green eyes bright with excitement.

His thin clever face reflected amusement. "I recognize that feverish expression, if not the cause for it."

It was absurd, and yet stranger things had happened—and to Grace and Peter.

"The mere *word* 'poesy' conjures his ghost."

"Surely not."

He was still joking. Grace was not. " 'In the still cave of the witch Poesy, seeking among the shadows,' " she quoted.

Peter appeared to consult some inner and extensive reference section. "Shelley," he identified. "Percy Bysshe."

"Shiloh," Grace agreed triumphantly. "Lord Byron's pet name for Shelley."

"Pet name?" he objected. "Must you put it quite like that?"

"Albé and Shiloh, that's what they called each other," Grace persisted eagerly. "Byron and Shelley. Two of the greatest poets of the Romantic Age." Two of the most intriguing, anyway; Grace had a private yen for the bad boys of poetry. The frail, sensitive, and iconoclast Shelley had always proved a huge hit with her freshman and sophomore classes.

Peter was unconvinced. "You can't be serious. An unknown work by Shelley? Where would this 'John' find such a thing—assuming that vague reference to Shiloh is meant to indicate Shelley and not some other Shiloh."

"What other Shiloh? I don't think he's referring to the American Civil War. It's not exactly a common name. Not even in the 1940s. I mean, there was that Neil Diamond song—"

"If this is a confession," he interrupted, "I'm not ready to hear it."

She laughed. "But it was Shelley's nickname, and a

name by which Shelley scholars know him. And just because we don't know where the letter writer might have found such a work, doesn't mean the work couldn't exist."

Peter said nothing, holding the paper up toward the light streaming through the front window. His black-winged brows drew together. Turning, he flattened the letter on the counter behind him and studied it closely.

"What do you think?" She joined him at the counter as he studied the yellowed paper.

"Even if this bloke managed to get his mitts on an original work of Shelley's, this was written over fifty years ago. The item, whatever it might have been, is long gone."

"But it might not be!" Grace gestured to the boxes still unopened, the stacks of partially sorted papers. "And the clue to its whereabouts might be here, maybe in another letter. It looks like some of this stuff hasn't been gone through in decades." The layers of magazines, newspapers, bills, circulars, letters, and other assorted paperwork formed a kind of pulp strata.

"My dear girl."

Dearest Girl . . .

Who was John? What Mallow daughter or sister had been his "dearest girl"? Grace adored the riddles of the past. Her idea of a good time was exploring an old churchyard or whiling away an afternoon in a library archive. Maybe that was why she was pushing thirty and still unmarried.

"It's not that far-fetched. There was a lost Mary Shelley story discovered in a wooden chest in Tuscany a few years ago. And what about back in 1976, when that trunk was opened in Barclays of London and a slew of previously unknown works by Byron and Shelley were found? It's not impossible."

"Mary Shelley lived in Tuscany," Peter pointed out. "And the Barclays trunk belonged to Scrope Berdmore Davies, who was a friend and confidante of Lord Byron. Correct me if I'm wrong, but did Shelley ever visit the Lakes?"

"I don't see how that matters. Thanks to Wordsworth and Coleridge and Southey, the Lake District was *the* center of the Romantic Movement, and Shelley was a huge admirer of Wordsworth. Perhaps he made a trip that no one documented." It was difficult to imagine that such a meeting wouldn't be recorded in those days of fanatical journal and letter writing, but it was possible.

"Or perhaps he mailed a copy to his idol," he suggested blandly.

"Yes! Or no." She saw that this brought them back to the original problem. If a poem had been mailed to Wordsworth or another literary figure, it would surely have turned up in someone's papers. Even in their own lifetimes, the most casual writings of these men had been valued and preserved by their friends and family. "It doesn't matter how it got here—assuming it is here."

"Here?" He seemed to consider the idea for the first time. "But the item, whatever it is, appears to have been in John's possession, and for all we know, John may have lived in London. Or Tuscany."

The man was most aggravating when he was right.

But Peter wasn't finished dashing her dreams. "Has it occurred to you that perhaps this is too much of a coincidence? A letter hinting of a work by Percy Bysshe Shelley just happens to turn up in an antique shop where you, a scholar of Romantic literature, just happen to work?"

Grace was to appear as guest speaker at the annual Romantic literature conference held at Amberent Hall in Carlisle. Nearly two years earlier, she and Peter had been involved in the search for a lost work by Lord Byron. She had written a book on their adventures, which had sold to an obscure press back in the States. Though the book was not yet published, word rippled quickly across the academic pond Grace paddled in, and she was basking in her fifteen minutes of fame.

As much as she disliked the notion, Peter had a point. "You think someone is . . . salting the mine?"

"I should be very skeptical of any unknown works by long-dead literary giants that mysteriously turn up on your doorstep," he said dryly.

The bells on the gallery door jangled, and Grace guiltily snatched at the letter. She was not quick enough. Unhurriedly, Peter slid it beneath the leather blotter on the countertop.

Footsteps heralded the approach of the customer or tourist who had found Craddock House on its shady country lane.

The man who rounded the giant carved confessional dominating the center of the gallery floor was a stranger to Grace. He was big, with wide, powerful shoulders straining the seams of his cheap brown suit. His hair had the wiry texture and color of a rusty Brillo pad. His bushy eyebrows and long red mustachios looked false, as if they were part of some outlandish disguise.

"So," he said to Peter.

Grace turned to Peter and was startled. He stood straight and motionless, a stone effigy with blue eyes burning. As she stared, his nostrils flared almost imperceptibly. But when he spoke, his voice was surprisingly easy.

"Hello, Harry."

"Toll ghoul go."

That was certainly cryptic. Was he speaking in code or some obscure dialect? She would have suspected a gag of some kind, except Peter's reaction was definitely unamused.

His eyes flicked to Grace and he made a gesture with his head. Aha. *Tell girl go*. Her cue. It seemed unbelievable that Peter would know someone like this, let alone take orders from him.

Doubtfully, she edged past the man crowding the narrow aisle.

He smelled . . . alien. Of cigarettes and body odor. She risked a curious glance. His gaze held hers, then looked her up and down with black insolence. The hair at the nape of her neck prickled.

Reaching the front door, she opened it and shut it

again hard, using the music of the bells to cover her stealthy return through the maze of Edwardian dining chairs, assorted cabinets, and overmantel mirrors. She eased open the door to the confessional and slipped inside its cedar-scented darkness.

The irony of her hiding place did not escape Grace. Her insatiable curiosity regarding Peter's past might not be a sin, but it was certainly a character flaw. Nonetheless, she pressed her ear against the wall.

The voices of the men were muffled, but she could just make out their words.

"Many year, eh?" That was Harry. He spoke with a deliberation that seemed threatening all by itself.

"Not enough." And that was most definitely Peter. If she hadn't had that glimpse of his face, she would have believed his flippant tone.

The man laughed harshly. "You think I no find you? Think I no . . . rozozes?"

Rozozes? Three syllables, sounds like . . . *resources?*

"I didn't give it much thought," Peter returned.

Another one of those laughs that had nothing to do with mirth. "We say in Turkey, 'Insolent man are never without wound.' "

"It's a bloody country, true enough."

Silence. It was about the size of a phone booth in the confessional, maybe seven feet tall and thirty-nine inches deep. The door had a pale green stained-glass window. Grace couldn't see out, and she trusted no one could see in. When she leaned against the outside wall, the wood creaked, and she sucked in a breath. She had a sudden vision of herself pushing the entire structure over, and had to bite back a nervous laugh. But the men outside were oblivious to her presence, as hostilities mounted.

"Enough. You know why I come."

"The usual? Fresh air, sunshine, Beatrix Potter?"

Harry's voice altered, grew tight. "You laugh? We siz who laugh when I am drag you like dog back in prison."

Nothing funny about that threat. She could hear the crackling of paper. Was it a warrant? She wished she dared open the door.

"Know what thiz are? The documents of extradition."

Grace gasped. Even after two years, she knew little of Peter's past. Only that he had spent fourteen months in a Turkish prison after a jewel heist had gone wrong. The full details of that job—Peter's last, he assured her—were still unknown to Grace. Perhaps unknown to anyone besides Peter. And possibly Harry.

"We had deal."

Peter said, as though deliberately baiting the man, "You know what they say about honor among thieves."

She winced and shook her head.

"Give me, or God be witness, I have you before week is out!"

What on earth could this man want? He sounded like the goblin in that Harold Munro poem.

Give them me. Give them me. Your green glass beads, I love them so. Give them me.

Her poetical musings were ended by a harsh scuffling from outside the confessional, followed by grating, as though furniture had been pushed violently across the floor. What was going on out there? Grace's hand went to the door, but she hesitated.

And then she heard the distinct silver shiver of metal. She knew that sound but couldn't quite place it. It reminded her of skewers scraping against each other, or a knife rasping against a whetting stone.

"Oh, I wouldn't do that, mate." Peter's voice was even.

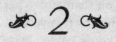 2

Grace couldn't help it—she cracked open the confessional door and peered around the corner. Her eyes widened as she took in the naked blade of the sword cane Peter held, rapier tip poised at Harry's quivering Adam's apple.

Harry drew back with a hissing sound. For a moment the men stared at each other, blue eyes to black—the only thing in common murderous hatred.

Then Harry turned. In the nick of time, Grace ducked back into the confessional as he lumbered past.

She heard the bells ring in discord and flinched as the gallery door slammed shut.

The silence that followed seemed to reverberate. She bit her lip, trying to decide on her next move.

"Come out, come out, wherever you are," Peter drawled.

Grace opened the door and stepped out of the confessional with an appearance of nonchalance. Once this kind of behavior would have seemed unorthodox, not to mention shameful to her. One could say it had been an interesting two years.

"How did you know I didn't leave?" She dusted off her hands.

In one swift, businesslike move, he slid the cobra-headed blade into its disguising scabbard and dropped the cane back into the umbrella stand beside the counter. Simply another day at the office.

"You didn't go upstairs. You didn't cross the lawn. I watched for you."

Afraid to ask, Grace asked anyway. "Who is he?"

"His name is Hayri Kayaci. He was a gendarme at the prison in Istanbul where I was held." His straight pale hair fell across his eyes; he raked it back absently.

"What does he want? Why is he here?" Despite Peter's calm tone, she picked up a certain edge. "You served your time."

His eyes did that evasive slant that she had come to recognize.

"Actually . . ."

"Actually what?"

"That's rather a gray area."

"A gray area?" Prison gray, apparently. "Are you saying you . . . escaped?" Now that she thought about it, he had never specifically told her he had paid his debt to society.

"It depends on how one views it."

"How do you view it?"

He grinned. It was a wicked grin, a little rueful, a little mocking.

"Swell," said Grace. "So what was this deal you made with Harry that you chose not to honor?"

"It wasn't really a choice. Nor was it a deal that Harry had the authority to make, you see?"

Only too well.

"Can he really have you extradited?"

"I don't think so."

"You're not sure?" Grace had spent much time and effort working out the intricacies of her own visa problems with the British Immigration and Nationality Directorate, so Peter's offhand attitude seemed provokingly blasé.

"I don't believe the United Kingdom has an extradition treaty with Turkey. There are certain . . . irregularities . . . within the Turkish penal system."

Not to mention gross human rights violations. Grace had done a bit of reading on Turkish prisons. They were horrific. She didn't blame Peter for escaping, regardless of what crime had put him there.

"Then he can't harm you."

Peter didn't answer.

"Can he?" The shop door jangled once more. "Crikey. We should be selling popcorn and peanuts," Grace exclaimed.

Peter arched an eyebrow. "I am running a business, you know. It can't all be lost manuscripts and menacing foreigners."

In fact, many of the shop's customers these days were savvy, young American collectors. The antique biz was booming, and Rogue's Gallery was the place to appeal to the American love of whimsy and tradition.

However, it was a young Asian woman in a chauffeur's uniform—complete with a billed cap and rather sexy-looking boots—who came around the corner of the confessional.

Peter's eyes laughed at Grace. "Can I help you, love?"

The lady chauffeur did not exactly click her heels, but the overall effect was the same.

"I am Kameko Musashi. I am here on behalf of Mr. Matsukado." Her glance inclined toward Grace. "My mission is of a somewhat delicate nature."

"We do get rather a lot of that lately," Peter murmured.

The young woman's gaze took in the crates and boxes of Mallow Farm. She was about Grace's height but slim as whipcord. Her hair was cut boy's fashion; however, she wore eyeliner and a discreet red lipstick. The red lipstick and glossy boots combined to give her sort of a dominatrix look—or at least what Grace fondly imagined was a dominatrix look.

"It is our understanding that Mr. Okada, acting as Mr. Matsukado's representative, arranged to sell you the contents of Marrow Farm for a certain sum. Mr. Okada made this arrangement without the permission of my employer, Mr. Matsukado." She rattled it off in typewriter fashion, and with about as much emotion as keys hitting blank paper.

She paused, but Peter said nothing.

"Mr. Matsukado has a proposition for you." She directed another of those pointed looks in Grace's direction.

Peter said, "Miss Hollister is my trusted associate."

All things being relative, Grace thought.

"Mr. Matsukado would like to repurchase his belongings. He will restore to you the original investment. As further incentive, he will give to you the new contents of the house."

Instinctively, Grace looked to the ink blotter on the counter where Peter had hidden the Shiloh letter. If Mr. Matsukado was requesting the return of all his property, the letter would have to be returned to him. Her disappointment was intense. For one brief, exhilarating moment she had pictured herself and Peter back on the trail of another lost work by one of her beloved Romantic poets.

"I'm in the antique trade," Peter said. "I'm afraid 'new contents' aren't of much interest to me."

"I have misspoken," Kameko said primly. "There are many fine Japanese antiques belonging to Mr. Matsukado's family. Many fine works of art. My employer does not wish to retain these. He wishes to exchange them for the original furnishings of Marrow Farm." Her English was flawless until she hit the double Ls of "Mallow." The mispronunciation was cute, although she was about as cute as a hungry mink.

"Why?" Grace asked.

Kameko ignored her. "If you will consider his offer, Mr. Matsukado would like you"—her almond eyes darted to Grace—"and Ms. Horrister to meet him at Marrow Farm."

"What, now?"

Her nod was crisp. She stood—if possible—straighter.

Peter considered her stiff figure, then offered a crooked grin. "I have the distinct impression things are going to turn nasty if I decline your charming invitation."

Kameko smiled a tight smile.

Grace studied her with renewed interest. Kameko's head, hands, and feet looked tiny, but beneath the fitted uniform was the shapely outline of muscled arms and thighs.

Kameko made an after-you gesture, and after locking the shop and setting the security system, they filed out to where the Matsukado car, a long blue sedan, was parked along the shady lane.

As they piled into the sumptuous leather interior, Grace reflected that if they had to be shanghaied, it was nice to do it in style.

"I think you could have taken her," she whispered as Kameko went around to the driver's side.

The corner of his mouth twitched. "Your faith in me is touching."

"Perhaps you didn't wish to compromise your position as a feminist." She was teasing him; while Peter was not exactly a chauvinist, he held some archaic attitudes, in Grace's view.

"Let's say I confess to a certain curiosity . . ." He fell silent as the chauffeur got in the car and started the engine.

The car glided soundlessly down the shady lane. After a time they left the canopy of trees. A golden haze of summer heat drifted over the lush, green fields; in the distance were the hills, "rock-ribbed and ancient as the sun." But Grace was oblivious to the pastoral charms of her adopted country. The afternoon was turning into a chapter out of Edgar Wallace. But even the weirdness of the situation, and the fear that Peter's past was once again rearing its ugly head—a particularly ugly head this time around—could not eclipse her excitement at the possibility that somewhere in the flotsam and jetsam of Mallow Farm was a lost poem by Shelley.

This was the dream of every literary scholar, to discover a hitherto unknown work. But even if the work were not completely unknown, if it were merely the draft of another poem, to be the one to reintroduce it to the world . . .

Grace's brain continued to spin sweet airy fantasy as though someone had left a cotton candy machine on overdrive.

She wondered from what period in Shelley's life the poem might be. The "Mad Shelley" days of his youth, the political activism of his years in Wales, when he had stuffed political treatises in bottles and thrown them into the sea, or the final days of his Tuscan retreat?

Kameko drove the big car with quiet efficiency, her small hands graceful on the steering wheel. Watching her, Grace noticed half of her little finger was missing. The Asian woman seemed too precise ever to suffer something as ungraceful as an accident.

At last they turned off the main road onto a weathered track that seemed to consist mostly of potholes and weeds. Grace had never visited Mallow Farm before, although she had ridden on its extensive grounds during fox-hunting season. The experience had not been one of unqualified delight.

They rounded a bend, and the rambling brick house stood before them. Blue wisteria framed its weathered facade. The hedges were overgrown; the lawns had a faded, threadbare look. Beyond the chimneys of the house were the spires of tall trees, and farther on, the wild tangle of Innisdale Wood.

The sedan made a lazy swoop of the cracked and broken circular courtyard and rolled to a stop.

Grace found herself curious about their "host." No one in Innisdale had met the Shogun so far.

Her curiosity was soon satisfied. Mr. Matsukado met them at the door, as if he had been hovering there since his curvy minion departed.

Contrary to her expectations, he was a young man about Grace's age, slender and refined-looking. He had gentle eyes and one of those scraggly mustaches that is always a mistake.

"Ah, the famous Mr. Fox." He greeted them with apparent delight. "A great pleasure, old chap." He bowed a brief bob and offered his hand.

"An unexpected one, I assure you," Peter returned.

Was it Grace's imagination or did the Shogun smirk?

"And the so-lovely Ms. Hollister. It is an honor," he said, performing another one of those combination bows and handshakes with Grace. "I read with great interest of your adventures regarding the"—he permitted himself a small chuckle—"gewgaws of Lord Byron."

As Grace's book had not yet been released, she

realized that Mr. Matsukado must have read one of the articles she had written for scholarly periodicals. Not typical light reading for the nonacademic. Did this mean that Mr. Matsukado was also a scholar of Romantic literature?

If that were the case, she was more inclined to believe in the legitimacy of the Shiloh letter.

As though theirs was an ordinary social call, Mr. Matsukado gave them a mini-tour of the farmhouse, which had been recently and comprehensively remodeled. Skylights and modern windows transformed the nooks and crannies of the original building. Clearly the transformation had been done with an eye toward comfort and practicality, but in Grace's opinion, much of the original character had been lost. The house was furnished in contemporary fashion, but filled with traditional Japanese and Asian artworks.

While Mr. Matsukado showed them around, he chatted inconsequentially about the important and influential people he knew. There seemed to be an awful lot of them, including a local magistrate and the regional representative of BADA, the British Antique Dealers' Association.

Grace paused to admire a snowy scene of a man on horseback followed by another man on foot.

"Jolly good, what?" Mr. Matsukado sounded as if he had learned English from 1930s stage productions. "The poet Teba and his manservant," he informed her. "Hokusai portrayed many poets and illustrated many poems."

"Lovely." She noted the painstaking detail, the

vibrant browns and blues of the woodcut, while wondering if there was anything pointed in the allusion to the "poets and poems" comment.

"Hokusai?" Peter inquired.

Mr. Matsukado looked pleased. "You are familiar with his work?"

Peter answered Grace's glance of inquiry. "Katsushika Hokusai is one of Japan's most famous artists. You've seen that woodcut of the giant wave and the men in boats?"

"Bang on, old chap," said Mr. Matsukado. "Much of the work of Hokusai has become cultural icon. His images appear in everything from advertising to *manga.*" To Peter, he added tantalizingly, "There are also several works by Hiroshige."

"I'm no expert on Asian antiques or art," Peter replied, "but it's obvious even to me that the market value of what you have here far outweighs the worth of Mallow Farm's original contents."

Mr. Matsukado's smile altered imperceptibly. Thanks to years of teaching devious adolescents, Grace recognized a disingenuous expression when she saw one. In the vernacular of the young ladies of St. Anne's, what up?

"The things that were sold to you have . . . great sentimental value for me, don't you know." There it was again, like a Noel Coward character caught in a time warp.

"How so?"

"It is difficult to explain, old chap. You must simply take my word for it."

Peter was silent. But then, he wasn't the sentimental kind.

"These things around us," Mr. Matsukado urged, "would bring great value in your trade. The items here"—he gestured to a complete set of elaborately costumed dolls arranged on what appeared to be a seven-tiered altar—"are worth many thousands of dollars."

That was no exaggeration; Grace had read enough reports on Japan by high school authors to know these *hina* dolls were valuable heirlooms passed down through generations. Mr. Matsukado's disregard for them was startling.

Peter said, "And you wish every item from Mallow Farm returned to you?"

Mr. Matsukado's eyes glittered. "Yes. This is most important. Every book, every . . . paper." He rubbed his hands in unconscious anticipation.

He knows. Grace didn't dare look at Peter. She was torn between jubilation that the letter did indeed refer to a work by Percy Shelley and the realization that they must in all decency return it—the letter *and* any other clues to the poem that might be concealed in the books and papers of Mallow Farm.

Peter said lightly, "This appears to be one of those offers one cannot refuse." Her heart sank as he added, "It's a deal."

❧ 3 ❧

They dined in the brick courtyard. Red pagoda-shaped lanterns illuminated the lingering English twilight. Silvery bells tinkled softly on the breeze. Menservants in white coats waited upon the table.

Sampling pork-flavored *butajiru* soup from a lacquered bowl, Grace recalled a line by Shelley. *Twilight and evening bell, and after that the dark.*

She could not help feeling the Shogun's insistence that they stay for the evening meal was designed to keep them from having extra time to sift through Mallow Farm's contents.

She replaced her soup bowl in position on her left. On the right sat another fragile bowl piled with white rice. Behind the two bowls were three flat plates, one with beautifully arranged *sashimi*, one a grilled dish, and finally, something that appeared to be stewed seaweed mixed with other greens.

"Delicious," she said, noting the expert way Peter set about using his black chopsticks.

Mr. Matsukado petulantly tossed his own chopsticks to the ground. The hovering manservant scurried to remove the offending utensils. "Mr. Okada made many decisions that I regret," the young man said. "I'm looking for a crackin' good English cook."

Peter's eye met Grace's.

"That shouldn't be difficult," she responded. She decided to forgo using her own chopsticks since their presence on the table seemed to offend their volatile host.

"It shouldn't be, no." Mr. Matsukado was curt.

Hastily she tried a bite of the crispy grilled dish. Inside, the meat was tender and had a rich, dark flavor like pâté. "That's different," she said.

"Grilled eel," Mr. Matsukado said. "They consider it a delicacy."

Grace swallowed hard. "Um. Mmm."

"They?" murmured Peter.

Mr. Matsukado continued to brood over the fare. Peter brought the conversation back to their earlier discussion, insisting that he would need twenty-four hours to check for items he had placed into stock.

"Is it possible you have sold some of these objects?" Mr. Matsukado could not hide his horror.

"I'm afraid so." Peter looked apologetic. "After all, the items were purchased to sell."

Grace, who knew they had not yet sold any of Mallow's contents, wondered if Peter was up to something.

"Worse luck, I'm afraid a number of articles weren't fit for resale."

The Shogun made a strangled sound—as though

he had swallowed a bit of grilled eel the wrong way.

"Mostly rubbish from the thirties and forties," Peter went on mercilessly. "By the way, who was the character with the mania for Egyptology?"

"John Mallow," the Shogun said faintly.

"John Mallow," Peter repeated cheerfully. "That's the bloke." As his gaze met Grace's, his lips quirked ever so slightly.

John *Mallow?* Was the John who had written the Shiloh letter the owner of Mallow Farm?

The meal was followed by brandy and dessert. The dessert, according their glum host, was called *anmitsu*. It seemed to consist of beans and a variety of fruit mixed with a sweet pale jelly. After the eel, Grace figured she had nothing to lose and bravely dug in. It was . . . interesting, she decided, and found herself craving a slice of old-fashioned cheesecake like her mother used to make.

She had been thinking that it was strange for Mr. Matsukado to reject his own culture in favor of the Anglo-Saxon, but it occurred to her that she, too, was in a sense dissing her heritage in her adulation of all things British. Lately she had begun to long for things she had taken for granted—things like screens on windows, central heating, and passing lanes.

When the uncomfortable meal was at last finished, Miss Musashi drove them home in the long sedan.

Behind rock walls and natural high hedges, the shining lakes swept by in the blue moonlight.

Peter spoke to Kameko in Japanese. She answered softly. Grace noted the glimmer of her smile in the rearview mirror. Whatever Peter had, it apparently translated into every language.

"I didn't know you spoke Japanese," she remarked, as they let themselves into Rogue's Gallery. The purr of the car's engine died into the warm night and was replaced by nocturnal sounds: crickets, whispering leaves, and the eerie screech of the barn owl that had recently taken up residence in Peter's little-used gardening shed. It was only after dark that Grace had a sense of how far from the village Craddock House was.

Peter cocked his head, and she added, "Oh, right. What I don't know about you would fill a book."

"I rather hope not. One book is quite enough."

For the first time, she wondered whether publishing an account of her exploits might draw more snakes from under the rocks in Peter's past.

It wasn't a happy thought. To distract herself, and possibly him, she chattered. "Kameko's an interesting character, isn't she? I could picture her as a Bond Girl."

"Interesting, yes," Peter said. "She's carrying."

"Carrying what?"

He smiled. "A gun. She's probably Matsukado's bodyguard as well as chauffeur."

"Why would he need a bodyguard?"

"He's a very wealthy young man," Peter said dryly. "And as naive as he is pampered."

"He knows about the Shiloh letter."

Peter sighed.

"Did you have to agree to sell him back all this stuff?" Her plaint was more routine than heartfelt.

"I don't wish my entire inventory tied up in legal

tape for the next twelve months. Besides, I'm making close to a quarter of a million on the deal." He sounded uncharacteristically irritable. "Look, I didn't tell him about the letter. Keep it if you like."

Because the idea was all too tempting, Grace reacted hotly. "That would be *totally* dishonest! He specifically requested all the papers and books and—"

"If he already knows about the Shelley, John Mallow's mention of it isn't going to help or hinder. Make a copy of the bloody thing. I don't care."

"But what's the point? If the Shelley exists, it will be somewhere in this pile of . . . of junk. And it's all got to go back to Mallow Farm within twenty-four hours."

"Then you've got twenty-four hours to search for it, haven't you?" He started up the stairs.

"Are you serious?"

Grace gazed into the shadows of the shop. The glass eyes of a slightly moth-eaten teddy bear gleamed at her from the gloom.

"Are you just going to bed?" she called after him.

He paused. "I'm going to have a nightcap, and then I am indeed going to bed." His smile was exaggeratedly lustful. "You're welcome to join me, old chap."

Laughing, she followed him into the upstairs flat, curling comfortably on the long red-leather sofa while Peter poured brandy into snifters.

It was a spacious room with Georgian windows and polished wood floors. A formal white fireplace stood at one end. There was a huge moon-faced grandfather clock, and several bronze lamps with translucent milk-glass shades cast a warm glow over the room's jewel-colored Oriental rugs and red-leather chairs. A mounted telescope offered a view of the starry night sky.

Grace sipped her brandy thoughtfully. "Suppose I did look for the Shelley, and suppose I did find it," she said at last.

"Then you would have to decide whether you were going to admit where you found it, or whether you were going to pretend it turned up someplace else." He raked a hand through his thick, straight, fair hair that immediately fell back across his forehead.

"Lie in other words. Cheat. Steal."

" 'Who Dares Wins,' " he replied, quoting the Special Air Services motto.

Not always, Grace reflected. Sometimes those who dared lost big. Peter looked tired. She realized that she had actually forgotten all about Horrible Harry. Though Peter didn't appear unduly alarmed, the threat of extradition must be weighing on him. At the least, the gendarme's appearance had to stir up dreadful memories.

His winged brows drew together. "What's that for?"

"What?"

"The look of melting sympathy?"

Grace felt her cheeks grow warm.

He leaned over and kissed her. It was a light and expert kiss. More compliment than seduction, but this was the pattern they had fallen into since the events of the autumn. Peter flirted, made the expected move, and Grace laughingly evaded what she was sure was a kind of reflex with him. She felt certain that when his heart was in it, so to speak, she would know. But sometimes lately she wondered if she wasn't making a mistake—if they had passed the point of no return, if their relationship had devolved into that of friends rather than potential lovers.

Isn't that my luck. The night I've been waiting for, the night he finally asks me to stay—and means it—is the night I have to spend prowling through eighteen crates of bric-a-brac, dust, and spiders.

Peter brushed his knuckles against her cheek, smiled an oblique smile, and said, "Be sure to lock up when you're finished, love."

Downstairs Grace kicked off her shoes, made a cup of tea in the stockroom, and settled down on the wooden floor surrounded by stacks of long out-of-date gardening manuals, magazines, cookbooks. She needed a system, a mode of attack, but there wasn't time.

Hurriedly she flipped through the magazines and books.

A perusal of the enormous family Bible gave her a better understanding of the Mallow family tree—and alerted her to the fact that there had been several John Mallows. Since Peter seemed to have struck a nerve this evening with his comment about "thirties and forties," she focused on those entries.

John Mallow, brother to Phillip and David. B. 1916 and D. . . . nothing.

Grace studied the tiny meticulous letters.

No mistake; there was no date of death. Ever.

Mallows continued to be born and die, but John Eldon Mallow, born in 1916, appeared to have vanished from the face of the earth.

That wasn't the only peculiarity.

As Grace sifted through sheet music, household account books, photos aged to sepia, and letters—years, and generations, worth of letters—she asked herself why, if John Mallow had mailed this letter, it was still with his possessions.

It did not take her long to realize her task was an impossible one. Most of the stuff, though haphazardly preserved, was not in any kind of order. Fashion magazines from the fifties were tossed in with livestock journals from the seventies. There were decades of bar chits (the Mallows had evidently been members of the drinking class).

Poring over hundreds of photos, sorting by costume and hairstyle, she squandered a couple of hours getting familiar enough with the distinctive Mallow features to tell them at a glance from those of their neighbors and in-laws.

She found several group photos staged in front of Mallow Farm, watching with fascination how the building changed through the decades, how small trees became tall trees, and the paint faded, and trim changed. At last she narrowed a stack from the forties. Three men close in age who looked too similar to be anything but brothers posed in front of the familiar brick and wisteria. *John, Phillip, and David* read the feminine writing on the back of the photo.

She singled out another marked *John*, and studied it.

There were several others of the lean, dark-haired man with a disreputable-looking terrier. Curiously, she studied the handsome face gravely smiling into the camera lens. In the last photo he wore a khaki uniform and—if she was not mistaken—a cap badge that looked very like the one they had found earlier. She thought that in this final shot he looked older, and there was something indefinably guarded in his expression.

Grace's tailbone smarted; she shifted on the hard floor. Out of the corner of her eye, she caught movement at the side window.

A tree branch moving in the breeze?

But there was no breeze on this warm June night.

Swallowing hard, she stared down at the pile of photos. There it was again, a white blur at the window seeming to float just out of the frame.

The perfect finish to a bizarre day. Why didn't I go home when I had the chance?

With great deliberation she set down the papers she was holding, picked up her mug, checked it, and rose. She walked toward the back room holding the cup out, playacting getting a refill. She hoped from across the room the watcher could not tell her hand was shaking.

Inside the stockroom she banged the cup on the desk, ran to the shelf that concealed the secret passage leading from the shop to the stairs that led to Peter's living quarters, and pulled hard.

The shelf swung out soundlessly.

Guided by the light of the stockroom, Grace darted up the stairs half-feeling her way. She tripped, but without losing speed continued on in anteater style till she came at last to the wooden panel opening.

Sliding the panel open, she crawled through the enormous grandfather clock case into Peter's dark living room. Light shone from his bedroom. She ran on tiptoe, sliding to a stop in his doorway.

Peter was sleeping, a book on the bed beside him. Even in her distress she realized that she had never had this advantage before. Never seen him out cold while she was up and alert. His chest was bare, lightly tanned and subtly muscled. She wondered if he was nude beneath the blankets.

As she realized what a strange time it was to be thinking about such things, she moved to touch his shoulder. He seemed to sense her presence. His lashes flickered, his eyes opened. He sat up although he was clearly not fully awake, his hand going for the drawer of his nightstand.

Did he keep a gun in there? It seemed to be a night for one revelation after another.

"Peter, there's someone downstairs," she gasped.

He blinked at her. "Inside?"

"Outside. Looking in the window."

"Ring the cops," he said, rolling off the bed and pulling on Levi's in what appeared to be one fluid motion.

He opened the door to his closet, stepped inside . . . and vanished.

❧ 4 ❧

*A*fter an astonished moment, Grace went to the giant wardrobe, and pushed aside the clothes that smelled of Peter and some wonderfully expensive aftershave. She took in the false back of the wardrobe and the door beyond, which stood wide open. Another secret passage. The house was full of them, but this one was new to Grace. She stared into the bottomless opening.

It was pitch-black in the passage, like a doorway into the netherworld. Peter had to have eyes like a cat to find his way. Instinctively, she moved forward, listening. His steps faded to ghostly footfalls, and then . . . nothing.

Now what? Would he be all right? She tried to think. He had told her to phone the cops. In her entire acquaintanceship with Peter she had known him to do almost anything possible to avoid attracting police attention, but now he wanted her to summon them.

Clamping down hard on rising panic, she knelt

beside the four-poster bed, and dragged the phone out from under it. Fingers shaking, she made the call, and reported a prowler to the official voice on the other end. All the while, she wondered frantically what was happening downstairs. It was so quiet. Too quiet?

She couldn't stand it. Ignoring the official request to stay on the line, she left the receiver off the hook and jumped to her feet. Making her way across the unlit living room, she peered out the window, but she could see nothing from the upper story.

She *had* to know what was happening.

Letting herself out of the flat, she stepped onto the shop landing. The bright light caught her off guard, though she herself had left the overhead on. Rogue's Gallery was lit up like a theater stage. She felt for the wall switch and doused the light.

The darkness felt sheltering and familiar, and Grace relaxed a fraction. She moved to the landing railing and stared down. There were no windows on the top gallery of the store, which was lined with bookshelves, but moonlight from the store windows limned the face of the mermaid ship's figurehead suspended from the vault ceiling. Nothing moved. All was silent.

Taking a deep breath, Grace crept down the stairs, holding tight to the banister to steady herself. She headed straight for the window on the lower level.

No sign of an intruder—or Peter. She inched along to the next window where she had seen the figure. Pressing close to the glass, she tried to angle herself so that she could see below the sill. A bulky figure rose out of the darkness, filling the window. Grace screamed.

The next instant, Peter's startled and exasperated face appeared in the glass. Grace made apologetic motions. He gestured that he was moving along the side of the house. Or at least, that's what she supposed he was indicating. Perhaps he was indicating he wanted Grace to move along the side of the house. Perhaps he was communicating something very rude indeed.

She craned her neck watching him navigate his way through the bushes and shrubs, then darted to the next window, waiting for Peter to appear.

No sign.

She waited.

Where was he?

She ran back to the other window.

Nothing.

What had happened? How could he disappear between the two windows? It was only about twelve feet from point A to point B.

Grace's heart pounded hard. What next? She listened tautly. No sounds of struggle. No sounds at all. She didn't dare open the door or a window, but what if Peter had been knocked unconscious?

She headed to the next window, peering out intently into the blackness.

Movement in the glass caught her eye. Something in the darkness. No . . . a reflection. Someone was coming up swiftly behind her! She whirled and shrieked.

Peter jumped and swore. "Damn. Stop doing that!"

The highly irritating implication was that Grace made a habit of unprovoked shrieking. "I'm nervous," Grace yelled back.

"As am I."

That was ridiculous; he didn't have a nervous bone in his body—although he did seem more snappish than usual.

Spots of red and blue lights slid across the wall behind them. Grace turned to the window and saw a silent police car parked on the roadside.

"That was fast," she said.

"Always there when you don't need them," Peter retorted, but perhaps he was thinking of other times and places. He went to meet the police.

Grace woke to a morning scented with apple blossom. For a few moments, she lay in bed reflecting over the odd events of the day before—and the even odder events of the evening.

Innisdale's Finest had been unable to locate the intruder, but Peter had found a set of small distinct footprints outside the window where Grace thought she had spotted someone.

"Small as in child-sized?" Grace had inquired, thinking of the diminutive Miss Musashi.

"That's right, Snow White," Peter drawled. "The dwarves are after you."

This drew a snigger from one of the young constables, but it occurred to Grace that Peter, quite easily following her line of reasoning, had, for reasons known only to himself, wanted to throw the police off the track.

Had the Shogun ordered his chauffeur to spy on them? If so, his worst fears had been confirmed. Well, maybe not his *worst* fears, because Grace's search had proved fruitless.

She cast off the sheet, which was the only covering she needed these warm nights. After a quick shower— the eccentric plumbing of the Gardener's Cottage did not lend itself to luxurious bathing—she brewed a pot of tea and sprinkled cinnamon and sugar on toast.

There was a time when cinnamon and sugar would have seemed as dangerous as cocaine, and freshly brewed tea would have felt like a silly extravagance. But since her extended and unplanned stay in the Lake District, Grace was no longer driven by clocks and calories.

Well, not most of the time, anyway. Old habits were hard to break. She would never face being "tardy" with anything other than dismay, and sometimes she found the slow pace of Innisdale's denizens more aggravating than charming. But it was pleasant to have thrown off the shackles of weighing herself every morning, even as she had cast off the notion that control-top panty hose were required wear for every ensemble.

Sipping tea and crunching her sugary toast, Grace planned out her day. She had decided, while driving home last night, to check out the Innisdale Historical Society in hopes of turning up information on John Mallow. Her search through the history of Mallow

Farm had raised more questions than it answered.

She had found nothing to support the hypothesis that there was an undiscovered work by Shelley in the papers of Mallow Farm. She had neither the time nor justification to keep digging—Peter would have to turn everything over to the Shogun in a matter of hours. But if she could figure out what had happened to John Mallow, perhaps she could retrace what he had done with the Shelley.

Assuming that there really was a Shelley, and that this was not some elaborate hoax.

It was a long shot, but with what was at stake, Grace was more than willing to commit herself to the hunt.

Finishing her breakfast while listening to a meadowlark in the tree outside the kitchen window, Grace donned a red Laura Ashley floral-print shift.

She decided to walk to the historical society, which was yet another difference between her old life and her new. Although she was very fond of the battered Aston Martin her landlady had sold her for a song, these days she walked everywhere it was practical to do so. She found she enjoyed walking, and often strolled in the village or the surrounding countryside for the sheer pleasure of it.

This morning she walked briskly, entering the tall iron gates of Cherry Lane Park and cutting through the booths and tents of the annual arts festival.

It was a lovely day. Fluffy white clouds gamboled through the blue field of sky, an occasional little black cloud hinting at one of the sporadic Lakeland showers. The air was sweet with the scent of cherry blossoms, and the strains of saxophone drifted from the gazebo in the center of the park.

As she hurried on her way, Grace resisted the temptation of colorful booths stocked with everything from ceramics to baked goods. Color photographs of Innisdale taken in the 1950s and '60s were on display at one tent, and she slowed down to have a look.

Despite the Brigadoonish character of the village, clearly time had not stood still there. She was leaning in to have a closer look at Renfrew Hall back in the days when it had served as the vicarage, when a heavy hand closed on her shoulder.

Startled, she turned to find Hayri Kayaci towering behind her. Grace was generally polite to a fault, but her antagonism to Harry was such that she couldn't—and didn't even try to—conceal it.

"What do you want?"

"You." He stuck his face in hers. Grace recoiled from the crumbs in his beard.

"Me?"

"Yes, I ask in village. Learn you am his woman." Apparently he had honed his technique by watching Igor in the Frankenstein films.

He smiled, which was even worse than his habitual scowl.

"His 'woman'?" She tried to shake off his hand.

His grip tightened. "Tell Fox, there iz no out for him. He honor our bargain, bargain I haf made in good faith. Or . . . I haf friend tell."

It took her a moment to translate. Grace glanced at

the busy stalls around them. No one seemed to be paying attention. Given what Harry seemed to be implying, she wasn't sure if that was a bad thing or not.

"Tell what?" She knew instinctively that she should not acknowledge any concern or interest in what Kayaci said, but she couldn't help it.

Her words brought a snaggle-toothed display of yellow. "My government pay lot of money to get him back. Your government not protect thiv of national treasure."

Grace thought of the Elgin Marbles, but held her tongue.

All the same her expression must have irritated Harry. His red lips pulled back in a smile that was more a baring of teeth. "He not so proud gentleman then, Peter Fox. Dirty. And starving. And afraid. Yes, afraid. They all afraid." He moved his shoulders like someone cringing from a blow, then laughed. He made a whimpering sound, then laughed again.

"Afraid like dog. Do anything. Say anything. But he keep his word to *me*."

Grace's throat seemed to close up. Her heart was thudding uncomfortably with something she was surprised to recognize as rage. Rage that men like this were allowed to operate . . . to *live*.

"*You* are the dog," she got out through dry lips.

He was cheerful. Apparently there was nothing like someone else's distress to brighten his day. "In Turkey is saying. 'Satan's friendship reaches prison door.'" Like a malevolent Confucius, Mr. Kayaci seemed given to quoting grim aphorisms.

Was he threatening her? She didn't know and didn't care.

"Yes, I've heard all about the prisons in your country. Children imprisoned for shouting antigovernment slogans. Hunger strikers shot. Writers, artists, and dissidents jailed and tortured for daring to question state policy. The visiting relatives of prisoners routinely threatened and humiliated. And human rights organizations warned that criticizing these policies is itself a criminal offense." She was shaking with anger and adrenaline.

Kayaci's fingers dug into her shoulder. "I want Serpent's Egg!"

"The Glen in Kendal serves a very nice breakfast . . ."

He shook her so hard, he nearly knocked her off her feet. Grace's head snapped back, and she cried out, afraid he might break her neck.

"Hi, you!" The vendor of the photography booth came around the tent flap, looking outraged.

That was the advantage of living in a small town.

Kayaci let her go so suddenly she nearly fell against the photo display.

"We see each other again," he promised, and departed though the rhododendrons.

"And that was the last anyone saw of the Croglin vampire," the stout, sensible-looking proprietress of the Innisdale Historical Society informed an enthralled group of Americans.

Grace, who had had her own recent vampire

experience, would have liked to hear more. She was mostly recovered from her unpleasant encounter with the Horrible Harry, and the hushed museumlike atmosphere of Landon House further soothed her nerves.

While waiting for the tourists to disperse, she examined the displays of old china and lace until at last the opportunity arose to waylay Miss Webb. She introduced herself and her mission.

"Must say this is a pleasure," Miss Webb said, her pale green eyes scrutinizing Grace. "Come upstairs, my dear, and we'll have a natter."

Miss Verity Webb appeared to be descended from the long line of traditional English spinsters that populated British crime fiction. She looked a hale and hearty sixty, her iron gray hair close-cropped, her broad face tanned. She reminded Grace of girls' hockey, spinster friendships, and . . . cats. In fact, there was a cat—a large, black cat—in the upstairs room where Miss Webb led Grace.

The cat was industriously occupied in reducing a hideous one-armed orange-and-green jumper back into a ball of yarn.

"Naughty puss!" exclaimed Miss Webb without heat, and shooed the unrepentant beast off. "Put the kettle on, shall I?"

Grace had a sudden and overwhelming craving for a mocha frappucino with a double shot of espresso. "Tea would be lovely," she said, taking the overstuffed chair Miss Webb indicated.

"Of course we're all so excited about your book,"

Miss Webb boomed from the kitchenette in the robust accents that must have called several generations of Girl Guides to order. "Been thinking that perhaps we could make arrangement to sell copies here at the historical society."

"Oh?" Grace, who had not been thinking much beyond earning some extra cash, couldn't think of anything to say to this unexpected and flattering offer.

"Something of a local celebrity, after all."

Grace didn't know what to make of that. Miss Webb bustled around in the tiny kitchen, and the cat, which was about the size of an armadillo, watched Grace balefully from across the room. Grace usually got on well with animals, but no amount of sweet talk would lure this one into petting distance.

Miss Webb returned with a tea tray laden with blue-and-white Willow Pattern china.

Grace sipped tea strong enough to strip varnish. "I'm a celebrity?"

"Course you are, my dear. To have made a discovery that sheds new light on Lord Byron's family connections is an amazing achievement."

"It was more or less an accident," Grace confessed. She became uncomfortable when anyone tried to make her the heroine of that particular adventure. "And I had a lot of help."

Miss Webb patted her hand. "So modest. Especially for a Yank." She offered Grace a plate of scones. Grace sampled one. It seemed to have been mixed with concrete.

"Understand you will be speaking at the Amberent Hall literary conference."

Grace touched her teeth with her tongue, feeling for chips. "That's right. Are you taking part in the conference?"

"Not my sort of thing. Afraid my notion of poetry is jolly old Edward Lear."

The author of such literary classics as "The Dong with a Luminous Nose" and "The Pobble Who Has No Toes"? Grace had no response to that.

Miss Webb poured some milky tea in a saucer and set it on the floor. The black cat swaggered over and began to lap it up, his tail twitching languidly. Watching him indulgently, she said, "You were interested in the history of Mallow Farm, was it?"

"Actually, I was wondering if you could tell me anything about John Mallow."

Miss Webb's green eyes, similar to those of her cat, narrowed. "John Mallow? Great many John Mallows, my dear. Any one in particular?"

"Well, yes. The John Mallow who was born in 1916. I'm guessing he must have died in World War II."

"Ah, the Great Patriotic War." Miss Webb was silent for a moment. "Any reason?" she asked suddenly.

It was an obvious question, and Grace was chagrined that she was unprepared for it. "Just curious—"

"Rattling skeletons in the closet, you know."

"I am? Am I?" She sounded like a parrot. Polly want a concrete cracker?

"Afraid what I know is only gossip. After twenty

years, I'm still something of a newcomer to Innisdale."
Miss Webb glanced down at the cat, which had made a
sound that in a human would have been a burp. The
cat looked at Grace as though she had made the
uncouth noise.

"Anything might be helpful."

"Really?" Miss Webb thought it over. "Suppose it's
almost local legend by now. From what I gather, this
young John Mallow was engaged to marry Eden
Monkton. You're familiar with the Monkton Estate?"

Grace nodded. She didn't wish to let on exactly how
familiar she was with the Monkton Estate, but several
months ago she had believed that circumstances war-
ranted her first attempt at B&E. Fortunately, no one
had ever learned of her one-woman crime spree.

"Sir Vincent Monkton was one of our more famous
Egyptologists. Did you know that, my dear?"

"No."

"Yes. Was discussing it with Mr. Sartyn only this
morning. He had an amazing collection of antiquities—Sir Vincent, I mean, not Mr. Sartyn." Miss Webb
chuckled at the mix-up.

"Mr. Sartyn?"

"New head librarian. Interesting young man.
Pleasure to see someone so young take an interest in
the past."

"I don't think I've met him yet."

"Oh, but you must. Believe he's about your own
age." Was there a matchmaking glint in Miss Webb's
eye? Now that *was* a scary thought. "The Courtship of
the Yonghy-Bonghy-Bó"?

"Pity of it was, Sir Vincent lost the whole kit and caboodle during the Blitz." Miss Webb poured more tea—or possibly paint thinner. "Quite a coincidence that you would also be asking about Sir Vincent."

Grace said tactfully, "It's really more John Mallow that I'm interested in."

"Of course, my dear. In any case, I believe Sir Vincent did not approve of the match. And his doubts turned out to be quite right. On the eve before he was to report back for duty, John Mallow went AWOL. Frightful scandal. Eden Monkton was pregnant, you see. The war created quite a bit of that in those days. Young couples believing each day might be their last—difficult to explain the frenzied atmosphere at the time."

Grace fastened on one point. "So no one knows what happened to John Mallow?"

Miss Webb said briskly, "Well, I don't, but that's not to say that no one does. He could never return here, you see. Would have been shot for desertion. Wartime, after all." She seemed to think this over. "He must have had friends and relations. Suppose someone might know what became of him. In the confusion after the war, it's possible he could have started a new life someplace else. Under an assumed name."

Grace felt sudden empathy for the girl who had fallen for a handsome and untrustworthy man. "What happened to Eden?"

"Disgraced. At least, I'd imagine so, remembering how intolerant we were back then." She shook her head. "Don't know, to be perfectly honest. Have an idea she did eventually marry." Miss Webb glanced at the clock on the fireplace mantel, and Grace realized she must be expecting another busload of tourists.

"What happened to the baby?"

Miss Webb looked apologetic. "No idea, my dear. The Monkton family still owns the estate, so perhaps you could contact their agent." She regarded Grace curiously. "Were you thinking of writing another book perhaps?"

"Oh, nothing like that," Grace said hastily, then could have kicked herself for giving up such a handy excuse for her nosiness.

Shortly afterward she thanked Miss Webb for tea and departed, aware that she had probably raised more questions in Miss Webb's mind than she had answered in her own.

5

"So what exactly is the Serpent's Egg?"

Grace tried once more to have the conversation that Peter had managed to elude all day. They were in Cherry Lane Park, enjoying a picnic supper and the Thursday evening concert.

"Try this." He held a chocolate truffle to her mouth. Grace nibbled, the tips of Peter's fingers delicately grazing her lips.

"Mmm. Mr. Fox, are you trying to—" She intended to say "sidetrack me," but somehow, as though she had seen too many reruns of *The Graduate*, the words came out "seduce me?"

"If you have to ask, I obviously need more practice."

"Any more practice, and you'd lose your amateur standing."

Peter laughed, and Grace realized that the odds of having a serious conversation were not in her favor.

In the gazebo several yards down the hillside, a local string quartet played songs that Grace's grandparents had probably listened to. Cherry Lane Park was over a hundred years old. She imagined that Eden Monkton might have sashayed its shady paths summer evenings with her faithless lover. Granted, those were the bleak days of blackouts and bombing raids, but life must still have gone on in some semblance of normalcy.

The gazebo was strung with white lights that twinkled like tiny stars in the fiery sunset. Beneath clouds of pastel cherry blossoms, people sat on blankets or park benches. The nostalgic music and drifting snowlike petals reminded Grace of a pretty scene in a musical glass globe.

"Seriously," she persisted. "Is it a jewel? Does he think you have it?"

Peter topped her wineglass again. "Nice vintage, this."

"Could it be something to do with the acoustics of the park?" she mused. "I can hear you, but you can't seem to hear me."

"I hear you," Peter said. " 'An echo and a light into eternity,' " he quoted Shelley, his tone mocking.

"As Time Goes By" floated on the breeze.

That really was a Golden Oldie. The 1930s, if she wasn't mistaken, and thanks to the film *Casablanca*, irretrievably linked with World War II in Grace's mind. Hearing it now almost seemed like a "sign," were she the kind of girl who believed in omens and talismans.

She burst out, "Surely the authorities could help us. Couldn't we go to the Turkish embassy?" She had described her earlier encounter with Harry. Peter had listened without expression and without comment: no satisfying display of outrage on her behalf, no comforting assurances that such a thing would never happen again.

He laughed. "The Turkish embassy? I don't think they'll be terribly sympathetic."

"But if it's simply a misunderstanding—"

He offered her another bite of truffle, his eyes amused—which was quite annoying.

She ignored the morsel of chocolate waved teasingly beneath her nose. "There must be some legal recourse."

"Grace, I'm sorry you were brought into it, but the situation will resolve itself shortly."

Even taking into account Peter's antipathy for any kind of law enforcement, this seemed to be taking self-reliance to extremes.

"What does that mean? How can it possibly 'resolve itself'?"

But Peter seemed to have nothing to add.

They dined on smoked turkey and mozzarella with pesto on focaccia bread still warm from the oven. Marvelous wine, chilled fruit, and chocolate truffles completed their repast. Grace knew that she was deliberately being distracted with wine and kisses and picnic basket goodies, but she was, alas, weak-willed or sleep-deprived enough to let Peter get away with it.

"How's the quest for the lost Shelley going?"

"I'm afraid it's futile." She sighed, lying back on the blanket. "If John Mallow did find a poem by Shelley, it seems to have been completely overshadowed by the scandal of his personal life."

"You've only started looking," Peter pointed out.

"True. But every direction I turn is another dead end. There's simply not enough to go on."

"That's never stopped you before."

"I suppose." She stared up at the pines trees, tall and black in the dusk. "I could try to contact the Monktons, but it's a bit awkward. I mean, what do I say? Remember the gentleman who got your auntie into trouble?"

"Auntie?"

"Granny? Actually, I have no idea of Eden Monkton's relationship to the surviving Monktons."

"Can't help you. I'm not familiar with the family."

"And even if there was a poem, Mallow might have sold it or lost it or donated it to a museum."

"If he donated it to a museum, the odds are good that someone would have heard of it."

"True."

He said with suspect easiness, "Well, once you figure out what became of John Mallow, you'll know what he did with the poem."

Grace made a face. "The old send-her-off-on-a-wild-goose-chase-so-she-doesn't-interfere-with-me routine."

"Not at all. I'm merely encouraging you to do what you love—and are so very good at."

"Uh-huh."

She thought of poor disgraced Eden Monkton abandoned by her lover. There had been a time when she had no patience with women who let such things happen to them. That was back in the comforting days when she believed all it took was a bit of self-control to master one's destiny.

The string quartet was having a bash at "When I'm Sixty-Four." Grace listened to the sprightly melody, feeling inexplicably pensive.

"Do you suppose you'll ever—that is, do you ever wish you'd had children?"

"Isn't this the sort of question the ladies' magazines counsel against?"

"Yep."

He studied her for a moment then shrugged. "I don't think I should make a very good parent."

She didn't respond, because she suspected he might be right. It was nearly impossible to visualize Peter in the role of father. She wondered what his own parents had been like. He never spoke of family, never spoke of his past. What kind of childhood had produced a man like Peter? Her own had been unremarkable except in its normalcy. She had envisioned much the same for her own eventual offspring.

"I love children," she said quietly.

"I know."

"I miss teaching."

He kissed her, and she felt it all the way down to her toes. She remembered seeing a film once where the movie heroine's shoes flew off her feet at the hero's kiss. If any man's technique could knock a girl right out of her socks, it would be Peter's. She was smiling beneath his mouth, and Peter raised his head.

"What's the joke?" His warm breath was scented of basil with a hint of chocolate.

She shook her head, and he sighed. "It's a wonder I have any confidence left."

Grace chuckled, and he kissed her again with a subtle insistence that robbed her of laughter and oxygen and reason.

Some delightful minutes passed beneath the sheltering canopy of trees. There was a kind of bittersweet pleasure in such moments. Though she longed to be like the Romantic poets she so admired, and live completely and intensely in the present, her nature was such that she couldn't help worrying about committing emotionally to an unknown future.

Perhaps he sensed her conflict, for after a time, Peter pulled back. He seemed to study her face in the dusk. Then he slipped his arm around her, settling back against the blanket. She rested her head against his surprisingly comfortable shoulder, her body relaxing against his. The wine and lack of sleep from the night before were catching up to her. Her eyelids felt weighted. The combination of music and twilight acted like a drug.

Peter's hand trailed lazily through the length of her hair. She turned her head, but found only the ascetic line of his profile. Looking past him, she stared up at the stars. *The white bees of the moon*, someone had written. Who? She couldn't quite seem to recall . . .

She woke to a symphony of frogs and crickets. Unbelievably, she had fallen asleep. Deeply asleep.

The music was silent. The night air was damp, chilly. Grace sat up stiffly and pushed her hair out of her eyes.

She hoped with all her heart she had not been snoring.

Not that she would have disturbed anyone, because she was alone.

"Peter?"

No answer.

She wondered how late it was, how long she had slept. The concert had apparently been over for some time. The gazebo and surrounding tables were empty. Though there were still people in the park, they were clearing off, moving farther and farther away, voices fading as they moved toward the entrance gates.

Grace threw aside the corner of the blanket that had been tucked around her to keep her warm, nonplussed that Peter had left her sleeping and defenseless. Obviously there must be an explanation. Perhaps he'd had an irresistible craving for a banger. Perhaps he had felt the call of nature.

After all, she was perfectly safe here. Nothing ever happened in Innisdale.

Beyond the occasional murder . . .

Scrambling to her feet, she scanned the trees that seemed to have suddenly grown several feet. Small sounds came from the underbrush.

"Peter?" She meant to call out in a strong, firm voice, but her words came out sounding tentative and hushed, as though she were afraid of being overheard by the wrong person.

She was scaring herself. Grace stooped, shoveling the picnic things into the basket, rolling the blanket, breaking camp as fast as though a posse were on her trail. Frankly, she would have welcomed a posse. Blanket wedged under her arm, lugging the heavy basket with the other, she hurried to catch the retreating voices and lights.

The picnic basket brushed noisily against the bushes as she picked her way down the uneven trail.

"Peter?" She couldn't explain the instinct that had her whispering his name.

There was still no answer. She went on, stepping carefully. She didn't want to fall or turn her ankle.

Something brushed against her face and she bit back a cry. It was only a moth.

The woods, which seemed a place of peace and serenity during the day, now seemed full of silhouettes and creeping odors.

She was nearly to the bottom of the hillside when her eyes picked out the dark shape of a log lying across the path. Her steps slowed, stopped.

The log had eyes.

She swallowed hard, her mouth suddenly dry, as the moonlight cast the shadows of leaves over the shirt and upturned face of Hayri Kayaci.

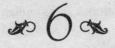

6

$\mathcal{G}$race supposed that it said something about her personal growth and professional development—or the crime level in Innisdale—that she did not scream. After a swift sharp inhalation, she knelt beside Kayaci.

Dark blood pooled beneath his head, soaking the path. His eyes—she averted her gaze, and gingerly touched his hand. He was still warm. There might be a chance. She must get help . . .

She rose on shaky legs and turned. A man's form loomed up before her.

Grace did scream, then.

The man did not move. The oval reflections of his glasses made twin white moons over his narrow face.

"What have you done?" he whispered.

"*I?*"

Voices drifted closer as others swarmed the hillside in response to Grace's scream.

The bushes moved and a tall, familiar figure

stepped out. A nimbus of moonlight circled his head like a saint's halo, or so it seemed to Grace's over-wrought imagination.

"Peter," she said with relief.

Peter stared down at Kayaci, then knelt and felt his throat in a perfunctory manner. The Turk's eyes gazed fixedly up at them.

"Is he—?" It was a silly question, and her voice faded away.

"Very." He wiped his hand on the grass, and rose. When he spoke, it was to the young man. "What happened?"

"I was headed down the path and found Ms. Hollister kneeling beside . . . it."

The nasal voice sounded accusatory, but Grace reminded herself that this was exactly what she had been doing.

"Who are you?" she asked. "How do you know my name?"

"Naturally I know who you are."

"Really? And why would that be?" She noticed that he still had not given them his name. She started to point this out, but Peter interrupted.

"What were you doing on the path?"

What were you doing off the path? Grace wondered, but kept her mouth shut.

The young man bridled. "It's a public path. Why shouldn't I be on it?"

"Just taking the evening air?"

"Not that it's your business, but I was on the hill-side listening to the concert."

If Peter had a reply to this, it was forestalled as another man crashed through the shrubbery. "I heard—" He looked from one to the other of them, noticed the body on the ground, and took a step back. "Mother of God. Is he—? What happened?"

"There's been an accident," Peter told him. "We need help."

An accident?

The newcomer lumbered down the hillside, calling, "There's been an accident!"

Peter took the picnic blanket from Grace's unresisting grip and tossed it over Kayaci's remains. Consideration for the living, not respect for the dead, Grace concluded.

"Perhaps it was an accident," the young man said slowly. He stepped farther down the trail from them. "Perhaps he tripped and hit his head on a rock." He sounded unexpectedly conciliatory.

Grace was reminded of the White Queen in *Alice in Wonderland:* "Why, sometimes I've believed as many as six impossible things before breakfast." Perhaps if they all put their minds to it, they could all believe in this particular impossible thing.

"Perhaps." Peter was noncommittal.

"I suppose it could have happened that way. The terrain is uncertain here. Visibility is poor." He took another of those sidling steps.

"Nonetheless, the police will want to question you," Peter said, "so do quit trying to scuttle away."

"Police!" And then the young man bit off whatever else was on his mind. He positioned himself out of arm's reach down the path and waited with them until the authorities arrived.

All the while they waited, Grace tried in vain to catch Peter's eyes. She would have liked to speak privately to him. It was not so much that she felt they should compare notes or "fix" their stories—well, actually, that *was* pretty much what she felt. But she was frustrated by the anonymous young man who kept watching them as though he suspected they might be planning to roll the body for cigarette money.

In short order they were joined by the emergency services—and the police. A stubby, rotund man pronounced Kayaci officially dead.

Grace heard the young man identify himself as Scott Sartyn before she was separated from her two companions. So this was Innisdale's new librarian. Fleetingly, she wondered how this buttoned-down type got on with Roy Blade, the motorcycle-riding warden of books.

Once the preliminaries were over, a constable guided her down the hillside to the now-abandoned gazebo for her account of the fatal accident. She hoped that the fact that they were being interviewed separately did not mean trouble.

Having had an embarrassing amount of experience with police inquiries, Grace answered briefly but as thoroughly as seemed wise. The constable took notes, but his questions were casual and his manner sympathetic. He did not seem to doubt the suggestion that Kayaci had suffered some kind of accident on the hillside, and Grace hoped devoutly that his faith would be rewarded by the coroner's findings. It would make everything so much simpler if Harry had simply tripped over his own giant feet and hit his head on a rock.

"Of course, the Village Council has been talking about improving the lighting on the paths since I was a boy," the constable confided to Grace, and she began to feel that perhaps they were home free.

Toward the end of her interview, they were joined by another man in jeans and a T-shirt. She did not recognize him, but the constable sucked in his gut and became slightly more formal. Was the newcomer a reporter? Another police officer—perhaps off duty?

The newcomer listened intently but without comment as Grace answered the constable's final questions.

She could not help glancing toward the man in jeans, although it was impossible to really get a good look at him as he stood out of the circle of lamplight. She had the impression of whippet-slim vitality, and his silence had a formidable quality to it.

"Well then, Ms. Hollister," the constable began in what was clearly conclusion. He was interrupted by the observer, who asked suddenly, "Did you know the deceased?"

Grace spoke politely to the shadows. "I'd met him on two separate occasions."

"What were the circumstances of those meetings?"

She answered carefully. "The first time I met him he came to the shop—Rogue's Gallery, that is—to see Peter. Peter Fox. He owns—"

"I know who Peter Fox is," the shadow said curtly. "Why did Kayaci visit Rogue's Gallery?"

"I've no idea."

Necessary lie number one. Or so it seemed to Grace. These days her moral compass seemed to have hit Magnetic North Pole.

After a heavy pause: "And the second occasion?"

It was ridiculous to feel guilty, Grace assured herself. She had done nothing wrong. And she refused to believe Peter capable of murder. If only she could trust that the police wouldn't leap to the obvious—and wrong—conclusion because of his record.

She lifted a shoulder. "It was—I don't know what it was. He stopped me in the park this morning. He was mumbling and incoherent. He grabbed my arm."

"Why?"

"Why was he mumbling and incoherent?"

Too patiently, he said, "Why did he stop you?"

"I don't know. But the vendor at the photography booth saw him harassing me. He yelled, and Kayaci took off. I never saw him again. Until . . ."

"You have no idea what he wanted?"

"He was raving," Grace said. "Mumbling about snakes and breakfast. It was all very weird."

"You had no subsequent dealings with this man Kayaci?"

"None."

The plainclothes officer—Grace was now convinced he was with the police—stepped forward into the light. She could read his T-shirt. *You have the right to remain silent, so please SHUT UP.*

Not bad advice, frankly.

"Was it your decision or Mr. Fox's to start down the hillside in that particular direction?"

"Mine."

She could see the gleam of his eyes in the lamplight and knew this was a trap. "That is to say, Peter wasn't with me. I woke up, and I was a little flustered. I thought it was later than it was, and I gathered everything together and started down the path."

"Mr. Fox left you asleep on the hillside?"

"I realize now he had only . . ." She paused delicately. "Stepped away for a moment, but as I say, I was feeling off-kilter."

The constable hastily erased and rewrote his notes, then looked to the other officer.

"Tell me exactly what you did upon spotting the deceased?"

"I think I just stood there for a moment or two. I thought it—he—was a log. The light was—that is to say, it didn't register at first . . ." She was talking too much. She sounded like she was trying to cover up something. "When I realized what I was looking at, I dropped everything and knelt to see if he was . . . alive." She shivered. "He was still warm."

"I see. And then?"

Something in his crisp tone made Grace uneasy. "Then I got up and Mr. Sartyn was standing there watching me. He startled me. I screamed, and a number of people started toward us."

"Including Mr. Fox."

He made it sound sinister. Was Peter's showing up

on the heels of Sartyn more or less suspect? "Peter showed up a second or two after Mr. Sartyn. He instructed someone to call for help."

"Do you have any idea why anyone would want to kill Mr. Kayaci?"

"Are you sure it wasn't an accident?"

He said smoothly, "We're exploring every possibility." Then he added, "You haven't answered my question, Ms. Hollister."

"I don't have any idea of who might have wished him harm. He wasn't from around here, you know."

She saw an unexpected glimmer of teeth. "But then, neither are you, Ms. Hollister."

Grace was relieved to find Peter waiting for her in the car park amidst a crowd of onlookers and emergency vehicles. He leaned against the hood of the Land Rover, arms folded, a slightly bored spectator at the circus that followed violent death.

It had to be an act, but if so, it was the role he had been born to play. He greeted her without concern, politely held the door for her, and moved around to his side without haste.

Grace observed him with something akin to exasperation. She knew it would not take the police long to connect Kayaci to Peter. Once that happened, it was impossible to predict what might follow. It seemed unlikely that anyone else in Innisdale would have a motive to kill the man.

"Was he murdered?" she demanded, as Peter slid behind the wheel and started the engine.

A news van pulled up alongside them, and she quickly turned her face away. She feared she was becoming a tad too well known at crime scenes.

Head turned over his shoulder, Peter reversed the Land Rover in a tight arc. She barely caught his cool "It does look that way."

Until that moment, she had been clinging to hope. "What *happened?*"

His eyes remained on the rearview and the commotion behind them. "How should I know?"

"I mean, where did you *go?*"

He shifted gears smoothly. His voice was smooth, too. "I realized we were being watched. I decided to circle round and see if I couldn't get the jump on our friend."

She couldn't tell by his voice if he was lying; she would need to see his eyes to be sure. "Thanks, by the way, for leaving me spread out like a virgin sacrifice."

"It's a lovely thought, but hardly that."

She made a sound that in a less well-bred girl would have been a snort. "Your concern for my safety is overwhelming."

She felt him look her way. "You were in no danger."

"That's easy for you to say. You were off in the woods playing . . . Natty Bumppo."

"And you, my faithful Indian companion?" Beneath the mockery, he sounded terse. Definitely not as calm as he pretended.

She bit her lip. "Do you know what happened to him? Harry, I mean."

"Is that your diplomatic way of asking whether I killed him?"

"Did you?" She closed her eyes and said a silent prayer.

"No." With a candor she could have done without, he added, "The opportunity never arose."

"Do you know who did?"

"Some civic-minded soul."

"You shouldn't even joke like that. The police—"

"I'm not joking."

She bit back whatever she had started to say.

Already they were turning down the side road that led to Renfrew Hall and the cottage Grace rented. She would have liked to have talked this out, discuss the possibilities, reassure herself that Peter could not commit murder, but he pulled behind the redbrick house and got out.

The silence between them was filled with unsaid things as he walked with her through the garden, pale flowers glimmering in the dark, their footsteps scraping the stone walk. The light she had left on burned cheerily behind the windows of the Gardener's Cottage.

Peter watched her unlock her door. She turned, starting to speak, but he gave her a peck on the cheek and was gone, moving with uncanny stillness through the trees.

$\mathcal{G}$race went inside, leaned against the door, and listened to the sound of Peter's car engine dying out down the village lane.

Too wound up for sleep, she made a cup of cocoa, pulled out the sofa bed, and curled up in the nest of pillows sorting through the day's mail. There was a fat registration packet from Amberent Hall. Slightly cheered, Grace tore it open and quickly read through it.

"Amberent Hall is situated in a beautifully restored nineteenth-century Gothic manor with charming gardens and a stunning view of Wastwater and the stern rugged mountains of Yewbarrow and Great Gable."

That sounded right up Grace's alley.

Academia seemed a safe haven from the violence of the night. It occurred to her that there was a chance she might find someone at this conference with some information on John Mallow and the Shiloh letter. After all, where better to start looking than at a meeting of Lake District experts on the Romantic period?

She shuffled through the papers. The program looked promising.

Friday, June 9
8:30 Tea and pastries. Drawing Room (armchairs for 19)

She would have preferred tea and crumpets or tea and scones, but decided to forgive this concession to non-British appetites and read on.

9:00–11:00 The Heart That Would Not Burn: The Life and Death of Percy Bysshe Shelley. Lecture Room (hearing loop installed)
   Dr. F. Archibald, *Blithe Spirit: The Life of Shelley*

11:00–12:30 Mrs. Prometheus: The Feminism of Mary Wollstonecraft Shelley. Parlor
   C. V. Keene, *Mary Shelley: A Life*

Feminists were divided as to whether Mary Wollstonecraft Shelley rightfully belonged amongst the sisterhood; Grace was certain it would be an interesting lecture. There were those who believed that the daughter of the author of *A Vindication of the Rights of Woman* should never have published her own efforts anonymously or allowed her husband to edit her work, and that doing so somehow diminished her.

12:30–1:30 Byron and the Bryon Complex. Cedar Room
   James Postit, *The Demon Lover*

1:30–2:30 Lunch in the Rock Garden

Grace hoped that the meals would prove something better than the usual interchangeable hot protein option, hot starch option conference fare.

2:30–4:00 Panel: The Pisan Circle. Lecture Room
Panel: J. B. Plow, *Circle of Sisters*
V. M Brougham, *Glorious Apollo*—CANCELLED
George Garfinkle, *Ariel & Endymion*
Quincy Ludlow, *Lord Byron's Doctor*

Moderator: Dr. F. Archibald, *Blithe Spirit: The Life of Shelley*

On Friday the program appeared heavily slanted toward Shelley, which was encouraging. And Dr. F. Archibald, the director of the conference, looked to be the reigning Shelley expert. Surely he would be aware of whether there had ever been a local discovery of a work by Shelley.

Smothering a yawn, Grace laid the papers aside, switched off the bedside lamp, and scooted down on the mattress.

The gnarled silhouette of the apple tree outside the window was projected across the wall like the slide in a magic lantern. In the silence and darkness, the horror of the evening crept into the small room. She could smell the damp decay of the woods, feel the watchful silence pressing in; once again she saw Kayaci lying sprawled across the path.

With a shudder, Grace banished these dreadful images. She debated sleeping with the light on, but managed to resist giving in to irrational fear.

Think of something else, she instructed herself, and immediately began to mull over Peter's role in the evening's events.

A few months earlier, she had made a decision not to pry into his colorful past—to let Peter tell her his life's story in his own time. It had not been an easy decision. Peter's mysterious history acted upon her the way an unopened jigsaw tempted a puzzle addict. She comforted herself with the belief that there was something sad and desperate about women who felt compelled to spy on their men.

Not that Peter was exactly "her" man. He was more like . . . public domain. Or maybe a national treasure.

She chuckled sleepily at this but sobered as she considered the truism that everyone was capable of killing under certain circumstances. What might those circumstances be for Peter?

The previous day at the gallery—just for a moment—there had been something in his eyes . . .

"Another murder? You've turned into quite the Miss Marple." Roy Blade, Innisdale's biker librarian, greeted Grace.

"Why is it always Miss Marple and never Sherlock Holmes?" Grace complained, and Blade grinned his pirate's grin.

"Maybe because your legs are so much better than Holmes's."

"But not better than Miss Marple's?"

He laughed. He was a muscular man with long black hair and an eye patch. He sported an impressive and probably dangerous collection of tattoos, and was not typical of Grace's acquaintances before she had moved to Innisdale. Not everyone would agree that expanding her circle of friends to bikers and ex–jewel thieves was a wise move, but it made for an interesting life.

She and Blade exchanged pleasantries, if discussion of murder could be classified as pleasant, as they made their way through the canyons of books.

The library had been built in the 1950s. It was not large, and the reading selection was mostly unremarkable, but Grace felt at home there. She loved the smell of old books, she loved the faded red carpets and the yellow and ruby pendant lights that hung over the long, battered tables.

Glancing across the mostly empty tables, she met the gaze of Scott Sartyn standing behind the massive front desk. Sartyn held her eyes for a moment, then looked away.

Following her gaze, Blade muttered an obscenity, more startling in his public school accents. "I see you've met the Boy Wonder."

"He was there last night. When I found . . . um . . . Mr. Kayaci."

"Was he?" Blade's good eye gleamed with malicious interest. "Was he indeed?"

"He seemed very suspicious. Of Peter and me, that is—although I find him rather suspicious myself."

"Do you?"

"Well, no. But something about him bugs me."

"Something about him bugs everyone." He slanted a look in Sartyn's direction that in another time and place might have forewarned of a knife between the ribs.

"Where did he come from? Who hired him? Is he actually in charge now?"

Blade growled, "And why not? He's the sort Village Council twats love. As for where he came from, your guess is as good as mine. Simply showed up one day with all his bright and shiny credentials."

"But how could they give him your job?"

His lip curled. "It never was officially my job. The Council could never quite bring themselves to make the post mine permanently. Maybe it's my image." Blade raised a black-leather-clad shoulder. He always seemed to wear black leather regardless of weather or occasion. At Grace's expression, he laughed a low and nasty laugh. "Don't worry, I've got the little punk's measure. He won't be content with our backwater village for long. I can put up with him for a bit."

She nodded, only partially convinced, and glanced Sartyn's way again. He was scowling as he shuffled through a stack of papers. Good. She didn't want to attract his attention any more than she had to. Part of her reason for visiting the library was to get Blade's opinion on the possibility of the Shelley document. Though he might not look it, Roy Blade was a scholar of Romantic literature.

She said, "Have you ever heard anything about the

local discovery of a work by Shelley? This would have been in the 1940s."

Blade's eyes narrowed. "No. What's up?"

"Maybe nothing. Probably nothing. Can you think of anyone who might know for sure?"

"Your friend and mine, Her Royal High and Mightiness."

"Lady Vee?"

Lady Venetia Brougham was the authoress of several lurid if thoroughly researched books on Lord Byron.

"She and her cronies used to call themselves the Cumbrian Circle or some such twaddle back in the day."

As they conversed, Grace felt a funny prickle between her shoulder blades. She recognized that feeling; it was the uneasy awareness of being watched. She glanced over her shoulder and sure enough, Scott Sartyn's eyes were drilling into her.

Blade muttered another obscenity, and said out of the corner of his mouth, "Later."

Grace nodded and moved off through the creaking towers of bookshelves. Feeling a bit foolish, she paused to peer through a space in the medical reference books to see Sartyn quietly but obviously taking Blade to task.

Blade's face was flushed and his powerful hands gripped the bookcart as though he wanted to smash it into the younger man. Patrons in chairs listened interestedly until Sartyn stalked off.

Clearly she would have to wait to talk to Roy when

he was off duty. Still, the morning's visit need not be wasted. Grace settled down at the computer bank to research what exactly might be a "Serpent's Egg."

She convinced herself that she was not prying into Peter's past so much as scouting out who else might have motive for getting rid of Kayaci. Whatever this Serpent's Egg was, it seemed to be Kayaci's reason for contacting Peter—possibly for being in the U.K. at all.

Her research uncovered a CD by a band named Dead Can Dance, a foreign film from 1977, and a couple of novels. Nine Internet pages later, she came across a small reference to an attempted robbery at the Topkapi Palace in Istanbul.

Topkapi? Vague memories of the famous caper film starring a befuddled Peter Ustinov in pursuit of a bejeweled dagger flitted through her brain. Oh, Peter, she thought. *Topkapi?*

Focusing her search on the former Imperial Residence of the Ottoman Dynasty, Grace was able to locate the full story—or at least as much of it as was Internet record.

Twelve years earlier, thieves had broken into the national museum located by the Bosporus Sea. Fortunately, depending on whose side you were on, the daring plan of the robbers had been foiled—how it had been foiled was glossed over—and nearly all the loot had been recovered with the exception of a national treasure called the Serpent's Egg. The suspected ringleader of the thieves had been arrested, and the authorities were confident the Serpent's Egg would soon be returned. However, subsequent stories were increasingly vague as to what became of either the Englishman or the jewel.

Grace paged on and on. There were many pictures of the *Kandjar*, the famous emerald dagger featured in the film *Topkapi*. There were photos of the *Kasikci* or Spoonmaker's Diamond, a few jewel-encrusted thrones, and a golden coffer that used to contain the poetry book of Ahmet III, a poet with whom Grace was unfamiliar. But none of these treasures had apparently interested the thieves.

And then finally she found it. Grace stared at a photo of the 140-carat egg-shaped diamond and caught her breath. It was both beautiful and repulsive. A thick vein of tiny blue sapphires and rubies ringed the center diamond like a glistening sac, giving the illusion that the egg had only moments before been laid by some terrifying mythological creature.

She scanned the short history of the piece. In the sixteenth century, Babur, a descendant of Genghis Khan, had invaded India and set up the Mughal Empire. Mughal rule technically lasted until the nineteenth century, and was ingenuously referred to as a time of "unrest." The disorganized and warring *Rajputs* were no match for the trained and well-armed—with primitive firearms no less—Mughals. News to Grace, but then, she was rather weak in Islamic history.

The rest of the story was legend. On one of many military campaigns, a favorite captain of the newly established sultan came upon a small provincial temple dedicated to Anant Nag, the thousand-hooded snake god. In the temple, the Mughals had discovered a ten-foot-tall snake statue. In Grace's opinion this would have been sufficient reason to get the heck out of that temple, but the Mughals were made of sterner stuff.

Apparently one of the statue's eyes had already been gouged out, and had no doubt been dishing bad luck for centuries, but in the other stone socket was a fabulous diamond. Despite the obligatory doom and gloom prophecies of the temple priests—whom they silenced by slaying—the Mughals had stolen the remaining diamond orb. And lo and behold, Babur's favorite captain had died of a cobra bite the very next day, proving that the gem was cursed—though not so cursed that it was returned to its rightful owners.

Shades of *The Moonstone,* thought Grace. She could see why this tale would appeal to the youthful Peter's romantic streak.

How the jewel had traveled from the hands of the Mughal Dynasty back to the Ottoman Imperial Treasury was lost in a blood-drenched history of war and conquest.

So that was it—the root of Peter's downfall? She peered at the larger-than-life image on the computer monitor.

Serpent's Egg or snake eye. It seemed to wink malevolently at her through cyberspace.

8

When Grace got back to the Gardener's Cottage, the light was blinking on her answering machine. The first two messages were from *The Clarion* requesting an interview. These she promptly erased. The third was Chief Constable Heron requesting her presence at the police station in order to "review her statement."

The chief constable was well known to Grace. She had dined at his home on two occasions, and had Heron and his wife Constance to dinner in her own small cottage. She liked and respected the chief constable, a shrewd and kindly man. Unfortunately he had filed Peter in the scoundrel category, which put certain constraints on their friendship.

Still, she was relieved that the official summons came from the chief constable and not the crisp executive of law and order she'd met the night before.

She did see the crisp executive, however, as he was leaving the chief constable's office as she was being ushered in.

He nodded without warmth, and Grace nodded

back with an equal lack of enthusiasm. She noticed that he was only a little taller than she was, very trim and straight as though he'd just "earned his colours," as the Regency novelists were wont to put it. His hair was dark and his eyes a light indeterminate color.

"Who is that?" she asked the chief constable, closing the door to his office.

Chief Constable Heron looked very much like a *Masterpiece Theatre* policeman, right down to his magnificent handlebar mustache.

"Detective Inspector Drummond. He transferred from the Metropolitan Police force a few months ago. Very able young chap."

"I'll just bet," Grace said with feeling.

There was a faint twinkle in Heron's black-cherry eyes, but he said, using his pipe to indicate the chair across from him, "Now then, Grace. Tell me what you know of Mr. Hayri Kayaci."

Grace seated herself with the sensation of one seeking a comfortable spot on a hot griddle. She knew that by then the police must have established the connection between Kayaci and Peter. If they hadn't, they soon would, and they would take a hard long look for the reason behind any lies or half-truths. If she could confine her answers to those things the police must already know, that would be the safest course.

"He was one of the gendarmes at the Istanbul prison where Peter was held," she replied.

Heron observed her beneath beetling brows. "You didn't reveal that fact in your statement last night."

"I was only asked what my personal relationship to the deceased was."

Heron shook his head disapprovingly. "Prevarication, Grace," he told her. "And well you know it. Why was Kayaci in Innisdale?"

"Now that I don't know."

"You must have some idea."

She could say with honesty, "Peter doesn't confide in me. Not that kind of thing, anyway."

Heron made a harrumphing noise.

Grace said tentatively, "I thought his reason for being here might be official. I know Peter escaped from Turkey."

Heron's cheeks puffed on his pipe in meditative fashion. "Kayaci was not representing the Turkish government in any official capacity," he said at last. "He was sacked a couple of years ago for dealing in the antiquities black market." He studied her shrewdly. "You seem surprised."

She was not surprised. She was elated that her deductions up to now had been correct. Kayaci was after the Serpent's Egg. He believed that Peter still had it. Kayaci himself had been nothing more than a crook.

She answered, "I was afraid he might be here to have Peter extradited."

The black eyes fastened on hers. "Did he threaten to have Mr. Fox extradited?"

"Um, not that I know of." She sidestepped, realizing that her decoy might give Peter motive for murder.

Heron studied her. "Then why would you fear such a thing? Surely Mr. Fox is aware that the United Kingdom has no extradition treaty with Turkey."

Everywhere she looked were land mines. She had to make sure nothing she said implicated Peter in the man's death.

"We didn't discuss it." She hated lying. Her skin felt flushed and prickly, as though she'd overdosed on niacin. Serve her right if she broke out in a rash. "And although I couldn't really make out what he wanted, he was clearly not a friend of Peter's."

"You're referring to your encounter with Kayaci in the park on Thursday morning?"

"Correct." She resolved to restrict herself to brief answers that couldn't possibly get her into further hot water.

"What precisely did Kayaci say to you in the park?"

"I can't be precise, because he was practically incoherent. He rambled on about prison, about how I should talk to Peter. He quoted something."

Heron's eyes lit up. "A quote? What did he say?"

Heavens. Then they knew all about the Serpent's Egg. But of course, when they ascertained Kayaci was no longer with the Turkish government, they would have put two and two together. The stone had never been recovered. The Turks would never have stopped watching for this national treasure to turn up.

But did Heron believe that, like in some old-fashioned pulp mystery, the solution to the stone's hiding place would be in a riddle or a quotation? She must be wearing off on him.

" 'Satan's friendship reaches to the prison door.' "

Heron mulled this over and seemed disappointed. "And you say here you never met Kayaci before Wednesday afternoon?"

An easy one. "Correct."

"Can you explain why Kayaci was inquiring after you in the village on Tuesday?"

Grace didn't have to feign surprise. "I have no idea. What kind of questions was he asking?"

But Heron declined to answer. He referred again to the file before him.

"According to witnesses, you spoke to Kayaci in the park for several minutes before the conversation appeared to turn ugly."

They were covering the same ground again. It was difficult to know what to say when she had no idea how much Heron knew.

"It was ugly from the start," Grace said. "He said he had asked around the village and learned that I was— that Peter and I were friends."

"But he already knew that from his visit to Craddock House, didn't he?"

"I didn't stay for their reunion. Anyway, Mr. Kayaci seemed to think that I could influence Peter. I suppose he believed Peter had information he wanted."

"Information regarding—?"

Why had she said that? Did that contradict what she had said earlier? It was hard to keep track.

"Information about the job Peter was arrested for in Istanbul. I don't know the details, but he was obviously looking for someone or something, and he believed Peter had the answers he needed." That much they already knew or could deduce.

Heron studied her for an uncomfortably long moment. Grace had never experienced this side of the chief constable. She decided she didn't like it. Nor did she like the feeling that she was disappointing him.

"You say you did not remain for the reunion between Kayaci and Fox, but isn't it true that you and Fox went to dinner at Mallow Farm shortly after?"

Grace's mouth parted but nothing came out. How could he know about that? And what could she say? *I was hiding in the confessional? I went home and came back?* "I stepped into the garden while they talked," she said finally, belatedly.

"I see." Heron made some notes. Grace would have given a lot to be able to read upside down.

"According to Mr. Sartyn you were going through the deceased's pockets when he arrived at the crime scene."

"*What?*"

"Not true?"

"I knelt to check his pulse. Why would he say such a thing?"

"Perhaps that was the way it looked to him."

Indignantly, Grace exclaimed, "He needs to have his eyes checked. You don't honestly think I had anything to do with that man's death?"

After a moment the chief constable's lips twitched. "Bridget Jones commits murder, eh? I don't think you killed Kayaci, no. But you're holding something back. I know you that well."

He paused as though to give Grace opportunity to change her course. When she said nothing, he said gravely, "There's some truth in that quotation of Mr. Kayaci's. A woman should pick her friends carefully."

"As should anyone."

Absently, he twisted the end of his handlebar mustache, his eyes assessing. "You might as well know, I've given DI Drummond lead on this case."

"Oh?" She preferred the kindly chief constable, even when he wasn't thrilled with her.

Accurately interpreting her expression, Heron added with dour satisfaction, "It may be you'll not find him as patient a man."

Grace picked up her purse, privately hoping that she would not have enough interaction with DI Drummond to find out anything about him at all.

It looked like moving day at Rogue's Gallery. An enormous lorry was parked out front, half-blocking the country lane, and men in overalls moved back and forth across the lawn lugging boxes. Kameko Musashi stood to the side supervising. Though she did not carry a whip, she managed to convey the impression that sluggards would be dealt with severely. The moving men kept a brisk pace.

Peter stood inside the doorway directing a procession of lacquered chairs.

"Welcome to the Bridge on the River Innisdale," he greeted her.

Grace ignored this. "It *was* murder," she informed him.

One black brow arched in characteristic fashion. "My dear girl, you'll frighten the customers with these cryptic utterances."

"That will make it unanimous."

"Whisht." That was Scots for "shut your gob." He jerked his head in the direction of a carrying Brooklyn accent inside the shop, and Grace took the hint and went in to deal with the usual summer crowd.

After she had answered the usual barrage of questions and rung up a sale for some small but pricey items, she headed for the back room to pour herself a cup of tea. *The Clarion*, Innisdale's local newspaper, lay on Peter's desk, its banner headline screaming bloody murder—as though violent death were not a normal occurrence for the quaint but disconcertingly perilous village.

She scanned the story, but there was remarkably little information. Mr. Hayri Kayaci, a Turkish national on holiday, had been found dead in Cherry Lane Park following the Thursday night concert. Kayaci appeared to be the victim of foul play, although the police had not yet revealed the cause of death. The police were equally unforthcoming about their possible suspects.

Grace folded the paper and replaced it on Peter's desk.

The day passed quickly and was a profitable one, at least for Peter. When he had closed the door on the last client, and locked the gallery, he sent Grace out to the back garden with plates, flatware, and a bottle of chilled Riesling.

Apparently they were dining al fresco that evening. She set the table, one of those wrought-iron constructions of another generation, wondering if it was her imagination that Peter seemed more lighthearted now that Kayaci was dead.

But after all, why shouldn't he be relieved that Kayaci was no longer a threat? He would have to be very noble indeed to regret the end of Horrible Harry, and one thing Peter had never pretended to be was noble.

Pouring the wine, she sat down in one of the heavy lawn chairs and took a sip. She loved this garden, as she loved every inch of Craddock House. The old iron chairs in a variety of paint-chipped bleached colors were made comfortable by plush cushions in faded florals. Discreetly concealed outdoor lights combined romance with practicality. Brilliant annuals burst from vintage pots; ivy and clematis trailed from urns. Flowering vines of wisteria, old roses, and clematis wound up the house. *Some of these flowers are older than I.*

Grace's thoughts were interrupted as Peter rounded the corner carrying a plate of freshly prepared salmon. The Lake District was famous for its salmon.

"I was a-thinkin' bar-bee-cue," he said in a Texas drawl.

It always amused Grace that when Brits imitated Americans, they invariably seemed to choose a Texas accent.

Peter did accents quite well, another of those small mysteries that intrigued her. She had developed an ear for regional pronunciations, but she couldn't place Peter's. He spoke what she considered "public school," with some transatlantic inflections. It reminded her a bit of Cary Grant's oddly regionless speech.

The paving stones beneath her feet were still warm from the afternoon sun, and she allowed herself to be soothed by the summery scents of newly mown grass and grilling salmon. Remembering other summers and other barbecues, she was suddenly, intensely homesick.

It was difficult to believe that she had gone nearly two years without seeing her parents or brothers. She missed them all so much. Not merely the family picnics and swimming pool parties, but the comfortable intimacy of being with the people who knew her better than anyone else, the people who accepted and loved her for who she was, and would never judge her for not being something she could not be.

"You're very quiet this evening," Peter remarked, setting a plate before her.

She smiled quickly, shaking off her preoccupation. "It's that police interrogation thing. It really takes it out of you."

"Ah yes. I remember it well." He smiled, and the afternoon almost seemed like an adventure in retrospect. "Never mind, Esmerelda. You're home with the gypsies now." He took his place across from her, and it seemed for a moment that this was how it had always been, and always would be.

The meal was a delight. The salmon was grilled to flaky perfection, and the nutty-flavored couscous and cucumber salad with mint and crème fraîche were the perfect accompaniment. For dessert there was blackberry cobbler. She'd had many such delightful dinners with Peter.

She wondered where and when in his strange and crooked career he had learned to cook. There was so little she knew about him. Where had he learned about antiques? He was very well read; where had he been educated? Oxford? Cambridge? She did not even know how old he was. She guessed he was in his late thirties or early forties.

"When is your birthday?" she asked suddenly.

"June. June 20."

"That would make you—?"

"Old." His mouth curved at her expression. "Or were you inquiring as to my . . . er . . . sign?"

"I don't believe in astrology." She put her fork down and leaned back, staring up at the night sky.

The keen stars were twinkling.

She glanced across the table. Peter was rolling the stem of his wineglass between his long fingers. He watched the glitter of the crystal in the candlelight as though it were fascinating.

"This murder business had nearly driven the Shelley from my mind," she said to break the silence.

"You take these things too much to heart."

She opened her mouth, then let it go. He was teasing her. At least, she hoped he was.

"I forgot to tell you. I think I found a photo of John Mallow wearing that cap badge we found—or one very similar."

He looked up then. "SAS, Special Air Service. A tough outfit. Lads in the Regiment don't desert."

"This one did, apparently. I just can't figure out why."

The candles threw shadows across Peter's lean face. "Maybe he couldn't face the idea of going back to that carnage."

"You said lads in the Regiment didn't desert."

His smile was twisted in the flickering light. "Given the right set of circumstances, anyone's nerve can fail."

"He didn't look like that type."

"What type is that?" His voice was unexpectedly bitter. "This is based on one photograph?"

"Several photos. He looked, oh, I don't know. Like Rupert Brooke. Young and gallant. Willing to die for his ideals."

"Yes, well, there's the ideal, then there's the reality of getting your arse shot off."

There was something in his tone that held her silent for an instant. Thinking aloud she said, "But to have left Eden . . ."

" 'Though he has Eden to live in, man cannot be happy alone,' " Peter quoted sententiously.

Grace chuckled. "No, Eden Monkton. They were engaged. She was going to have a baby. When he disappeared, he abandoned her, too. She was disgraced."

"A rotter through and through." But his tone was derisive.

"But that's what I mean. Can you picture the man who wrote the letter we read disgracing himself and his family, abandoning his fiancée and unborn child, deserting everything he valued and believed in?"

"Had you considered that your John may not be John Mallow? Perhaps he's . . . hell, I don't know. John Smith."

"Who's John Smith?"

"Who's—?" Peter's brows drew together. "You do have a one-track mind. I meant only that we don't know that your letter writer *is* John Mallow. We don't know to whom the letter was addressed."

"His dearest girl."

"There are other dearest girls in this fair land. You, for example, might be my dearest girl."

"I might," she returned lightly. "But there've been so many, you might have me confused with another girl."

He laughed, but there was something in his voice as he retorted, "You underestimate yourself, Esmerelda. And possibly me."

Maybe he was right. She had to stop making those smart-alecky comments every time he tried to pay her a compliment.

She said, groping for the first safe topic she could find, "Until Sam Jeffries, no one but Mallows had lived at Mallow Farm. All this stuff came from Mallow, ergo the John who wrote the Shiloh letter must be John Mallow. The letter is dated 1943, only two years before the end of the war, which makes it circa John Mallow."

"Except that the letter was apparently still in John Mallow's possession when he disappeared."

"But there are possible explanations for that."

"Such as?"

"Perhaps it was a rough draft."

"Of a letter?"

"Letter writing used to be an art."

"Shaky."

"Maybe the letter was returned. Maybe he decided not to mail it."

"Maybe."

"It seems more reasonable than that there should be another John with knowledge of the Shelley."

"Take nothing in this life for granted." Peter spoke as one who knew.

❧ 9 ❧

"**P**OLICE SEEK MYSTERY WEAPON," blazoned *The Clarion*'s headlines the next morning. Grace realized that the police had ruled out any possibility of accidental death. Cinnamon toast seemed to lodge in her throat as she read that the murder weapon, as yet unidentified, was being searched for in Cherry Lane Park. She swallowed hard. She reminded herself that this was not news, and that the paper was merely reporting what she had already deduced.

In a reflective mood, Grace bathed and dressed in a summery pale green Ralph Lauren dress that she had bought on clearance in a Lakeland boutique. She had been illogically pleased to discover the dress, as though it were a familiar face in a crowd of too-short, too-bright, too-trendy aliens.

The truth was, she had found many lovely things in English shops (most out of her limited budget's range) but her loyalty to American fashion was strong—although much of what she loved about "American" fashion was based on British traditions:

jodhpurs, lace blouses, tweed jackets, and vintage accessories. In any case, no matter what Grace wore, she still felt that she looked unmistakably American.

She was considering this indefinable American-ness as she twisted her hair into a neat coil and studied the result. Reaching for a couple of hairpins, she started thinking once more about that mystery weapon. Surely that ruled out lead pipe, rope, wrench, revolver, dagger, and the ever-popular candlestick.

What mystery weapon would, for instance, Peter have access to on a picnic? A wine corkscrew? No, Grace had tossed that into the basket herself when she was gathering up the remains of their picnic.

There were any number of possibilities in Rogue's Gallery: wicked daggers, lethal-looking hair ornaments and hatpins—even antique chopsticks. The Grace in the mirror looked wide-eyed at this, and the Grace on the other side of the looking glass shook her head scornfully.

She felt sure that if Peter were to commit murder—which was unlikely (because she could not imagine Peter that panicked or desperate)—he would arrange for something quick and uncomplicated. Something that could be mistaken for an accident.

Macabre thoughts for such a beautiful day! She switched off the bathroom light.

Grace generally had weekends off, although she frequently spent them with Peter. That Saturday she had received an invitation to lunch with Mr. Matsukado. She had toyed with the idea of accepting, but in the end decided to pursue another avenue.

Resisting temptation, she had returned the Shiloh letter to its hiding place in the sheet music. It seemed the fair thing. But more than this she could not bring herself to do. She didn't dislike Mr. Matsukado, but she didn't trust him, either. Grace had experience with fanatic collectors. Better the devil she knew than the devil she didn't know, and she resolved to, in the words of Shelley himself, "dare the unpastured dragon in his den."

Except this dragon was a lady dragon, and her den turned out to be the pasture-sized garden behind Brougham Manor.

As Grace was escorted across the expanse of velvet lawn she spied Lady Venetia Brougham, her niece, Allegra Clairmont-Brougham, Scott Sartyn, and a young woman she did not know engaged in what appeared to be a croquet death match.

The butler ducked as the young woman sent a croquet ball smashing through an elegant topiary like a blue cannonball. There was a splash as the croquet ball entered the goldfish pond and sank from sight.

The young woman laughed merrily as Grace and the butler continued toward the tableau stationed around the croquet hoops.

The Honorable Allegra, looking the classic English rose in white linen, waved languidly.

"If it isn't our own Miss Marple. Do you play croquet, Grace?"

Scott Sartyn turned at Allegra's greeting and stared at Grace.

Meeting his affronted gaze, Grace decided it was

better to be regarded as a Miss Marple than Public Enemy #1.

"Of course she does," Lady Vee said around the ivory cigarette holder clamped between her teeth. "Americans love sports. I've no doubt that Grace is a *mahvellous playah*." The gay straw hat trimmed with blue roses was startling in contrast to the shriveled face beneath, sunken eyes glittering like some prehistoric creature's.

Grace shook her head, smiling. "I'm afraid I don't play."

Lady Vee's penciled brows drew together in disapproval, but she said, "Still, how *delightful* of you to pay us a visit, my *deeeah*. Would you believe I was planning to ring you up? I do not believe you've met my little grandniece, Cordelia."

Grace judged that Lady Vee's little grandniece was about seventeen and nearly six feet tall. She was a thin, sallow-faced girl with a tangled mop of black hair. Her eyes were her best feature: large and deer-like, although her expression was more faun than fawn. Cordelia's dark gaze was disconcerting in its intensity.

"How nice to meet you," said Grace, offering her hand.

Cordelia shook hands. Her grip was hard, her hands bony, nails badly bitten. "You're the school-teacher." Her brown eyes were frankly curious, and Grace was not surprised if the girl had heard Lady Vee and Allegra's version of their peculiar acquaintance-ship.

"Guilty." Grace added to Scott, "Of teaching school, that is," and was pleased to see him redden.

After an awkward moment, he greeted her stiffly. Grace sympathized with the etiquette dilemma. How *did* one greet a person one had basically accused of murder?

"And to think she buzzed into the web all on her own," the Hon. Al murmured.

What did that mean? Lady Vee's expression remained bland.

"Do let's play," urged Cordelia, swinging her croquet mallet and narrowly missing Sartyn's legs. He made a move that would have done Jean-Claude Van Damme proud, and Cordelia giggled. Grace felt herself warm toward the girl.

Lady Vee looped her arm in Grace's and retreated with her to the terrace, settling into comfortable white wicker chairs. This unexpected cordiality made Grace a little wary, but Lady Vee seemed content to make small talk in between shrieking encouragement to the players.

Grace chatted about village news and tried to think of a subtle way to introduce the topic of the Shiloh letter.

There was a loud yelp—something close to a shriek, in fact. Tail between its legs, one of Lady Vee's dilapidated Irish wolfhounds bolted across the green as Cordelia sent another colored ball rocketing through a hedge. Lady Vee mused, "A most intelligent child, but . . ."

"But—?"

"There have been some difficulties," Lady Vee murmured vaguely.

"That's adolescence," Grace said, and to her surprise—and unease—Lady Vee turned that reptilian smile upon her once more.

"You understand so much, my *deah*," she said. Hissed, really. Sort of like Kaa the snake in *Jungle Book*. "You have such affinity for young people."

Grace was unmoved by this praise, since Lady Vee had never seen her with anyone remotely resembling a young person until that afternoon.

"You must miss teaching very much."

"I do," Grace admitted.

At last the bout of Extreme Croquet ended, and the flushed and perspiring combatants made their way to the terrace, where lunch was being served on a table set with crisply ironed linen, crystal glasses, and polished silver.

Chilled white wine sparkled in the glasses; the scent of herb-roasted chicken mingled mouthwateringly with the sorrel, leek, and mushroom tart. Grace, seated next to Sartyn, sampled the endive-and-pear salad with sherry vinaigrette. It was all satisfyingly exquisite. Even the butterflies fluttering overhead seemed more elegant than the usual flying insects.

"This is the life," Sartyn said, reaching for his wineglass.

Grace decided she did not like his aftershave, and smiled politely at him. His eyes slid away from hers. What a wacko, she thought, and happened to catch

Cordelia's interested gaze. She hoped her face was not betraying her.

To Lady Vee, she said, "I was sorry to see you canceled your appearance on the Pisan Circle panel. I was looking forward to hearing your talk."

"A bad impulse," Lady Vee said. Did her ladyship mean her initial agreement to do the panel or the decision to cancel?

"You people do seem to revel in your literary bibble babble," Sartyn remarked indulgently.

This seemed an odd attitude for a librarian.

Allegra's black brows rose. "It *is* the Lake District," she pointed out.

"So I've been told. Supposedly it was discovered by a poet." Sartyn's tone implied this was an amusing fiction.

"Thomas Gray," Cordelia chimed in, and looked to her aunt for approval. Lady Vee was occupied in spearing a piece of endive, scarlet lips pursed with the endeavor.

"Damned if I know. I've never heard so much rubbish about poets and poetry as since I moved here," Sartyn informed them, and pitchforked a mouthful of salad too large for his admittedly big mouth. He proceeded to chomp away in a self-satisfied manner.

"Where are you from?" Grace inquired. She was thinking the planet Mars was a strong possibility. Or—here was a thought—perhaps, like the *Brontosaurus* he resembled at the moment, Sartyn wasn't quite the genuine article. She couldn't quite put her finger on it, but there was something about him . . .

He ignored her question, assuring them all through lettuce and vinaigrette, "I can't think of anything more useless than poetry."

"You're not trying, *deah* boy," Lady Vee murmured without looking up. "I can think of several things."

Cordelia snickered. She was eating her salad with her fingers. But then, she had probably been raised by wolves. Well-read wolves, naturally.

"Even that great lout of an assistant of mine is a nutter on the subject." Sartyn forged on with his diplomatic mission.

Grace nearly choked in her hurry to swallow and answer that one, but surprisingly Allegra beat her to the punch.

"Wasn't Blade a candidate for professor of poetry at Oxford?" Her airy inquiry did not seem to be directed to any one person, so perhaps it was rhetorical.

"For what it's worth. I can't understand how someone like that could have been hired in—"

"I believe I prefer the creamed endive salad," Lady Vee cut across to Allegra, and Sartyn fell silent.

Apparently the line had been crossed at last.

Allegra returned equably, "I imagine you're thinking of the creamed spinach."

"Possibly."

And so they went on, effectively preventing Sartyn from any further confidences. Very Anthony Trollope. Or possibly Agatha Christie, given Grace's suspicions. All that was missing were the vicar, a big-game hunter, and a breathless, panting ingenue on a bicycle— or possibly a unicycle, taking present company into account. Cordelia was a token ingenue, although of the Addams Family sort.

"If you're not interested in literature, what is your field?" Grace inquired of Sartyn when there was a pause in the conversation.

He gave her a supercilious glance. "Archaeology."

"Really? Where did you do your fieldwork?"

"Cyaneae." He went on to fill them in on his credentials earned while working as reference librarian in a university library.

Grace fastened on one point. "Cyaneae? That's in Turkey, isn't it? I was reading about the Roman sarcophagi in the rock tombs on the cliffs."

"That reminds me," put in Lady Vee. "Has Peter found me my mummy case yet?"

Sartyn looked ready to phone Scotland Yard's Art and Antiques Squad on the spot. Grace hastened to say, "Well, no. It takes time. There are proper legal channels that must be followed."

Lady Vee seemed disgusted with this lack of initiative. "Surely the *deah* boy has certain *connections*?"

"Patently." Sartyn sneered.

Grace turned on him. "By any chance, did you know the man who was murdered? I understand *he* was from Turkey."

Sartyn looked offended. "I did not." He reached for his wineglass.

"Oh, *do* tell us all about your latest case, Grace," Allegra invited with more than a hint of mockery. She turned to Sartyn. "Grace is something of an amateur sleuth."

"So I've heard." He downed his glass of wine.

He was not the only one putting it away. Unless Grace did not know her young ladies, Cordelia was quietly getting crocked on the white wine. Forget Agatha Christie; comparisons to P. G. Wodehouse were probably more apt.

Meeting her gaze, Cordelia chirped, "You're the one who found those buttons." She giggled. "Lord Byron's buttons. You seem awfully young."

"For what?"

Cordelia giggled again.

Oh boy, thought Grace. "It sounds like you're interested in the Romantics, as well."

"I like Shelley," Cordelia said. "He believed in Free Love."

"He believed in many things," Grace replied. She hoped that didn't sound as prim as she suspected. From the gleam in Cordelia's eyes, it did.

"But he especially believed in Free Love. He ran off with Mary Shelley when she was only sixteen, and his first wife drowned herself."

"She was not Mary Shelley at that time," Cordelia's aunt corrected, entirely missing the point, in Grace's opinion. "She was Mary Wollstonecraft Godwin."

Cordelia said with relish, "First Shelley wanted Mary to live with him and his wife Harriet, but when Harriet refused, he ran off with Mary. He was also the lover of her half sister Fanny and her stepsister Claire."

And probably one or two others, Grace thought wryly, but she didn't think it a good idea to encourage Cordelia's interest in this direction.

Dessert was served, but Grace barely had a chance to sample the light-as-air daffodil cake garnished with rose geranium leaves before Lady Vee made their excuses and hied them both off through the French doors that led from the terrace.

The room was stuffed with Empire furniture and gilt-framed pictures of handsome young Moors. Lady Vee poured two doses of the inevitable sherry, and Grace braced herself for trouble.

"Grace, my *deah*, what do you think of my little niece Cordelia?"

"She seems a nice girl," Grace said. She had no idea what Cordelia seemed like. "I didn't realize you had another niece."

"Great-niece, actually. She's my brother Hugo's granddaughter. I'm keeping her for the summer."

Since Grace had never heard of Hugo before, this didn't clarify much. She couldn't imagine any sane person sending their teenage daughter to stay with Lady Venetia, who sounded like she was boarding a puppy in her kennel.

"I could not help but notice the way the child took to you."

"She did?"

"She wishes to be a writer, you know. She's a *deah* sweet child. Perhaps a bit headstrong, but with the proper guidance . . ."

Oh my God, thought Grace. She wants to engage me as governess. "I really don't think—"

"Ah, but I do. In fact, I've given it a great deal of thought. Don't you Yanks have something called the

Big Sister Foundation?" The kohl-lined eyes fastened on Grace. "Perhaps we could reach some arrangement. You could take little Cordelia places, places of cultural and academic interest. You could share the occasional meal with her. At my expense naturally."

Terrific. As though her life were not complicated enough.

But since she needed information from Lady Vee, Grace was hesitant to refuse her outright. She hedged. "Have you spoken to Cordelia about this yet?"

Lady Vee looked ever so slightly guilty.

Grace's heart sank. She thought of those badly bitten fingernails and the impudent but hopeful way the girl looked to Lady Vee for approval. "I promise to think it over," she said firmly. "Right at the moment, I'm preparing for the conference. By the way, did you happen to know any of the Mallows, Lady Vee? Did you know John Mallow by any chance?"

Lady Vee knew when to hold them and when to fold them. She poured herself another thimbleful of sherry and mused, "Johnny Mallow. I hadn't thought of him in years."

"He was engaged to Eden Monkton?"

"You seem very well informed, my *deah*." She made a face. "But of course you're right. We were all great friends, knew each other since our prams. Johnny was engaged to Eden, but Sir Vincent disapproved of the match."

"Sir Vincent Monkton, the Egyptologist?"

Lady Vee's penciled brows rose in surprise. "Right

again, my *deah*. Yes, Johnny was quite interested in Egyptology himself, but it didn't do him much good with Sir Vincent." She gave a laugh that sounded like a sneer. "What an old terror the man was."

And who would know better? Grace finished off her sherry as Lady Vee reminisced.

"There was a crowd of us. Bunny Hooper-Smith, Johnny Mallow, Eden, old Fenwick, Aeneas Sweet, Cherry Ford—"

"Fenwick?" Grace fastened on this. "Fen?"

Lady Vee smiled a snarky smile. "Fenwick Archibald. What a *charactaah!*" Which was surely yet another instance of the pot calling the kettle black.

"Do you mean Professor Archibald in charge of the conference? Or would this be his son?"

"The same." Lady Vee added dryly, "Don't plant us all six feet under quite yet. As I recall, Aeneas Sweet was in relatively good health until you came along."

That remark was beyond outrageous, but Grace refused to be sidetracked. "I take it you're no longer on good terms with Professor Archibald?"

"Paugh!" In one word Lady Vee summed up both her professional and personal opinion of her old chum.

"What happened?"

The faintest smile touched the scarlet lips. "We *diffaahed* over Byron's decision to put the child Allegra in the convent at Bagna Cavallo. Fenwick believed that Byron acted selfishly, that he should have handed the child over to her mother, in effect to Shelley's menagerie."

Clare Clairmont, Byron's lover, had been Shelley's sister-in-law. As Cordelia had noted at lunch, Clare (who changed her name from Jane to Clara to Clare to Claire) enjoyed a ménage-à-trois with her half sister Mary and Percy Shelley—when she wasn't in pursuit of the ever-elusive Lord Byron.

Grace deduced, "Professor Fen was a Shelleyan?"

"Correct."

There could be no doubt, then. Professor Fenwick Archibald was the expert that John Mallow had relied on to authenticate the poem.

"He was a tad older than the rest of us," Lady Vee reflected. "He must be a thousand years old by now. The son of the Nether Wasdale vicar. Poor as church mice, but good stock." She shrugged a bony shoulder.

Grace barely paid attention to this, too excited over the knowledge that "tetchy old Fen" was indeed still alive and could possibly shed light on the Shiloh letter. She need no longer worry about what had become of John Mallow. Still, curiosity prompted her to ask, "No one ever discovered what happened to John Mallow?"

"After he ran off with Arabella Monkton, you mean?"

"Who?"

"Bella Monkton." The beldam's eyes glistened. "Don't tell me you imagined there was some mystery to Johnny's lope?"

"Isn't there?"

Lady Vee chortled. "Not a whit. At least, none except how Johnny could prefer Bella. She was a rather intense girl, though pretty enough. Not a candle to Eden, but some men do go for those gypsy types."

"But he deserted, didn't he?"

Lady Vee looked nonplussed. "I . . . I really don't . . . he was in the Special Air Service, you know. Newly formed."

Which meant exactly what?

That she believed John Mallow had rejoined his regiment after running away with Bella Monkton? That while the notion of infidelity could be entertained, the idea of desertion was too scandalous?

"Did they marry, then?"

"Who?"

"Arabella Monkton and John Mallow."

"I suppose they might have done."

"You mean no one knows?"

"I'm quite sure *I* don't know."

"What became of Eden Monkton?"

Lady Vee relaxed perceptibly. "She married Aubrey Mason. Nice chap. Pots of money. Not our crowd."

Damned with faint praise, Grace thought.

Lady Vee seemed to look back in time. "Eden died in '68, a couple of years after Mason."

"I see." She hesitated then plunged. "Do you suppose the family—?"

Lady Vee made an exasperated sound. "Do stop trying to be discreet, my *deah*. You're no good at it. You want to know about the baby, Jack. Eden kept him. There were two other children by Mason, Marcus and Sophia. The house and everything else went to Jack. Satisfied? Now, what *is* your interest?"

Good question. Grace was torn. There was a strong chance Lady Vee could shed light on the Shiloh letter, but Lady Vee had proven a persistent and unprincipled rival in Grace's first adventure. Where academic glory was concerned, Lady Vee could not be trusted any more than a junkie could be trusted with a gold watch.

And so Grace . . . lied.

❧ 10 ❧

Zipping down the highway in the Aston Martin, Grace tried to convince herself that she enjoyed the summer wind through her hair, but she actually found having that mop in her eyes sort of annoying. She shifted gears, and the car easily overtook a dawdling Ford Mondeo packed with children and dogs and parcels. Tourists—the Lake District roads were congested with them this time of year. Then Grace grinned. She was beginning to sound like a native.

As she overtook another car, she caught a glimpse of herself in her rearview mirror. Her hair had entirely escaped the morning's hairpins. It looked like Cousin It would be meeting Peter for drinks at the Cock's Crow.

A scarf, she thought vaguely. She needed to invest in a couple of chic silk scarves à la Audrey Hepburn. If only her other problems were as easily taken care of. But after all, the problem of what had become of John Mallow *was* already resolved.

Mallow had not mysteriously departed with the Shelley poem. He had simply run off with his fiancée's sister and—probably wisely—dropped out of sight. Grace supposed she could verify whether he had ever returned to his regiment, but what had become of him was no longer an issue.

The issue was the Shelley poem. And the most obvious explanation for why no one had heard anything about it was that tetchy old Fen had taken one look and dismissed it as a fake.

Still, it couldn't hurt to ask him. It would be interesting to hear his thoughts, and perhaps he knew the ending to the story. Grace was a girl who liked all the loose ends tied up. She could hardly wait to tell Peter what she had learned.

Peter, it turned out, had news of his own.

Not that he gave any hint when he rose to greet her as she came into the pub. As always, Grace's heart lifted at the sight of that tall figure. There was a sort of silly pleasure in being the companion of the most attractive man in the room.

He greeted her with a casual kiss and pulled out a chair. Whatever other qualities he might lack, he had lovely manners.

"I thought we might eat here tonight."

"It's fine with me." They usually did have one meal a week at the pub. Grace had come to enjoy the casual evenings socializing with their neighbors and catching up on local gossip.

Tonight the talk revolved around the murder of

Hayri Kayaci. Local opinion was that the Turk had been dispatched by someone in town for the arts festival. It was clear that no one wished to consider the possibility that he had been killed by one of their own.

Grace received sympathy for having discovered the body, and some gentle ribbing. She was coerced into giving her account of finding the body for the crowded room, which she did, uncomfortably aware of Peter's ironic gaze.

When they were at last able to move to a table of their own to eat their steak-and-mushroom pie, she filled him in on what she had learned from Lady Vee. Peter drank ale and ordered Grace drinks and listened. He was a very good listener.

"I'll be gone for a few days," he mentioned casually, as they were on their way out the front door after their pleasantly uneventful evening.

Grace stood stock-still. The decision seemed a sudden one; he had given no hint of it at dinner. Not that it would have been easy to get a word in edgewise; she did tend to dominate the airspace when the subject turned to literature or her beloved Romantic poets.

"Oh?" She couldn't help a flash of unease.

Peter's thin mouth twitched with humor. "Don't fear. I'm not pulling a runner. It's merely a buying trip."

"Oh. Okay." She wondered how the police would view this sudden jaunt.

He leaned forward and kissed her. "Be a good girl."

Then with a mocking smile, he added, "Ah, but then you're always a good girl, aren't you?"

Sunday's church bells pealed sweet and silvery in the cool morning.

Grace had taken to going to church during the last few months, though she wasn't sure what her Unitarian parents would make of her Church of England connection.

Generally Grace found inspiration and peace in the homely sermons of the vicar. That morning she was intrigued by his argument that the lost sheep was dearer to the Lord than the sheep that followed unquestioning, although her thoughts kept straying from the spiritual plane and back to the morning edition of the paper.

Kayaci's murder was still front-page news in *The Clarion*, where the usual lead stories had to do with the condition of local roads and the struggle to preserve the endangered native red squirrel.

According to *The Clarion*, the police had interviewed local antique dealer Peter Fox and—gulp—visiting academic scholar Grace Hollister.

The paper had gone on to detail Grace's role in two previous homicide investigations and her part in restoring a valuable article of historical and literary interest to the British Museum.

There was a smudgy and not very flattering photo of Grace taken at the previous year's Christmas pantomime.

She couldn't decide if she was more rattled at being

connected with yet another murder investigation, or the fact that the photo made her look about ten pounds heavier than she was.

Why was all this attention being focused on her and not Peter?

Not that she wanted Peter to be the focus of anyone's suspicions, but she felt uncomfortable with her center-stage role.

Remembering the teasing at the pub the previous evening, she wondered if others were taking note of how often she had been the first to arrive at the scene of a crime. In crime novels the person who found the body was always considered a prime suspect; Grace hoped that was not true of real life.

She recognized Detective Inspector Drummond as she was filing out of the church. He nodded with distant courtesy, and belatedly, Grace nodded back.

She had never noticed Drummond at the services before, and she thought she probably would have. He was awfully good-looking in a lantern-jawed way, and he did have a sort of stiff-necked presence. She wondered briefly if he was there in some official capacity. But no, he left the church, got into a silver sedan, and drove off. With relief, Grace watched him navigate the narrow crowded street and disappear. She was fair-minded enough to know her antipathy was mostly due to a guilty conscience—though not as guilty a conscience as Drummond was liable to imagine.

Grace got in her own car and headed out of the village. She had started supplementing her income by writing articles for literary and small magazines back in the States. With Peter out of town, it seemed the perfect afternoon to make a long-postponed visit to Hill Top Farm, the home of beloved children's author Beatrix Potter.

As Grace drove, it occurred to her that this would have made the ideal outing for Cordelia. Briefly she considered phoning up Brougham Manor, but at the last minute she decided to hold off making any commitment to Big Sisterhood.

Hill Top Farm was located in Near Sawrey in Ambleside. The trip from Innisdale to Ambleside was definitely not for the fainthearted. Although it was only about an hour's drive, the winding road was hair-raisingly steep and had several hairpin bends. In many spots the road was only wide enough for one vehicle. Blind curves made passing impossible for all but the most reckless drivers.

Grace was a confident driver, but she resolved to start for home before it was dark. She did not fancy trying to negotiate these curves half-blind.

At last she reached Near Sawrey. Putting the top up on the Aston Martin, she left it in the car park next to the Tower Bank Arms and walked the hundred yards or so to the museum.

The farmhouse looked like something out of a Beatrix Potter storybook, and in fact, Grace soon discovered the seventeenth-century stone house and classic cottage gardens had provided inspiration for Potter's work.

Potter bought Hill Top in 1905 with the royalties

from her first books, written while she still lived with her parents in London. Many of her first and best-loved stories were written in the small house with the rambling rose framing the front door.

It was a charming place. Grace wandered around the gardens, which were sweetly and nostalgically scented by honeysuckle and other blooms. Foxglove, sweet Cicely, lupine, peony, lavender, and philadelphus grew in luscious abandon. Like all true cottage gardens, this one was a combination of pretty and practical. In the kitchen garden, vegetables, fat strawberries, raspberries, currants, gooseberries, and rhubarb looked ready for the picking. The air hummed with bees and the murmur of literary acolytes. Grace made notes and waited her turn to go inside the tiny house.

Once inside, she filed through the rooms that had been home to Potter and her husband William. The cottage was crowded with Potter's wonderful antiques, and Grace paused to admire the oak spinning wheel stationed before the fireplace.

She had the odd sensation that someone was watching her and she glanced up from the spinning wheel. The room was packed with sightseers, but no one seemed to be paying Grace any special attention.

She moved on to a display of photos, watching the glass for the reflections of the people behind her. But there was nothing to see. No one showed any interest in her.

Grace moved on, noting the collections of Chinese and English porcelain, oil paintings and tinsel pictures, the antique dolls and children's tea sets. Hill

Top had been left to the National Trust in 1943 with the proviso that it be kept exactly as Potter left it, complete with her furniture and china. It remained the most visited literary shrine in the Lake District.

Afterward, she went next door to the gift shop and bought copies of Potter stories for her nieces. She had not seen the girls in nearly two years, and as she painstakingly picked out the little books, she was again swept by that yearning for home and family.

Studying the delicate watercolor illustrations brought back fond memories of these gentle tales. Grace smiled faintly, glancing through *The Tale of Jemima Puddleduck*. She had nearly forgotten the story of headstrong but naive Jemima who had had a life-changing experience after making the acquaintance of a civil-tongued and foxy, but decidedly dangerous, stranger.

Flipping through the familiar pages, she read, *When she reached the top of the hill, she saw a wood in the distance. She thought that it looked a safe quiet spot.*

Think again, Jemima, Grace thought wryly.

After making her purchases she went next door to the Tower Bank Arms for a late pub lunch. The Tower Bank Arms had appeared in *The Tale of Jemima Puddleduck* as "a small country inn."

She ordered ale and pheasant pie. The pheasant was interesting and not, in Grace's opinion, in the least like chicken. She jotted down notes on her visit and relaxed, sipping the last of her ale, listening absently to the local chatter.

It was easy to lose track of the hour, and by the

time she walked back to her car it was nearly six, and the long, lingering English twilight threw shadows across the grass.

Again, Grace had that odd feeling that she was being watched. Unlocking the Aston Martin, she glanced around the car park, but again there was nothing to make her uneasy. Families were loading children into car seats; cars were pulling out onto the highway.

She got in the Aston Martin and started the engine. It purred into life, and she shook her head at the vague notion that had formed there.

The evening sky had deepened to indigo streaked with yellow. In the distance, the silhouetted mountains looked black and volcanic.

Grace ignored the scenic beauty around her and concentrated solely on her driving. The road home staggered up and over Greencrag Pass, uncoiling in a treacherous descent around Lake Swirlbeck. It would not smooth out until the homestretch, at least forty-five minutes away.

She cruised along, testing her brakes several times before she reached the really steep part of the road. There was no logical reason for her nervousness; she was a competent driver, the car was handling well, and it was not as though she had actually seen or heard anything strange.

The only other cars on the road grew impatient with her caution and passed her, red taillights disappearing into the dusk.

The road grew steeper, rising up, up, up, and falling

sharply away. She was reminded of the Hokusai woodblock of the men in the fishing boat trying to crest the great wave.

Concentrating on the tricks and turns of the road, it was some time before she noticed headlights growing larger and larger in her rearview mirror. Grace slowed, looking for a place to pull off, but the road was too narrow, with a lake on one side and mountain on the other.

The other car was now right on her tail, headlights blinding in her mirror. Grace tapped the gas, making the Aston Martin leap ahead. The road wound sharply; she could see the lake sparkling behind the bushes and trees. She spared a glance in the rearview but it was too dark to discern the make or model or the car. She had the impression of a large dark sedan, but most cars seemed oversized in comparison to the Aston Martin.

Headlights blazed behind her once more, and there was a sudden, appalling bang. The Aston Martin rocked, then righted.

Grace's breath let out on a half sob, her hands tightening on the wheel. She forced herself to stay focused on her driving. One mistake could land her in the water or the mountain, and at that speed, either could be fatal.

She accelerated to stay ahead. Another bump could send her into a spinout that would send her fishtailing into oblivion.

Thank God I didn't bring Cordelia, she thought, sailing around another curve. A detached corner of her brain noted how beautifully the sports car cornered each turn. She would never have dreamed of putting it to this kind of test.

Decelerate in, accelerate out. She could almost hear her father's voice, recalling her earliest driving lessons.

Would they never be past the lake and onto straight highway, where she might be able to put some distance between herself and the other driver? The road continued to snake through the hills as far as her headlights could reach.

If they met another vehicle on the narrow track, it would be over for all of them.

There was a second horrendous bang, and the Aston Martin's tires went off the embankment. Grace wrenched the wheel, and the car regained the road.

They whipped around a curve, the other car falling a few seconds behind, then catching up to her. Grace had a dizzying view of the lake below.

Half-remembered stories of survival started her fumbling for the window lever. Clumsily she cranked the window down an inch or two. Unfortunately, this distraction from the road caused her to misjudge the hairpin turn that came out of nowhere.

The Aston Martin's right tires went off the pavement, and the car plunged off the road and down the woody hillside.

Shock held Grace in a kind of suspended animation as the car crashed and bounced through brush and tree limbs. Rocks and dirt flew up in the cracked light from her headlamps and rained down on the windshield and roof. Then the bushes turned to reeds and rushes, and Grace saw the inky black bulk of the lake.

Instinctively she braked, jamming her foot down on the pedal, but even if the brakes had still been working, the velocity of the car's momentum could not be stopped.

The Aston Martin slammed down hard, the black water flying up in a great wave.

The car began to sink.

11

Silver bubbles streamed up in the green-gray water, then the headlights went out.

Icy water spilled into the open window and through the joints of the convertible top. Grace could hear the sickening slop of water as she frantically unrolled the window next to her. Many games of worst-case scenario informed her decision, yet as the lake gushed in, she screamed in mingled fright and panic.

The theory was that the water would enter the car and equalize the pressure between the inside and the outside. That would make it possible to shove open the door or escape through a window. But the car seemed to tilt forward and list sideways as the water flooded in, and Grace was trapped beneath a waterfall.

Her hands went to her seat belt. To her relief, it snapped open. She was free to move out from under the torrent of water, although the car's cramped interior did not make it easy. She climbed over the gearbox and tried the passenger-side door.

Several tons of water pushed against the door. She gave up and unrolled that window, too. Water surged in.

She could not see, which was the worst part, but Grace could feel the water was already up to her chest.

There was still enough air to breathe. Grace forced herself to calm down and think. She remembered Peter saying once that most people would rather die than think. That was *not* going to happen to her.

If she could not push open the door or swim through the cascading water, she would simply wait till the car filled, then the pressure inside and out would be balanced. It was a simple matter of physics. She refused to let herself think about how far the car had sunk. She refused to think about the fact that many of the lakes were so cold and deep that prehistoric fish still lived in them.

She groped in the frigid water, feeling and flinching from something slimy. At last her fingers closed on the strap of her purse. She jerked it out of the water and pulled it open. Inside she found her pocket flashlight and flicked it on.

The pallid ray of light illumed the car interior awash in a murky tide. Leaks seemed to be springing everywhere. Maybe that was a good thing, or maybe the car would be torn apart and she would be crushed. Better not to think about that.

The water was by then up to Grace's chin. The torrent of water had stopped, and the Aston Martin seemed to float in a kind of eerie stillness. Except they were not floating, they were diving steadily and swiftly to the bottom.

"Oh God," Grace prayed between chattering teeth.

She switched out the light, looped her bag over her shoulder as though she were starting out on a walk, and reached for the door handle.

"One, two, three." She took a deep breath. Her fingers clamped on the handle, and she used her shoulder to push the door open. She had to push hard; even so, she was surprised when it gave way.

Disoriented, she half fell, half groped her way out of the confines of the car and into the water. Instinctively she felt with her foot for the ground, but there was no ground. There was nothing below her but water, and she was falling through it, falling through water so pitch-black and so cold that the air seemed to freeze in her lungs.

Blindly, she began to kick toward the surface.

How far . . . how far . . . ?

Her lungs burned. She struggled to stay calm, to keep swimming. She hoped she was heading toward the surface, that she had not got so turned around that she was swimming down, deeper.

Her lungs felt as if they were going to explode, her body was screaming for oxygen. She *had* to breathe . . .

Grace's head broke the surface. The balmy night air caressed her wet face as she gulped in sweet lungfuls of oxygen. She had made it! Treading water, she continued to suck in deep breaths. She was alive. She had never felt so alive.

She could not have sunk as far as she feared, although it was surely deep enough to drown. The Stygian water around her glittered with points of light. Starlight, she realized, looking upward. She struck out for the shore, quietly kicking beneath the surface, dipping her hands softly through the water.

She was not far from the land. Her eyes raked the tree-studded hillside above, but it was too dark to see if anyone waited there. The road looked empty. No car idled there, headlights searching for her.

No cars at all.

A few strokes brought her into the reeds and floating weeds. She squelched through the mud and dropped down, panting and weak, on the spongy turf.

The smell of wet earth and dank water filled her nostrils. It was wonderful. A mosquito whined in her ear. That was wonderful, too. It was wonderful to be alive. To be unhurt and in one piece.

Someone had tried to run her off the road. Someone had deliberately forced her into the lake.

It made no sense. She had no enemies. Maybe some people found her a little annoying, maybe one or two women were jealous of her relationship with Peter, but actual *enemies*?

Who could possibly want to harm her? Memories of the previous year returned. Perhaps someone from Peter's past?

But that seemed far-fetched, even taking into account the strange turn her life had taken since first setting foot in Great Britain.

It must have something to do with Hayri Kayaci's

death. Someone must think she had seen something in the woods that night. But if she had seen something, she would have told the police; common sense should tell the killer that. If she knew anything, the police already knew it; so what would be the point of eliminating her after the fact?

Unless she knew something she didn't know she knew. Or . . . unless her attacker knew for a fact that she hadn't told what she knew. Because her attacker was Peter.

"No *way*," she said aloud, and the frogs, filling the night with their raucous chorus, fell silent.

Grace shivered. She refused to consider Peter, but looking at the thing objectively, the only person she was protecting by remaining silent was Peter. Peter knew that she had so far told the police nothing. He knew that she was uncomfortable lying. He could probably surmise that the police suspected her of withholding information.

And what? she asked herself angrily. Peter was trying to kill her before she cracked and confirmed for the police what they already suspected? That wasn't objective thinking, it was plain old ridiculous.

No, if anyone was trying to kill her, it was more likely to be someone who actively disliked her—like Scott Sartyn. He had been on the hillside that night. True, he behaved as though he believed Grace had something to do with Kayaci's death, but that could be a smoke screen. Grace had plenty of experience with devious adolescents who tried to throw her off the track by accusing her of everything from prejudice to cruel and unusual homework assignments. There was something about Sartyn that roused her suspicions, something she couldn't put her finger on.

Then again, just because Sartyn disliked her didn't automatically mean he was evil.

She closed her eyes, too exhausted to think about it anymore.

Instantly she saw again that glimpse of the car interior flooded with murky water and debris. She thought of Shelley, who had always feared drowning, and who had finally drowned off the coast of Italy.

Finally, she believed she understood Peter's horror of confined spaces. If she hadn't gotten out . . .

The ground was cold and hard. She was soaked through, her wet clothes clinging to her shivering body.

It sank in on her that she was not reacting normally. She should not be lying there thinking about Percy Bysshe Shelley's last struggles for breath, or what fourteen months in a Turkish prison had done to Peter. She should be trying to get help. She was probably in shock.

She peered at the face on her watch. It was too dark to read the dial.

Grace made a great effort and sat up, rifling through the soggy contents of her purse. She found her cell phone and tried it. It chirped forlornly twice, then nothing.

She gathered herself and pushed up to her feet. Every muscle in her body screeched in protest. Sweat broke out on her forehead, and her teeth began to chatter. So much for being unhurt and in one piece. The initial numbness had worn off, and she felt bruised and battered from head to toe.

She stared up the uneven hillside and nearly sat down again. There was no way she could get herself up that cliff.

But what was the alternative? She couldn't sit there all night, and it might be all night before anyone found her. And who would be looking for her?

Something crackled in the underbrush, and she caught her breath. Someone *might* come looking for her—the person who had driven her off the road.

12

Years afterward, Grace used to dream about climbing that hillside. At the time, it felt like a dream. Her sodden clothes seemed to weigh a ton, her trembling muscles felt like overcooked spaghetti as she scrabbled her way up, grabbing at bushes and jutting roots to keep herself from sliding back down. She climbed and climbed but never seemed to reach the top.

She kept climbing, promising herself a warm bath and a soft bed. Though the evening was mild, she felt chilled to the bone. She promised herself a hot drink and the entire next day in that soft bed. By the time she groped her way over the top of the hillside and crawled onto the paved highway, she had committed to a week in bed and a visit to a masseuse.

The road was empty of everything except a lone sheep, who expressed a woolly surprise at her appearance. Grace picked herself up and started off down the narrow lane, and the sheep followed at a prudent distance, baahing at her every so often.

Perhaps he was the lost sheep that the vicar had spoken of at this morning's service. Grace bit back a hysterical giggle, and trudged on. And on.

She began to wonder if she was dreaming after all. Perhaps she was lying in her soft bed, and this was merely a strange dream. Nightmare. She had had dreams like this, everyone had. Dreams where you walk and walk up hills and down hills and never seem to get anywhere.

Behind her, the sheep bleated.

She did not remember having a sheep in her dream before, but perhaps she had been counting sheep in her nice soft bed when she fell asleep, and this one had persisted into her sleep.

The *clip clop* of his hooves on the road seemed to echo through the night.

Far down the highway, Grace could see headlights coming toward her. She tried to decide whether to flag it down; but in the end, the fear that her attacker might be coming back for her sent her off the side of the road and into the woods.

The sheep followed, still bleating inquiry.

Through the bushes, Grace watched the car zoom by. Absently she patted the sheep, now nibbling at her damp clothes. She realized that she had reached Innisdale Wood, and that the village was only a few miles down the road.

That was the good news. The bad news was that she could not walk any farther. She turned and saw the friendly lights of a farmhouse twinkling through the trees. Mallow Farm, she realized. Just a bit farther . . .

She dragged on, coming at last to a wooden stile. There, she and her woolly companion parted ways. Grace clambered over the fence and dropped to the ground. The sheep baahed forlornly after her as she waded through the deep meadow grass. She passed deteriorating barns and crumbling stone walls, and the weeds and wildflowers underfoot gave way to patchy grass. She was weaving through an orchard of ancient apple trees when a figure stepped out of the shadows to intercept her.

Grace stood stock-still, speechless at the apparition of Kameko Musashi in black spandex leggings and a white muscle T. Her trim, muscular body glistened with sweat. What struck Grace speechless were the elaborate and amazing tattoos that covered Kameko's arms and as much of her chest as was visible in the poor light. Red-eyed dragons and poisonous-looking flowers spiraled up her sinewy upper arms and shoulders.

Grace's exhausted brain tried to place those tattoos.

"Yakuza," she said faintly.

"Hush." Kameko Musashi looked swiftly over her shoulder.

What was she doing out here? Chauffeur boot camp? Ninja training exercises? Grace was still trying to work it out when the Illustrated Woman's hand closed on her arm. "Ms. Horrister, what is the meaning of this?" Her small hard hand felt along Grace's sleeve, then her tone changed. "You are wet through."

"Someone ran my car off the road," Grace said. "I need to call the police." Her legs began to fold.

What happened after that was a bit fuzzy in Grace's memory. Somehow Kameko got her into house, gave her a stiff brandy, and summoned the police.

The other servants observed these proceedings with silent suspicion. Seated at the long kitchen table, brandy snifter cradled in both hands, Grace watched them watching her, and foggily wondered what was going on.

Somewhere in the midst of all of that, the Shogun burst into the kitchen. The servants began bowing. Mr. Matsukado waved them off and insisted on taking charge. Despite Kameko's calm explanation and Grace's protests, a doctor was called and more brandy was poured. Mr. Matsukado gave a great many orders, contradicted a great many more, and had a brief sharp exchange in Japanese with Kameko.

Grace was whisked upstairs and installed first in a hot shower, then in a scalding hot sunken bath.

By the time she was permitted to dry off, she felt parboiled and more than woozy. She was given a very large silk dressing gown with an embroidered dragon on the back—and another brandy. Thanks to all the alcohol or perhaps the hot bath, she had stopped shaking and felt pleasantly numb.

She sat down on the four-poster bed and checked out the room. The furnishings were probably original, but the windows were all new, and the walls had been freshly plastered and repainted.

For all she knew it might be John Mallow's bedroom, although thanks to the extensive renovations, it was doubtful John or any of the Mallows would have recognized a single room in their ancestral home.

A soft knock on the door interrupted her thoughts. She called, "Come in."

Kameko, now modestly garbed in a tailored pant-suit, stepped inside and informed her that the police were waiting downstairs.

It was interesting to Grace that Kameko evinced no interest in Grace's accident. In her place Grace would have been asking all kinds of questions, but perhaps this reticence was a cultural thing. Or perhaps this was a house where such incidents were a common occurrence. Kameko hadn't hesitated to call the police, so there could be nothing nefarious in her lack of curiosity.

Kameko escorted her to the drawing room with its red-velvet draperies and Tiffany lamps. Grace was less than thrilled to recognize Detective Inspector Drummond accompanying a constable.

She was sure Drummond was an efficient officer, but something about him put her on edge. She didn't have the energy to be clever; she was exhausted phys-ically and mentally; and the brandy was affecting her emotional reflexes. She knew it, but she still couldn't help the antagonism that crept into her greeting.

"Do all the other policemen have the night off? Or do you work every case?"

"Every case you're in involved in," Drummond retorted. He was wearing jeans and a yellow polo shirt, so maybe he had been off duty and had been called in. She was not flattered at the idea.

She sat down, wishing she did not have to face the

detective inspector in her dressing gown—worse, a dressing gown that looked like it belonged to a sumo-sized geisha girl. She pulled the tie of the dressing gown tight.

After hinting unsuccessfully that Mr. Matsukado and Miss Musashi should depart, Drummond started off by asking Grace where her car was. That indicated to Grace that either she had not previously been too coherent or everyone's listening skills left much to be desired. On the whole, she chose to believe everyone else was the problem.

After she had explained yet again the whereabouts of her car, there was a sharp silence.

"Are you saying your car was forced off the road into Swirlbeck?"

"Give you enough time, and you'll get there eventually," she told him, and propped her chin on her hand—except she ruined the effect by missing the edge of the table with her elbow so that she did a little drunken lurch forward.

The constable cleared his throat. It was very aggravating, although Drummond couldn't have looked more poker-faced.

"I see," he said. "I'm afraid this is the first I've heard about your car being forced into the lake."

"I say," exclaimed the Shogun, "are we to understand that your car is at the bottom of Lake Swirlbeck?"

"My beautiful little Aston Martin," Grace agreed, and burst into tears.

The tears caught her by surprise. She mopped her face hastily with the flowing sleeve of the blue dressing gown while the gentlemen exchanged uncomfortable looks. Kameko poured brandy into a snifter and brought it to Grace.

"*Baka* men," Kameko said under her breath.

There was no trace of the Tattooed Lady beneath the dark, mannish suit. Kameko was a girl who clearly loved dressing up.

"I think I've probably had enough," she told Kameko. "I had a late lunch at the Tower Bank Arms. It's in *Jemima Puddleduck.*" Her voice wavered on the name of Jemima Puddleduck. She hoped that she was not like Jemima Puddleduck, cozily ensconced in a feather-lined trap.

"Drink," Kameko ordered.

Grace gulped down the brandy, sneezed, and got control of herself.

She was aware that DI Drummond watched her every move. He said at last, "If what you say is true, you showed amazing resource getting yourself out of that car alive."

"Thank you," she replied, although he had not phrased it as a compliment. She wiped her eyes again, relieved to be mistress of herself once more.

Then the questions began in earnest. Did she see the other driver? Could she read the number plate? What make of car? How long had the car followed her before the attack? Had she noticed anyone following her earlier that day? Had anything happened at Hill Top Farm that made her suspicious? Had she had any arguments or disagreements with anyone recently?

"Only you," she told the detective inspector.

Drummond looked taken aback. "Naturally I don't count," he objected, sounding testy.

"I don't see why not."

Mr. Matsukado giggled.

The questions started again.

"No, no, no," answered Grace tiredly. She couldn't think about it anymore. The oversize dressing gown slipped from her shoulder, and she pulled it up hastily. She met Detective Inspector Drummond's light eyes. They were the shade of blue that looks gray in certain light.

They looked gray in that light.

Another of the Shogun's servants appeared in the drawing room doors and announced that the doctor had arrived.

"I think that's about it," Drummond said, and the constable flipped closed his notepad. "Naturally you'll ring us if you remember anything else."

Grace nodded.

They rose to leave, but the detective inspector paused on his way through the double doors.

"Where is Mr. Fox this evening?"

Grace glared at him. "He's on a buying trip."

"Convenient."

She opened her mouth, but another sneeze interrupted her. She felt as if her head had been stuffed with pepper.

"We'll be in touch, Ms. Hollister," Drummond informed her. "In the meantime, if I were you, I'd watch my back."

❧ 13 ❧

Just because I'm paranoid doesn't mean my boyfriend isn't out to kill me. Grace was not in good spirits, having woken at Mallow Farm with a raging head cold and a collection of bruises more colorful than Kameko's tattoos.

Or had she dreamed up those tattoos? The night before had taken on a distant surreal quality. Had someone really tried to run her off the highway, or was it simply a case of mistaken road rage? Did they *have* road rage in England? More importantly, did they have NyQuil?

She didn't really believe that Peter was her attacker, but it was obvious that DI Drummond did. She understood that the detective inspector had a policeman's jaded view of human nature, but she didn't think much of his detecting skills. Did she really seem like the kind of woman who couldn't tell the difference between a sociopath and a . . . a perfectly decent scoundrel?

Perhaps Drummond was a fan of gothic romances.

She liked the idea of the humorless, uptight—and too-good-looking—inspector kept up late at night, poring over the adventures of damsels in negligees.

Breakfast was served on a tray in her room. Grace studied the lacquered bowls doubtfully, but the miso soup proved to be hot and salty and soothing to her scratchy throat. She hadn't appetite for the rest of the dishes, but two cups of tea gave her the strength to drag her aching body out of bed and scrutinize her reflection in the mirror.

What is it with thee, sister? Thou art pale.

She looked like something that spent a lot of time underwater: blanched and dark-eyed. Her hair looked flat and lifeless. There was a bruise along the side of her neck where the seat belt had jerked tight. Her eyes were red, and her nose was pink.

Very depressing. She was further depressed to think of her beloved car at the bottom of Lake Swirlbeck. Would the police retrieve it? How expensive would such an operation be, and would her insurance cover it?

No doubt DI Drummond would be happy to give her the bad news.

She dismissed the annoying Drummond from her thoughts and set about getting ready to face the day. Her clothes would never be the same again, but they were freshly laundered. She dressed and opened the door to her room.

She was startled to find Mr. Matsukado in the hallway. She had the distinct impression he had been hovering outside her door waiting for her to wake—an unsettling thought.

"Oh, good mordning," Grace said thickly.

The Shogun, dressed in flannels and a Fair Isle pullover that made him look like an overage schoolboy, looked sympathetic. "Ms. Hollister, you are unwell."

"I may have caud a chill." She sneezed, and Mr. Matsukado's hand went to the banister as though to steady himself in the typhoon.

"Ms. Hollister, I must speak to you," he said urgently.

Grace's sole ambition was to get home and into her own bed. She groaned inwardly, but, after all, she owed Mr. Matsukado and his household for their hospitality of the night before.

Obediently she followed him into the library, wincing at the bright glare flooding down from the giant skylight. The room looked as if it had been ransacked the night before. Papers were everywhere, strewn on every available flat surface as well as scattered across the carpet. Her host waved off Grace's expression of dismay with that disconcerting giggle.

"No, no. All is in order. There is method in my madness, don't you know!"

She didn't know, but she hadn't the energy to worry about it. Grace sank into a comfortable club chair that she recognized from its brief stay at Rogue's Gallery. She would have liked nothing better than to close her eyes and go to sleep in the honey-colored sunlight flooding through the skylight.

Mr. Matsukado was all solicitousness, ordering grapes and ice water for her. He rang for one manservant to fetch a pillow and afghan, and another to supply a box of tissues.

"Really," she protested feebly, "if we could judst . . ."

Mr. Matsukado waved at her as though warning her to silence. Grace's voice died, and he went over to a wall safe, unlocked it, and removed an oblong object. He brought the object to Grace. She stared down at a leather journal embossed with a compass.

It looked old. Not 1800s old, but old. The faded leather was genuine. She traced the compass with a gentle finger and looked inquiringly at her host.

"I'm afraid I don't . . ."

"It is difficult to know where to start, what?"

"Why not start at the beginning?"

He nodded curtly, then began to stride up and down the room with restless energy. Grace did not know what to make of it. She sipped her ice water and resisted the temptation to open the journal or ledger or whatever it was.

Suddenly Mr. Matsukado swung on heel and faced her. "Ms. Hollister, you and I share a great passion!"

"Uh . . ."

He giggled at her reaction. "Ours is a passion for the writings of your English Romantic poets, what?"

"What? I mean, yes."

He gave her a cunning look. "I believe we share a secret, Ms. Hollister."

"We do?"

"It is the secret of the Sphinx."

Grace sat very still, as still as the Sphinx had

through centuries of sand and sun. Whatever he read in her face he took as affirmation.

"For many years, it was my dream to find an original lost work by one of these great men and present it to the world."

A tickle between her eyes had Grace reaching for a tissue to muffle her sneeze. "I guess id's everywad's dream," she managed with the insular view of the academic.

He approached her chair and leaned over her, his face close to hers. Grace withdrew. Uncomfortably, her eyes rose from his mouth working beneath the Shredded Wheat mustache to his incandescent gaze. She hoped he was not going to spontaneously combust.

He said in an undervoice, "For many years now I put out my tentacles—"

"Your *whad*?"

Mr. Matsukado looked uncertain. "My—how is it you say, *feelers*."

"Oh."

He straightened and began again to pace up and down the length of the room. Grace felt her forehead—107, 108? She wondered if she wasn't a bit light-headed. She sipped more ice water.

"One day in a shipment from England I found something most interesting. It was a journal by a man named John Mallow." He stared at Grace.

She coughed politely into her fist.

"He had a friend in Italy, this John Mallow. When war came, the friend sent many books and papers back to England for safekeeping. But the friend died, and John Mallow, sorting through his belongings, found what he believed was a poem—a sonnet—by the great English poet, Percy Shelley."

Grace could hear her own somewhat asthmatic breathing in the silence that followed. "How do you know all this?"

He pointed to the leather-bound book she held. Did young men even keep journals these days? Grace's fingers itched to open the book on her lap.

"The sonnet was titled 'Sate the Sphinx.' Have you heard of it?"

"No."

He breathed a relieved sigh. "I thought not."

Grace's mind was racing. Sate the Sphinx? Probably Sat the Sphinx; Shelley's spelling and punctuation were always a bit iffy—although perhaps it was sate. Impossible to know without reading the poem.

Matsukado was continuing. "I bought this house, the house of John Mallow, and I made up my mind to search for this poem."

"Bud surely the journald would tell you where the poemb is—was?"

"The journal ends in December 1941, when John Mallow returned to his regiment."

Two years year before Mallow had disappeared. The year the Japanese had bombed Pearl Harbor. She glanced at Mr. Matsukado, wondering if he was aware of any irony in his obsession with a lost English soldier. Except, like herself, it was not the lost soldier that interested him, it was the lost poem.

"There's no hint of what became of the poem?"

Mr. Matsukado shook his head regretfully.

"Was there proof that the poem was Shelley's?"

Another shake.

Grace bit her lip. No, because in 1943, Mallow had been waiting for "tetchy old Fen" to authenticate it. Had he given the poem to Fen to keep, and if so, had Fen ever returned it?

Mr. Matsukado advanced on her again. "I believe that somewhere in this house, perhaps in the items that you and Mr. Fox returned to me, is this poem." He looked as feverish as Grace felt.

"It's possible."

"I wish to propose a partnership." Mr. Matsukado bent over her and spoke in a heavy stage whisper. "A partnership between you and me."

"I—"

"If you will help me locate this poem, I will share with you all remuneration, all fame and fortune."

She stared, her hand unconsciously stroking the embossed leather. "Why?"

"Because you are an expert on these matters. And because you have a knack for finding what is lost." His eyes gleamed. "And because it would be nice to have someone who understands and can share in my triumph."

Grace didn't know about that, but she wasn't about to debate her credentials. She wanted in on this quest.

She opened the journal.

* * *

It was a relief to be home where she could give in to feeling miserable. Her head felt like the Statue of Liberty's torch.

She pulled out the sofa bed and, despite the warmth of the day, cocooned herself in pillows and bedclothes. The sofa did a couple of slow and sickening swoops. Hectic images flooded her mind, memories of the terrifying drive with headlights burning like comets in her rear window, of the car plunging into the blackness of what might have been her watery tomb, of Percy Shelley's battered body burning on a funeral pyre while Byron and Trelawney looked on.

Grace's eyes jerked open.

That last image wasn't memory. It was sheer imagination triggered by the Shogun's amazing revelation. Was it possible that the sonnet still existed, that it was genuine? She tried to imagine the first line.

"Solemn Sphinx, were I as stedfast as thou . . ."

"Hail to thee, blithe Sphinx . . ."

Well . . . probably not.

She woke up from an unpleasant dream in which she was arguing with Detective Inspector Drummond. It occurred to her that she never dreamed about Peter. Was that significant? He certainly filled a large portion of her waking thoughts. Just than she was wondering where he was, and what he might be up to. He had said he was not pulling "a runner," but would he tell her if he was? Might he someday disappear out of her life without a word of warning?

In the midst of these none-too-pleasant reflections,

her landlady, Sally Smithwick came around with a pot of chicken soup and something called Beecham's All-In-One. Grace dosed herself with soup and the yellow syrup, and sank into a deep dreamless sleep.

When she woke, she lay quietly listening to the doves cooing under the eaves with what her poets called "sleep-drowsed senses."

The danger and fear of the previous night seemed a lifetime ago.

Grace flipped through her edition of *The Great Romantics*, and was lost for a time in the delicate seduction of Shelley's verse.

And the sunlight clasps the earth,
And the moonbeams kiss the sea—
What are all these kissings worth,
If thou kiss not me?

Of all the Romantics, it was Shelley whose work most touched her. She thought of those heartbreaking fragments Mary Shelley had published after his death. Poems to his little son William, following the child's death from malaria at age three. Half-started poems to Mary, whose own grief had left Shelley feeling shut out and abandoned.

She read over her notes for her talk at the conference and slept some more, waking to the soft tap, tapping of her front door.

Miss Webb, a vision in lime green and tangerine polka dots, stood on the cottage stoop. "Oh, jolly good. You're home. I was afraid you might be at Rogue's

Gallery this afternoon. You will pardon the intrusion, my dear. I've had a rather odd experience."

Grace realized she hadn't given the shop a thought all day. She hoped Peter's finances could stand losing another day of business. Not that he didn't take a day off whenever he pleased.

"Please come in," she invited, trying to sound gracious but wishing that she had never opened the door.

Taking in the mussed sheets on Grace's foldout bed, Miss Webb said, "Under the weather, my dear?" Unlike Sally Smithwick, she had apparently not heard of Grace's adventures the previous evening.

"Actually, I'm feeling much better," Grace lied politely, sweeping up her bed, box of tissues, and books with ruthless efficiency. "Tea?"

Miss Webb assented, and Grace went into the kitchen, washed her hands, and put on the electric kettle. She cut two slices of chocolate sponge cake and fixed a tea tray.

From outside the kitchen window, she could hear the Smithwick children playing. "Not last night but the night before, twenty-four robbers came knocking at my door . . ."

Smiling faintly, she put the tea things on the small kitchen table and beckoned to Miss Webb. She was surprised to find that she was ravenous. She ate every bite of her cake and drank several cups of tea. Miss Webb also seemed to appreciate the sponge cake, and Grace ended up dividing up the last of it between them.

When they had finished their tea, and Grace was clearing up, Miss Webb dusted the crumbs off her cardigan and came at last to the point. "Mr. Sartyn paid me a visit this morning."

"Did he?" Grace's nose tickled. She managed to raise her bathrobed arm in time to shield the tea tray and Miss Webb from her sneeze.

"Gracious," murmured Miss Webb.

"Sorry. Summer colds are the worst, aren't they?" she managed thickly.

"It's I who should be apologizing, my dear. You should be in bed."

You're telling me. Grace kept smiling, though she feared it was a gruesome effort.

Miss Webb's own smile was rueful. "As I was saying, Mr. Sartyn was asking about you, my dear. Afraid I made the mistake of thinking perhaps he had a romantic interest in you."

Grace's hands froze on the tea things. "Something changed your mind?"

"You see, I realized that he wanted to know what you knew about Eden Monkton. As a matter of fact, he was asking all kinds of questions about the Monktons."

"Like?" That made absolutely no sense to Grace. Why should anyone, let alone Sartyn, care about the Monktons? Could Sartyn be interested in the Shelley sonnet? It seemed unlikely, given his disparaging comments on poetry and poets. Besides, his field was archaeology.

"Afraid I didn't pay a lot of attention. I was . . .

well, troubled. He seemed like such a nice young man, but he was saying rather awful things about you." She fastened Grace with her pale, pale eyes.

"About me?" She wished her mind were sharper. She poured another cup of tea and gulped it down. "I can't imagine why he would be interested. In either myself or the Monktons."

"Can't imagine why *you* would be interested in the Monktons either, my dear." Miss Webb sounded amused.

"I'm not. Not per se. It's just . . ." Now that she and the Shogun had formed their partnership, was there really any reason to conceal the possible existence of the lost Shelley? "Miss Webb, did you ever hear anything about the local discovery of a lost work by Percy Bysshe Shelley?"

Miss Webb stared at Grace. "A lost work," she said at last. "By Shelley?"

Grace nodded. "A sonnet."

"No," Miss Webb said slowly. "No, I don't believe that I have. Forgive me, but your interest is in Lord Byron, isn't it?"

"I'm interested in all the Romantics." If she'd had to pick one to date, Grace would have gone for Keats. Shelley's obsession with death and his tendency to drift with life's tides was against her nature. And she certainly didn't kid herself that she could have held the interest of a notorious rake like Lord Byron.

"Shelley." Miss Webb smiled. "He was the one who ran off with the sixteen-year-old girl. The one who wrote *Frankenstein*."

"That's right. But you never heard anything about a poem being discovered locally?"

"Well, you know, I might not have paid much attention to such a thing, my dear. I don't say that I don't enjoy the occasional limerick, but I'm not much of a poetry aficionado. And, despite what you might think, I'm still a relative newcomer in these parts. People don't talk to me the way they do to one of their own." Her smile faded as she pointed that out, and she left not long after.

Grace, analyzing her expression, thought Miss Webb had looked like a woman who suddenly remembered something she wished she had tried harder to forget.

❧ 14 ❧

$\mathcal{P}$eter phoned that evening.

"There you are," he said in his lazy, slightly husky voice. "I was beginning to wonder whether you'd run off with the till money."

"I didn't work today."

"I know, I've been ringing the shop all afternoon." His tone altered, though he still spoke lightly. "Everything all right? You sound like you've been crying."

"I'm okay. I've got a cold. I—er—had an accident."

"What sort of accident?" She thought he sounded genuinely startled.

She filled him in on her experience. A resounding silence hummed down the line.

"Are you there?" she demanded finally when he said nothing after she finished her tale.

"I'm here." He sounded preoccupied, like someone making a sharp left turn and hoping his coffee didn't spill into his lap.

"A little sympathy would be nice."

"And you have it, my darling." That was worse

than the silence. That was like someone reading from a bad script.

Grace opened her mouth, but the exchange came in. A voice spoke in heavily accented French.

"Are you in France?" demanded Grace. Not that there was any reason he *shouldn't* be in France . . .

"No. That is, yes," Peter said, and for the first time in their acquaintance, he sounded flustered.

What the . . . ? Grace caught sight of herself in the mirror over her bureau. Her mouth was hanging open. Not a good look. She closed it sharply.

"Peter—?"

He said hastily, "Grace, I can't talk. I'll ring you back."

Dial tone.

Slowly Grace replaced the receiver on its cradle. What was *that* about? She remembered previously thinking that Peter would never have been panicked or desperate enough to kill, but he had certainly sounded off-balance and guilty right then. Not at all like his usual cool and confident self. She couldn't understand it.

He had been nonplussed to hear of the attack on her, she was sure of that. But then she had asked him if he was in France and he had lied, and then thought better of it. Why? What about France made him skittish?

The obvious answer—that France was the last place they'd had word of his murderous ex-girlfriend Catriona Ruthven—she instantly rejected. That was over and done, she was quite sure.

Or was she reading something into a bad connection? That was the most likely explanation.

But he didn't ring back that night.

"My *deah*," Lady Vee said, "we were so *shocked* to *heah* of your unfortunate accident."

Grace adjusted the phone beneath her ear. It was the second day following her accident, and she was making the most of her convalescence by spending the afternoon in the garden, reading over her conference notes. It had been a while since she had spoken to a classroom, and she wanted to be sharp.

The garden was particularly beautiful on that sunny day, or perhaps it was the relief of feeling back to normal. Her bruises were fading, and the worst of her cold seemed to have passed.

She made suitable noises in response to this sympathy from such an unexpected quarter. Her eyes followed two hummingbirds exchanging words over the heavy purple clusters of a Buddleia bush.

"If it would help you to have the loan of one of our vehicles, you know you would be most welcome. The Citroën is out there gathering dust. I could have Bartleby drop it off later today. You have to be able to get around."

She did need to arrange transportation, and fast. She hadn't a car to get to work in, and Rogue's Gallery was too far to walk, even for one who had newly discovered the joys of perambulation.

"That's very generous of you." Suspiciously generous. Grace wondered what Lady Vee was up to.

"Then that's settled. And in the nick of time! We were *so* hoping you might be feeling well enough to take Cordelia on the guided walking tour of Hadrian's Wall this week. The *poor* child is bored to *tears* with us."

Grace sighed.

Oh, well. She was not averse to the idea of a walking tour of the Roman ruins. She would have preferred to go with Peter, and perhaps turn it into a picnic, but what were the odds of that? Crowds were not really Peter's thing, nor guided tours. Cordelia would provide company, and Grace would be doing a good deed. If she earned the use of a car, so much the better.

Hoping she was not going to regret it, she said, "I should be feeling well enough by Thursday. Peter will be back by then, and I'll ask for the afternoon off." She thought of her recent adventures, and added, "If you're sure you trust her with me."

Lady Vee chortled at the idea that her kith and kin would not be safe with Grace.

They finalized the arrangements, Lady Vee rang off, and Grace returned to her reading. Though her lecture would focus on Byron, Grace found herself reading through all the sections concerning Shelley. She was hunting for any references to sphinxes in his work, but found nothing. Shelley was not especially interested in Egypt or Egyptology, despite the success of poems such as "Ozymandius." He had never traveled to Egypt.

That didn't mean the sonnet was a fake. Though

she had not been able to take as much time as she would have liked examining John Mallow's journal, the bit that she'd read indicated that he had believed the sonnet was legitimate. John's excitement, despite the understated manly tone of his journal, had been tangible across the decades and faded pages.

Judging by the account of how the poem had come into his keeping, it seemed as though it must have been written during the final stage of Shelley's life in Italy.

That had been a troubled time for Shelley. Ill health, the recent deaths of his children, particularly William, Mary's nearly fatal miscarriage and her subsequent withdrawal from him, all conspired to depress him. He had dreams or possibly hallucinations of his own death, in particular the famous vision of the naked child rising from the sea.

Yet despite claims that his own writing days were behind him—"I do not write—I have lived too long near Lord Byron and the sun has extinguished the glow-worm"—he wrote prolifically. As well as "The Triumph of Life," he was working on a political play in verse, an erotic drama, translations of Goethe and Calderón, and several lyrics and ballads—mostly dedicated to Jane Williams, the wife of Edward Williams, Shelley's friend and companion on that final fatal boat trip. An overlooked sonnet might easily have been penned at that time.

It was tantalizing. Too tantalizing. Reluctantly, Grace turned back to her notes. But her wandering attention was caught by the copy of *The Clarion* that

Sally Smithwick had been kind enough to drop off for her. There was a brief account of her accident, but the murder was still the lead story. There had been no new developments, but *The Clarion* continually found different ways of reporting that.

Bored, Grace flipped through the pages, pausing briefly at the horoscopes. Like most people who did not believe in astrology, Grace invariably read her daily horoscope.

"An opportunity to make a difference to a friend or a youngster is present. The more you do to help someone out, the better you will feel about yourself. Love is in the air."

Something's in the air, thought Grace skeptically.

She scanned for Peter's birth date. June 20 made him a Gemini. According to the horoscope, Gemini, the sign of the Twins, was dual-natured, elusive, complex, and contradictory. "To Gemini, life is a game. The sign is associated with mutable Mercury; adaptable and versatile, the Gemini character can prove restless and fickle."

"Swell," she murmured.

"Quick-thinking, quick-witted, and fast on their feet like the messenger god of Roman mythology that rules their sign, it's that very curiosity and cleverness that can lead this sign into trouble . . ."

This is pathetic, Grace told herself. Now I'm looking to the stars for guidance?

This sage character analysis was followed by a Chinese proverb: "Better to be deprived of food for three days than tea for one."

I'll drink to that, thought Grace, returning to her books.

By Wednesday, Grace was feeling nearly normal. She went to work her morning shift at Rogue's Gallery, chugging along in the Citroën on loan from Lady Vee. Bartleby, Lady Vee's minion, had informed Grace that the car was a genuine classic, but something about the faded yellow hue and odd shape reminded Grace of a pear. Still, it ran—after a fashion.

Peter must have returned during the night, for he came out to examine the car as Grace was parking in a cloud of exhaust beneath the trees in the lane outside Craddock House. He opened the car door for her, nearly detaching it from the car.

Slamming the loose door back into place, he said, "Ah, it's you. I thought someone had started a bonfire."

"I'll have you know that this is a classic Citroën 2CV."

"I do realize that. Did you knock over a museum?"

"That's more your line, isn't it?" she inquired tartly.

He had been midmotion kissing her hello, but that stopped him. He drew back, his black brows rising. "Blimey," he murmured, and rubbed his jaw as though she had socked him.

Grace had to fight a smile. It was so *aggravating*, the effect he had on her. Despite her doubts, despite her irritation with his odd behavior, despite her better judgment, she was happy to see him.

"How was France?" she inquired as they walked up

the flagstone path to Craddock House. "Buy anything interesting?"

He held the door to the gallery open for her. "Hinting for presents?" he inquired without a hint of the discomfiture he had displayed on the phone.

"No!"

His mouth quirked with amusement.

When she went to fill her tea mug, she found a small parcel wrapped in gold-starred tissue. She opened it and found a beautifully bound volume of *Poems of Passion and Pleasure* by Ella Wheeler Wilcox.

She bit her lip. It really was a gorgeous little book. The light brown binding was embossed with gold decorations and lettering. There were sixteen luscious art deco color illustrations. She checked the copyright. Published in London in 1920.

Gently, she turned the yellowed pages.

And it is not the poet's song, though sweeter than sweet bells chiming, Which thrills us through and through, but the heart which beats under the rhyming.

"Ella Wheeler Wilcox," Peter said behind her, and she turned. "American poet, journalist, and Free Thinker."

"It's beautiful. Thank you."

He smiled, but it was an odd smile, almost uncertain. Some emotion flickered in his eyes that she couldn't read.

The morning went quickly. They were inundated with customers early on, but between customers

Peter questioned her about the attack, and Grace filled him in on all the details.

"Are you absolutely certain it couldn't have been an accident?"

She nodded.

"It doesn't make sense."

They were interrupted before he could complete the thought, but it occurred to Grace that if Peter had killed Kayaci, that might explain why he couldn't think of a reason that anyone should want her out of the way. He was the only one with a motive.

The good news was that her faith in him was justified. The bad news was that Peter had probably murdered Kayaci.

15

The moon was a curved and razor-sharp crescent, glinting like the horns on a samurai's helmet. Kameko pulled the heavy draperies shut, closing out the night, and unobtrusively withdrew from the library.

Mr. Matsukado muttered something, the first words either of them had spoken in over an hour, and Grace looked up from reading John Mallow's journal.

"Find something?"

"I'm beginning to believe there is nothing to find," he said shortly.

Having sifted through much of the "archives" of Mallow Farm once, Grace left it to her partner to pore over the photos and account books with fresh eyes while she read John Mallow's journal. She felt it was important to read John's own account of finding the sonnet; she wanted to understand everything she could about Mallow.

She suspected Mr. Matsukado did not feel that theirs was a fair division of labor, but he had not so far expressed this. It was the first night since Grace's accident that they had been able to get together and search. She was still undecided about this hastily formed alliance. She had not had good experiences with these obsessive collector types—naturally she did not count herself among the obsessives.

As she read, Grace had to remind herself that she was no longer interested in what had happened to Mallow. It was difficult, because the more she read of his private journal, the more she spied into the dreams and thoughts of this long-dead soldier, the more she cared about him.

John Mallow had only been in his twenties, but there was strength of character and a tough-mindedness one didn't often find in young people these days. He also had a strong sense of the ridiculous. Grace found herself chuckling at passages in the browned fragile pages that brought vividly to life the dark-haired man with grave eyes in the old photos.

He wrote of the war, but although he displayed the revulsion any thinking person would, he did not seem afraid. In fact, he seemed to possess an almost serene fatalism. He wrote of the antics of his dog Tip, of the men he served with in 'L Detachment,' and of Egypt.

Having "read" Egyptology at Queen's College Oxford in 1938, he had seemed destined for a career in archaeology, but then the war came. Mallow had seemed to make the best of it, and being stationed in Egypt was clearly something of a dream come true— world war notwithstanding.

He wrote nostalgically of England, of home and family, fretting a bit over his younger brothers, who were also serving in other "theatres." He wrote of Mallow Farm, which one day would be his—if he survived the war.

None of it seemed to fit with the young man who could desert his duty and the girl he loved.

And he did love Eden Monkton, if Grace was any judge. It was one of those long-standing childhood friendships that gradually turned into something else. At the beginning of 1941, John had still been thinking of Eden as a skinny kid with "fringe" in her eyes.

But after being injured in a November raid, Mallow had come home on sick leave and attended a Christmas party at the Monkton Estate; and John had fallen hard for the new and improved Eden Monkton.

Eden, seen through John's eyes, seemed an extraordinary girl. Beautiful, intelligent, charming, sensitive, witty, civic-minded, a fine sportswoman, et cetera, et cetera. The litany of her qualities went on even after John had left the country and returned to Kabrit in the Suez Canal Zone.

Cynically, Grace began to wonder if Eden had done John in. No one could be as perfect as he believed her to be.

Raising her head out of the journal, she stared unseeing at the wall of glass-fronted bookshelves. "I wonder what did happen to him?"

"It doesn't matter," Mr. Matsukado said. "They would all be dead now in any case."

"Not necessarily "

"The man would be nearly a hundred years old."

"Eighty . . ." Grace did some quick calculating. "Nine."

"That's practically dead."

Grace laughed. "Come on, Lady Vee and this Professor Archibald are both alive and still kicking." She set aside the journal and went to sit beside Mr. Matsukado on the floor. She picked up a stack of old magazines. They were mostly dated from the sixties, and she thought they could safely skip them. All the same, she found herself fanning through the pages.

She wondered what had happened to John's journals from 1942 and '43, and where Eden's letters were. John referred to them in his journal.

Mr. Matsukado sat back on the polished floor with an air of one whose race has been run. "We will approach this Professor Archibald at the conference. So far he has refused my calls."

"Your calls? I didn't realize you had contacted Professor Archibald."

Mr. Matsukado seemed slightly uncomfortable. "Yes, I mentioned it to you, old thing."

His eyes avoided hers, and he turned back to the papers before him.

Grace was quite sure he had not mentioned contacting Professor Archibald. But that didn't concern her so much as the fact that he was lying about it.

"I think it's necessary as a writer to experience everything life has to offer, don't you?" Cordelia confided.

"Within reason," Grace said cautiously. "Life has

things to offer that would do neither you nor your writing much good."

Cordelia made a face that indicated Grace was speaking in the predictable tongue of all adults.

The Citroën labored and puffed along like the Little Engine That Could. It was Thursday afternoon, and as promised, Grace had arrived at Brougham Manor to pick up Cordelia for the afternoon's outing.

Cordelia had taken one look at the pear-colored Citroën and suggested they take Auntie's Silver Cloud Rolls-Royce, which was not being used that afternoon. Grace had declined. She had taken one look at Cordelia's black fingernail polish and the plunging red midriff top that emphasized the girl's bony chest, and nearly suggested an exchange of her own. Was anyone paying attention to Cordelia? Certainly no one was in evidence that day.

Cordelia climbed into the Citroën and unfolded a newspaper. Was she planning to catch up on world events while Grace chauffeured her around? But no, it turned out that Cordelia was not quite as enthusiastic about Hadrian's Wall as Lady Vee had made it sound. A *deah*, sweet child she might be, but she definitely knew her own mind.

"That old wall will always be there. We can see it anytime."

Ignoring this sacrilege, Grace inquired, "Okay, what exactly did you have in mind?"

Cordelia quickly scanned the paper. "An Evening of Wine with Jane Taylor."

Grace opened her mouth, but intervention was

unnecessary. In disappointed tones, Cordelia added, "But that's next Tuesday." She brightened. "Hey, maybe we could . . ."

"I don't think so." Grace focused on her driving while Cordelia flipped through the paper.

"Cruise with a Lake Ranger. *Hey . . .*"

"No." Grace had the uneasy sensation that she was rapidly losing control of the situation. If only she didn't suspect that this was the first outing Cordelia had had all summer.

Cordelia grimaced. Then she sniffed the air. "I think we're on fire."

"This car always smells like that."

Cordelia gave her one of those classic teenage looks, which manages to convey a superior being's tolerance of adult absurdity, and went back to perusing the paper.

"Evening Jazz Cruise on Lake Windermere." She added, "With buffet."

Grace made a mental note to see if she could persuade Peter to join her for that one. "Probably not what your aunt had in mind."

"All Auntie has in mind is to get me out of her hair for a few days. I want to go someplace with people."

"The tour of Hadrian's Wall will have people."

"Not those kinds of people," she said scathingly. "People my age."

Boys, translated Grace.

"Here's something. Boot Beer Festival."

Now there was a visual: a drunk and boy-crazy

Cordelia set loose upon the unsuspecting denizens of Boot.

"Definitely not."

Silence while Cordelia thumbed through the paper. "Tango Geno with Geno Fabrosi."

"Serve you right if I let you in for that one."

On impulse, Grace decided to stop by Rogue's Gallery. They parked out front, and Cordelia led the way up the flagstone path, critically sizing up the male half of a pair of customers who were carrying their purchases out of the shop.

The kid was going to reach critical mass at any minute, and Grace had the uncomfortable feeling she was the one who was going be left to deal with the resulting fallout.

"Oh good," said Peter, as they walked through the front door of Rogue's Gallery. "It wasn't a car bomb."

"*So* funny," Grace returned.

"One tries." He turned to Cordelia. "And this will be Cordelia." He smiled.

Cordelia flushed. As her hand jerked out to shake Peter's, she brushed against a green-glazed ginger jar on one of the spindly ebony nightstands. The nightstand tipped, the vase pitched forward.

Grace and Cordelia gasped in dismay like a mini Greek chorus. But Peter made a swift yet unhurried dip, steadying the table with one hand and catching the jar with the other a moment before it crashed onto the floor.

"Wow!" exclaimed Cordelia.

"Now *that's* a marketable skill," Grace agreed.

"It's proved useful once or twice." Peter replaced the ginger jar on the nightstand. He smiled at Cordelia. "No harm done."

She gazed at him as though she'd only just noticed his shining armor.

Uh-oh, thought Grace. She'd had plenty of opportunity over the last two years to observe the bewitching effect of Peter's seemingly effortless charm upon her sex. At misanthropic moments—generally following reading some self-help or relationship-oriented book—she wondered if something in Peter's emotional makeup demanded constant reassurance of his attractiveness or proof of his power over other women. Cordelia was young and emotionally vulnerable.

She explained that they were trying to find a suitable diversion for the afternoon, something edifying but diverting, something educational but . . .

"You sound like Jane Austen," Cordelia gurgled.

Peter murmured, "Doesn't she? I could listen to her for hours." He winked at Cordelia, and she blushed again.

Amused, his eyes met Grace's. "Had you thought of the Curwen Fair? It's a Medieval festival, but they do plays and operas." He added enticingly, "Shakespeare."

"Oh, yes!" Cordelia clapped her hands together like a small girl. "Please!"

Peter looked inquiringly at Grace.

"It's not exactly . . ." She caught sight of Cordelia's hopeful expression and conceded defeat. She hoped that Peter might suggest going with them, but he did not. His strong sense of self-preservation kicking in, no doubt.

As Craddock House disappeared in a cloud of exhaust fumes, Cordelia asked very casually, "Are you sleeping with him?"

"I'm sorry?"

"Peter Fox. Are you sleeping with him?"

"Why?"

"Just curious. Al says you are. Auntie says no. She says you're a *skittish fillehh*." She mimicked Lady Vee's affected accents perfectly.

Grace said quellingly, "I can't believe this would be of interest to any of you."

Unquelled, Cordelia commented, "Why not? I think he's hot. For his age." She added slyly, "Al still fancies him."

Grace bit back a retort and told herself that discretion was the better part of valor.

She tuned back in to hear Cordelia prattling. "I think it's very important to have a wide variety of lovers before one actually settles down."

That seemed to be a popular theme with Cordelia. Grace said mildly, "That sounds like a rationalization for emotional sloppiness, to me."

"What does *that* mean? Are you saying you've never slept with anyone?"

"Of course not. But I haven't slept with anyone merely to be able to say I had sex. Doesn't that seem sort of predatory to you?"

"Men do it."

"Some men do."

"It's important to experience things, to experience *life*, if you plan to write about it." Cordelia made a broad gesture, her hand knocking against the window. The glass rattled and slipped down an inch in its track.

"Are you planning on writing romance novels?"

"Of course not! Sex need not be romantic."

At Cordelia's age Grace had been devouring Georgette Heyer and Barbara Cartland novels, so that withering worldliness took her aback.

"True," she said neutrally, "but sex without any kind of emotional connection is merely physical exercise. You might just as well play tennis. Or croquet."

"I thought you were interested in the Romantics."

"I am. I never pretended to be one."

"Yeah, right." Cordelia snorted.

Grace shook her head inwardly and devoted her attention to her driving.

Workington was an ancient market and industrial town dating back to Roman times. It was originally a fishing village, but coal and the industrial revolution had turned Workington into the largest town on the Cumbrian west coast. Grace found Portland Square, the cobbled center of the town, enticing, but could not lure Cordelia into sightseeing.

"Too many churches," she said disapprovingly. "Too much architecture."

Grace sighed, but knew when she was defeated. She pulled hard on the steering wheel, and they made their way east to Curwen Park.

"Are you going to Scarborough Fair," Grace murmured, observing what appeared to be two monks walking alongside the road.

"This is the place!" Cordelia rolled down her window, which promptly fell into the door track, and hailed the men.

Following the monks' advice, they parked beneath the trees and walked through the gatehouse into the old courtyard, which was crowded with tourists and festival participants clad in lavish Medieval costumes.

While Cordelia scoped out a broad-shouldered young man in a jester's outfit, Grace looked about with interest. This might not be too bad, after all. Workington Hall had once been one of the finest manor houses in the region. The Curwen family gave shelter to Mary Queen of Scots following the defeat of her forces in May 1568, before her imprisonment and execution in Fotheringay Castle in Northamptonshire.

"Sweet cakes!" shrilled a plump young woman lugging a heavy basket and a still-heavier bosom. She loomed up in Grace's face. "Sweeeeeeet cakes!"

Grace dragged her gaze away from what looked like eminent exposure of the sweet-cake seller's private wares. "Um, did you want to tour the Hall?" she inquired of Cordelia, who had locked eyes with the bell-capped and brawny jester and was apparently using some kind of traction beam on him.

The traction beam broke. "Everyone's out here," Cordelia protested.

Everyone did seem to be outside, including refugees from the Renaissance and Victorian periods, judging from the mélange of costumes.

"We could catch one of the plays," Grace suggested. "They're performing *Romeo and Juliet.*"

"Ugh. What light through yonder window *blows.*"

Grace wasn't that keen on high drama teen romance either, so she gestured for Cordelia to lead on—and lead on Cordelia did, making a beeline for what appeared to be a sheep-shearing contest.

The girl seemed to have an uncanny sensitivity to testosterone: all the sheep shearers seemed to be tanned muscular young men built on the lines of Jude the Obscure or Angel Clare. Not that Grace didn't find all those sweat-glazed biceps interesting, but after a time she became aware of that uncanny feeling of being watched.

She glanced around the crowd but saw nothing out of the ordinary—beyond an excess of falconers, Knights Templar, and ladies-in-waiting. Didn't anybody want to be a plain old peasant?

When the sheep-shearing exhibition ended, Grace and Cordelia weaved their way to a food vendor through madrigal singers, jugglers, and colorful tents with tempting displays. Grace ordered two lemon squashes. She was reaching for her pocketbook when a male hand reached past her, and a familiar voice said, "I've got it."

"Oh," Cordelia said in pleased accents.

"Oh," Grace echoed in less-pleased accents.

DI Drummond's smile was more of a grimace,

apparently recognizing Grace's tone for what it was. "No, I'm not following you," he said.

"Just seeing the sights?"

"Why not?"

She remembered the chief constable's saying that Drummond was new to the Lake District. She shrugged. It was possible that the DI was merely enjoying the sun and fun, but it seemed quite a coincidence that he would pick the Curwen Fair on the exact same day that she did.

"Who are you?" Cordelia inquired with her usual diplomacy.

Grace started to make the introductions, but Drummond cut her off.

"Brian Drummond. I met your mother through her work."

Grace nearly spilled her lemon squash, and Cordelia burst out laughing.

"She's not my mother!" She proceeded to explain in great detail who she was and what Grace was doing there. Drummond listened attentively. Observing him, Grace thought he had played that hand very nicely. He had managed to switch attention from himself—and the fact that he was a policeman—while finding out whatever he wanted to about Grace's trip and her connection to Cordelia.

"Glad to see you've recovered from your accident, Ms. Hollister."

"Shrink-resistant and watertight, that's me," Grace said lightly.

"And very, very lucky."

"That, too."

"I understand that Fox took charge of your car after it was towed out of Swirlbeck. Nice to have connections."

"No doubt you find something suspicious in it."

"Haven't said so, have I? Still, it would have been helpful if he'd let us know that he was retrieving the car. The insurance company hadn't time to really examine it."

Grace had merely been impressed by how quickly Peter and the local towing company had acted to salvage what could be saved from the wreck.

"I told you I drove into the lake myself. What good would examining the car have done?"

"You never know till you try."

She brushed this off a bit impatiently. Drummond, apparently noticing Cordelia's attention to their exchange, did not pursue it.

Professing an interest in the ruins, he accompanied them through the old manor house. Cordelia seemed to have lost her objections to architecture, and chattered happily whiled Grace consulted her information brochure.

The Hall had been built around a pele tower dating from the fourteenth century. Pele towers were fortifications built by the people of Cumberland and Westmorland to protect themselves from the invading Scots. In 1345, Robert the Bruce marched from Scotland to England with 30,000 men, and the Lake District had been directly in his path. Farms had been burned, people and cattle slaughtered, churches and abbeys plundered.

Grace stared out through the crumbling walls at the pastoral landscape, and tried to imagine a world of fire and sword.

"Why so grim?"

Grace glanced at Drummond, smiled, and shook her head. They went through the archway opposite the gatehouse and walked up the stairway to their left. At the top of the stairs was a doorway. According to the brochure, this was the room where Mary Queen of Scots had spent her last night of freedom.

Grace consulted her brochure. "It says here that Mary gave the Curwens an agate wine cup that guaranteed their good fortune so long as the cup was never broken."

Cordelia studied the room, open now to the wind and elements. "Someone must have dropped the cup."

"No," Drummond said absently. "The family still holds the cup."

Grace flipped the brochure over. "How do you know that?"

He moved his shoulders. "I must have read it somewhere."

Not in the brochure, thought Grace.

They left the room, moving along the hall to the right toward the banqueting room.

"There would have been a large wooden table for feasting running the length of the room," Drummond told Cordelia. "And an enormous open fire."

"You seem to know your way around," Grace remarked.

"I'm interested in history."

"Is this what you do on your days off? Or is this a day off?"

He gave her a level look. "This is my day off."

"We *are* honored."

He laughed.

Drummond kept them company for the rest of their tour, and even Grace had to admit that he was informed and pleasant. He made no references to crime or murder or Peter, for which she was grateful, and when they parted company at the end of the afternoon—Drummond declining Cordelia's invitation to join them for a late pub lunch—Grace was startled to realize that she was maybe the tiniest bit disappointed.

16

"I forgot to tell you," said Grace. "I think Kameko Musashi is Yakuza. I saw her in her workout clothes and she's covered in what look like mob tattoos. Does the Japanese mob have women members?"

"Not that I know of," said Peter. "Yakuza is an all-male society. Yakuza believe in a traditional role for women. There are 'comfort women' of course."

"Of course."

"I don't make the rules, love." He took a pull on his beer, and added reflectively, "I did wonder about that missing bit of little finger."

Grace dipped a cracker into the white cheese and tomato dip. "You're referring to the Yakuza tradition of cutting off the last joint of the little finger in apology for some transgression against the boss?" At Peter's expression, she said, "I do go to the movies, after all."

"Yes, but I assumed it was merely to catch remakes of *Emma* and *Wuthering Heights.*"

They were dining at a new place just outside of

Innisdale called the Sahara. This was the latest of several culinary incarnations. The restaurant had been a seafood shack only a few months previously. The nets and dried starfish had given way to old travel posters of Egypt and wall murals. The waitresses in yacht caps had been replaced by waiters in red fezzes. The menu seemed a Middle Eastern hodge-podge. It occurred to Grace that although Peter was exceedingly discriminating about the food he prepared, she had never heard him complain about a meal or anyone else's cooking. Was that the result of fourteen months under less than Club Med conditions?

"Cheers," said Peter, and clinked his mug against hers. Grace sipped cautiously. The beer was an Egyptian brand called Stella. She had read that a Japanese brewery had recently re-created the beer of the Egyptian New Kingdom by interpreting hieroglyphics. The ancient beer was 10 percent alcohol and, rather than being brewed by using hops, was flavored by dates, mandrake, and various spices. Bira Stella couldn't compete with that, but at 5 percent alcohol, it was getting the job done.

"Do you think Mr. Matsukado is Yakuza?"

Peter said carefully, "I think he's the offspring of a wealthy and influential family. Beyond that, I don't know."

"But you could find out."

His eyes, very blue in the smoky light, met hers. "I could. That sort of inquiry wouldn't go without notice."

"Now you've piqued my interest."

"You were born with piqued interest."

Grace chuckled.

The Shorbet Araneb rabbit soup arrived. It was a rich, slightly greasy-looking mixture. Peter tore off chunks of the fried brown bread and added it to his soup. Doubtfully, Grace followed suit.

"How is the quest for the lost Shelley going?" he asked.

She sighed. She had told Peter all about "Sate the Sphinx." This did not stop her from running through all the possibilities again. She paused when the waiter brought their dinners: lemon-flavored lamb served over basmati rice for Peter, and shish kebab rubbed in cinnamon clove for Grace.

"We'll have another." Peter tapped his mug, and the waiter nodded.

"I think John would have loved this place," Grace remarked, nibbling her shish kebab. It was unexpectedly spicy. She licked her lips and found Peter's gaze on her mouth. Heat flooded her face, but maybe it was the spices.

"John? Oh, right. Mallow." He raised one brow. "Don't tell me I'm now competing with ghosts as well as dead poets."

She laughed at the idea of Peter competing with anyone. The waiter brought another round of drinks, wished them *"Bel hanna!"* and departed.

"It is odd that he just disappeared," Grace mused.

"Perhaps he had to."

"What do you mean?"

"I mean, he may have got in over his head."

"With what?"

His lashes lowered, concealing his thoughts. "How much do you know about Mallow? You've read one letter and parts of a journal. If he'd any brains, he wouldn't commit anything incriminating to paper."

"He wasn't that k—" In time it occurred to Grace that this might not be a very tactful comment. "Well, what are you suggesting?"

"You said he was stationed in Egypt. He lived next door to a collector of all things Egyptian."

"Your theory is that he was involved in smuggling antiquities?"

"It's one of any number of possibilities." He smiled sardonically at her expression. "You don't like that theory."

"No, I don't. I think I'm a better judge of character than that."

"Do you?"

She considered her involvement with him, and knew that he read her thoughts accurately when he questioned, "Did Bullhead Drummond really suggest that I was trying to off you?"

"He thinks you killed Kayaci."

"As do you." He was still smiling, but his eyes were watchful.

"No."

"Strive to get a little conviction into it, darling."

"No pun intended?"

He laughed and signaled for another round.

That was surprising. She had never seen Peter drink to excess. She suspected it was partly because he liked always to be in control, but he was definitely knocking them back. Not that it seemed to affect him.

The conversation moved to less hazardous topics as they finished their meal. The final order of drinks came with *Basboosa*, semolina cakes with lemon and honey. The restaurant was crowded by then, and the smoky air and tinned music was contriving to give Grace a headache. She ordered Turkish coffee, and as far as she could tell it was simply ordinary, very strong, very sweet coffee.

Peter seemed steady enough when they left the restaurant, but he looked up at the starry sky, and said, "Perhaps we should walk."

"To Rogue's Gallery?" Despite her newfound enthusiasm for walking, Craddock House was a good twenty miles. "I can drive."

"I'm not drunk. I thought we might talk."

That sounded ominous.

"Haven't we been talking all evening?"

His look was quizzical, and Grace realized she sounded as if she were afraid to be alone with him. She offered her hand as they crossed the wide country road, walking in silence across a meadow of moonlit buttercups and bluebells. The scent of dust and flowers lingered in the warm air.

As the woods loomed somber and dense before them, Grace was reminded of the Tinker's Dam in Kentmere where they had first met. What a very long time ago it seemed.

She was glad that Peter did not continue into the woods, heading instead for a strange rock formation that stood in the middle of the field. The three tall outer stones were slightly bent, like robed figures hunched against the wind. In the center was a long slab that looked as though it might have been the roof of a prehistoric temple.

They entered the circle of stones.

"What is this place?" Grace stroked the nearest sandstone form, still warm from the day's heat. There was a perfect hole in the top of the rock about the size of a face.

"It's called the Monk's Supper."

"They do sort of look like hooded figures from behind."

She sat down on the fallen square in the center of the ring, slipping her shoe off and rubbing her foot. She was not really dressed for an impromptu hike.

Having dragged her out there, Peter seemed to have nothing to say. The chirp of crickets filled the night.

She studied his profile, etched in silver. No Egyptian relief had ever looked more remote and aristocratic. It was at moments like those that he reminded her of the maddening and mysterious heroes in those Barbara Cartland novels she had secretly devoured in her teens. Something he would no doubt be appalled to learn.

"When you said the situation with Kayaci would soon resolve itself, what did you mean?" she asked abruptly.

It was a moment before he turned to her. "Are you sure you want to know?"

"Tell me anyway."

A muscle moved in his jaw. "I felt, shall we say . . . confident that some interested party would take care of the problem."

"What interested party?"

"There's a large Turkish expat community in London. Turks, Turkish-speaking people, Kurds—people with scant love for Kayaci and the Turkish government. People who have lost sons, brothers, fathers and mothers, daughters, and sisters, for that matter."

"You have friends there?"

"You meet people in prison." He spoke evenly. "You form . . . alliances."

Like the alliance he had formed with Hayri Kayaci?

"You think one of those people found out Kayaci was here?"

He smiled, and it was a chilling thing. "I'm quite sure the news traveled quickly."

"And one of them killed Kayaci?"

He said nothing.

Grace shivered and hugged herself. Staring at her shoes, at the gleam of moonlight on the toes of her dusty pumps, she asked softly, "Did you go to France to see Catriona?"

"Yes."

He didn't hesitate. She wished she could read that brusque tone, but perhaps there was nothing to read. She said lightly, "How is the Bride of Dracula?"

"I don't know. I didn't see her. Apparently she's in the States."

Was that an alibi for his crazy ex-girlfriend? Grace

could imagine Catriona dispatching Harry and anyone else who got on her wrong side.

"You acted so . . . odd on the phone the day you called me. Why?"

"I don't know." She turned her head, and he was looking at her, smiling. He sounded genuinely perplexed.

"You once said you'd never lie to me."

"I don't think I said that, Esmerelda." His smile was a twist of self-mockery. "I said I'd try not to."

Grace made an unamused sound, and he said, "There it is, that little Mary Poppins sniff. I can always tell when you're displeased."

"Newsflash. I'm not trying to hide it."

He laughed, sounding more like himself.

"Right. Well, I haven't lied to you. I've never been keen on the idea of commitment. I think you know that."

She nodded.

"Steady relationships, routine—that's never been for me."

It wasn't really a surprise, and she supposed it was as well they were getting it out into the open, although why right there and right then?

"I haven't asked for anything."

"You don't have to ask. You're that kind of girl."

She found that a little insulting, although he probably didn't mean it to be. And he was right, after all. She had no quarrel with routine or steady relationships or reliability or responsibility, or all the other "R" words.

"I went to warn Catriona. I wanted her to know about Kayaci. I wanted her to know that the vermin is gnawing its way out of the woodwork."

"You don't owe her—"

He interrupted flatly, "I do. But when I phoned you, and you asked whether I were in France, I felt . . ."

"Guilty?"

"Uh . . . yes."

She didn't say anything. She could have said, "You don't owe *me* anything," but she couldn't help feeling that he did, since she had essentially stayed on in Britain because of him. And she certainly didn't want to hear him agree that he didn't owe her anything.

Because she didn't know what to say, she said nothing. Peter did not speak, either. And after a time, the silence between them changed and softened like the mist rising from the damp ground.

It seemed to Grace that whether he knew it or not, the fact that Peter was explaining himself to her was a positive sign. She knew he cared for her. Perhaps it would simply be a matter of time before he came to realize that his feelings for her were the lasting kind.

Or she came to realize that they were not.

17

Grace glanced up from Ceram's *Gods, Graves and Scholars* in time to catch Scott Sartyn passing her with that habitual scowl he seemed to save for her. Grace scowled back at him.

She turned back to the book but there was nothing about Sir Vincent Monkton in it. She moved on to the next book, Weigall's *Tutankhamen and Other Essays*. Weigall had been Inspector General of Antiquities with the Egyptian government and on the staff of the Egyptian Museum in Cairo back in the 1920s. She was hoping he might have something to say on the topic of the irascible Sir Vincent Monkton.

But mum—or perhaps mummy—was the word there, too. Grace moved to the next tome. *Letters from Egypt and Palestine* by Maltbie Davenport Babcock, written in 1902. For a moment Grace paused to consider parents barbarous enough to name a child "Maltbie."

She noticed that Sartyn was making another pass, apparently trying to see what she was researching.

If only she knew what she was researching, how much simpler it would all be.

The problem was that because there was little information available on John Mallow, she had to resort to secondhand sources. Mallow had been engaged to one of Monkton's daughters and had run off with the other. Monkton was comparatively well known. It was not inconceivable that a reference or two to Mallow might crop up in connection to Monkton. It was slim, but she was running out of options.

The connection seemed to be Egypt. John Mallow was fascinated by all things Egyptian. His neighbor was a famous eccentric Egyptologist. John Mallow had been stationed in Egypt. The Shelley poem was about the Sphinx.

On the other hand, Scott Sartyn's archaeological dig had been in Turkey. Peter had been imprisoned in Turkey. Hayri Kayaci had been a prison guard in Turkey. So maybe the connection was Turkey.

Egypt or Turkey, somehow all of these threads wove a tight web around Innisdale, which was about as far from the sands and sun of the Middle East as one could get.

But there had to be another connection. Why did Sir Vincent Monkton disapprove of John Mallow for Eden? Sure, he had ended up running off with Eden's younger sister, but it didn't seem like there was any indication of trouble before that. Mallow had referenced Monkton in his journal, but the references had been casual and friendly enough.

What had changed between them?

And why had John Mallow run off with Arabella Monkton? There hadn't been more than three passing mentions of her in his journal. Of course, Grace had access only to the year before Mallow's disappearance. Maybe something drastic had happened in the following year. Something to turn Monkton against John, and make John abandon Eden.

And something *had* happened: John had had the Shelley poem authenticated. And John had disappeared.

An hour later Grace did not know much more about Sir Vincent Monkton, but she had expanded her knowledge of the early days of archaeology in Egypt. She found it engrossing. The first systematic exploration of Egypt had been undertaken by French scholars accompanying Bonaparte's military expedition through the Nile Valley in the eighteenth century. When the French turned Alexandria over to the British in 1802, all their work, including their discovery of the Rosetta Stone, was handed over as well.

Fascinated, Grace read on, learning about the discovery of the legendary Serapeum, where generations of the sacred bulls of Apis were buried; the unearthing of the temple of Abu Simbel by circus strong man Giovanni Belzoni; the amazing find of a cache of over fifty royal mummies in Deir el-Bahri. As Egypt and its fabulous antiquities became "fashionable," a Wild West period of plunder-and-pillage archaeology began, which gradually slowed but did not effectively stop until 1914. Even in the twenty-first century, Egyptian antiquities meant big money on the black market—thus encouraging Lady Vee's hopes of one day owning her own mummy case, Grace thought ruefully.

Monkton's own contribution was the discovery of the Tomb of the Sorceress in 1921. The "sorceress" was actually a minor princess, but her ornately painted tomb had yielded, among other treasures, a collection of literary, magical, and medical papyri within a mummified leopard.

Unfortunately, Monkton's discovery had occurred during a decade for monumental achievements in Egyptology, and the appearance of the sorceress was eclipsed by the previous year's discovery of the fabulous riches in Tutankhamen's tomb.

"Have everything you need?"

Grace returned from the windswept dunes and the lost tombs, and blinked up at Roy Blade.

He waved a hand in front of her. "Ground control to Grace Hollister."

Slipping off her specs, she leaned back in her chair. "Actually, I've been looking for a book called *Kingdom of the Dead* by Sir Vincent Monkton. It doesn't appear to be checked out, but it's not on the shelf."

Blade jerked his head toward the counter where Sartyn, arms folded, stood observing his domain. He reminded Grace a bit of those statues of ancient pharaohs. That wrinkled lip and sneer of cold command.

Was Blade cautioning her? She couldn't read his profile; the eye patch covered the eye facing her.

"I'll have a look," he said casually, and pushed off the desk.

He returned a short time later and handed her a faded red volume. "I've checked it out in your name."

"Terrific!"

He grinned and put a finger to his lips. "Best keep it under wraps. Someone else had it in his private collection." He jerked his head back toward the desk where Sartyn stood.

Grace shoved the book in her knapsack.

"If anyone is behaving suspiciously, it's Sartyn," Grace informed Peter at Rogue's Gallery later that afternoon. "You should see the way he watches me."

Peter, who had been trying for twenty minutes to wrestle a suit of samurai armor into a shipping crate, grunted noncommittally.

"And I think he's been following me."

"And why do you think that?"

"Someone's been following me. I can feel it. I can feel someone is watching me."

Peter swore under his breath and sucked the blood welling from where his knuckle had scraped the mouth of the black battle mask.

"You've probably just ingested sixteenth-century hibernating microbes."

"So long as they continue to hibernate . . ." He gave the metal face a long, level look.

"Anyway, I'm not *that* imaginative. It's a very real, very primitive sense, the ability to tell when someone's watching you. I don't know if it's animal instinct or what, but it's real."

Peter did not argue with her.

"You'll break your hand if you punch that thing."

"Do I look like the kind of chap who resorts to brute force when frustrated?"

"At the moment? Yes. What I can't understand is why Sartyn would deliberately try to throw suspicion on me. And he definitely did; he told the police I was going through Harry's pockets."

"Perhaps he thought you were going through Harry's pockets. It was dark on the path. Or perhaps something about you raises alarms. It should do."

She ignored that last crack. "According to Blade, he swiped the library copy of Monkton's *Kingdom of the Dead* and tucked it away on his own bookshelf."

Peter directed a droll look her way but said nothing.

"Fine, but why that book? Miss Webb said he was asking all kinds of questions about Sir Monkton. Why?"

"You said his field was archaeology. What could be more natural than interest in a famous local archaeologist? He may be planning to write a book." He added dryly, "It's been known to happen."

Grace admitted, "He'd make an interesting subject—Sir Vincent, I mean. He was kind of a cross between Lawrence of Arabia and Heinrich Schliemann. Apparently he dressed and lived like an Egyptian noble, even at home in England. His first wife was one of these doughty lady archaeologists, but after she died, he married an Egyptian girl who was young enough to be his daughter."

"And this shocks you?"

"Not that. There are rumors that he wasn't exactly strict about keeping track of finds, but that, unfortunately, was par for the course in the early days of Egyptology. And he wasn't uncovering treasures on the scale of Howard Carter or Flinders Petrie or even George Reisner. Still . . ."

Peter's eyes held a certain gleam. "Ah, Petrie. The hidden treasure of Princess Sithathoriunet. Gold, amethyst, lapis lazuli, and turquoise jewelry from the Middle Kingdom, as well as ceremonial vessels of alabaster and obsidian."

Trust Peter to know his lost treasures. "Petrie's finds ended up in the Eqyptian Museum in Cairo, but Monkton was like a lot of his contemporaries, and accumulated a private collection. Unfortunately, almost all of it was lost in the London Blitz."

"It's possible. Incendiary raids destroyed sections of the British Museum and the National Portrait Gallery. To this day, the west side of the Tate is scarred by wartime explosions."

"The thing is, Monkton and Egyptology aside, there's no reasonable explanation for Sartyn's hostility toward me."

"Perhaps he's shamming."

Grace considered then discarded this. "I don't get that impression."

Peter finally succeeded in maneuvering his bamboo-and-metal foe into the crate. He began to tuck packing materials around the armor.

"You could always ask him," he said, in the tone of

one growing bored with the subject. Used to being the object of everyone's suspicion, he probably couldn't relate to Grace's grievance.

Glancing over his shoulder, he caught her expression. "I'm not serious."

"Actually, it's a very good idea. Maybe there's a simple explanation."

"Such as?"

"Such as maybe *he* killed Kayaci."

"Were you planning on asking him that?"

"If the moment presents itself. Didn't you once say you admired my frank and direct manner?"

"Did I? How extraordinary of me."

He slammed shut the wooden lid to the packing crate.

"According to the War Office, John Mallow never returned to his regiment. We can eliminate that possibility, at least." Grace pulled out a dresser drawer and began knocking along the bottom.

Three evenings after her conversation with Peter, she was back at Mallow Farm with her unlikely collaborator, Mr. Matsukado. She had spent her last two visits checking furniture for false bottoms, fake fronts, and hidden compartments. It was a slow and tedious process, made slower and more tedious by the fact that she was doing it on her own.

He said, "But we knew that already."

"We didn't know it for a fact. Now we've had our suspicions confirmed."

Mr. Matsukado did not look as appreciative as Grace felt he should. He seemed to grow more impatient and petulant as the days passed and they were unable to find the sonnet.

Watching in silence as she tapped along the drawer bottom for a few moments, he said, "We have searched these rooms, these cabinets already."

"That doesn't mean it isn't here."

Aside from secret compartments in the furniture, there was a possibility that the sonnet's hiding place could have been plastered over during the renovation, but she didn't say this aloud. She did not want to further discourage Mr. Matsukado—or herself. After several nights of searching, she strongly suspected that John had taken the poem with him when he left Innisdale.

Having read much of his journal, she was convinced she knew him—at least as well as any biographer could know her subject. But it was confusing. The John Mallow she had come to know would not be capable of running out on Eden Monkton and his unborn child. But perhaps he had not known about the child. There were occasional references to Bella Monkton, and Grace could not help reading between the lines.

"Your Mr. Fox could be of help to us, could he not?"

A certain inflection in Mr. Matsukado's voice brought Grace's head up. "I don't see how. This isn't really his field."

He smiled unconvincingly beneath that sparse mustache. "He has connections to the underworld. He is like the archrogue of your popular fiction, is he not? The Gentleman Thief. The Raffles."

Archrogue? What was that, Regency cant for the chief of a gang of thieves? "He's reformed." She turned back to the drawer and knocked again. No one home. She moved on to the next drawer.

"Anyway, no one can do this for us. There's no shortcut possible. The poem is either here or it's not." The drawer sounded perfectly normal. It sounded like all the other drawers, nice and solid. They built furniture to last, back in the old days. "What is it you imagine Peter could do?"

"Something! It takes a thief to catch a thief; that is one of your sayings, isn't it?"

Grace knelt, pulled out the last drawer, and began knocking at the edges. Her knuckles were getting sore.

She slid the drawer in and sat back on her heels, inspecting the face of the rosewood cabinet. There was quite a bit of bottom cabinet that wasn't utilized by the drawers. She pulled the shallow bottom drawer all the way out and examined the apparently solid bottom slats. She knocked along the top. Hollow.

She sat back again.

"You are not listening to me, Miss Hollister."

"Hmm?"

The center portion of each drawer was inlaid with pale, carved wood. Grace tried pressing against the lacquered surface, tried to slide it to one side, up, down, tried to slide it the other way. Nothing. She traced the raised wood carving, seeking a hidden button or latch.

She felt under the cabinet.

Mr. Matsukado fell silent and came to watch her.

Grace's fingers hesitated over a tiny tongue of metal. She pressed, and the side of the cabinet swung open soundlessly.

"There is something here! You have found it."

Heart beating fast, Grace reached in and lifted out what appeared to be an old sketch pad. She felt around in the compartment, but there was nothing else inside. With unsteady fingers, she turned back the cover of the sketch pad and saw a sheet covered in tiny ornate script.

"What is this?" demanded Mr. Matsukado.

"Hieroglyphics, I think."

Mr. Matsukado nearly danced up and down in his frustrated excitement. "What do they mean?"

"I don't know. There are pages of them. I think someone was experimenting, maybe learning to write in hieroglyphics."

"Someone? You mean John Mallow."

"We don't know who this sketchbook belonged to." Not for sure, although Mallow had been stationed in Egypt and had been fascinated by all things Egyptian.

Grace paused over a sketch of a young woman with dark hair and exotic eyes. Not quite how she pictured the matchless Eden Monkton. "These are really good. Whoever did these had genuine talent." She turned the page. There were several smaller sketches of the same woman.

"This cannot be all there is! Why would anyone hide this?"

Grace turned to a sketch of a piratical-looking terrier. She knew that dog, she had seen enough photos of him.

"Tip," she said. "John Mallow's Tip."

Mr. Matsukado cast up his hands. "Dogs and hieroglyphs? What is the point of this?"

"Oh, my God," whispered Grace as a thin sheet of paper slid out between the pages and landed at her feet.

Mr. Matsukado fell to his knees beside her.

Grace's fingers were unsteady as she picked up the paper at the corner. A familiar hand had written, "Ode."

"Is it? Is it?"

She read aloud, "If thou forsake me, let it be for love . . ."

"It is!" cried Mr. Matsukado, jumping to his feet. "We have found it at last."

But a quick read-through had Grace shaking her head.

"It's not Shelley."

"It must be!" Mr. Matsukado stood over her, hands in fists.

She shook her head. To have her hopes ascend so fast only to plummet back to earth was disorienting. "It's not. This is—oh, it's all right, but it's not Shelley. Look, the paper is completely wrong, for one thing.

And the handwriting is John Mallow's. We've certainly read enough of it to recognize . . ."

There was a second sheet stuck to the first. Grace separated it and glanced at the title. "Though I Must Leave."

Mr. Matsukado snatched the papers from her, read them over, then crumpled them up.

"What are you *doing?*" cried Grace. She picked up the crumpled papers and gently smoothed them out.

"You said yourself they are of no value."

Grace glared at him. "I said they aren't what we're looking for. I never said they weren't of historical or cultural value. Or sentimental value. John Mallow's son is still alive. He might like these."

"Amateur scribblings," he said scornfully. "In any case, they're mine to do with as I wish."

Yep, Grace was beginning to get a bit fed up with Mr. Matsukado.

"That may be true, but if you want my help, you're going to handle yourself in a professional manner."

"You have not been of help so far."

"Really? Who discovered the secret compartment?"

"And what use is it?"

"Don't you see what this means? If there's one secret compartment, there could be another. If John was deliberately hiding things like this sketchbook, it must have been for a reason." Or maybe John was by nature secretive. Maybe there had been a hidden side to his character—but Grace did not want to believe that.

"Perhaps John believed someone would try and take the sonnet." She was convinced that John's own attempts at sonnet writing and his efforts at concealment indicated that they were on the right track, but she could see from the Shogun's expression that he wasn't buying it.

"I do not need you to tell me this." Mr. Matsukado grabbed the sketchbook from Grace and placed it on a table as though putting it out of her reach. "Our partnership is at an end."

18

*F*rom her vantage point behind the Feminist Studies section (shockingly limited, even taking into account the size of the village and surrounding environs) Grace had ideal opportunity to observe Scott Sartyn in action. She had been doing so for fifteen minutes while she tried to make up her mind.

It was like watching the latest in androids. Though capable enough, he operated without any sign of warmth or interest. Not that there was any crime in having personality deficits, but what was he doing here in Innisdale? Why would a young, ambitious man settle for being head librarian in a remote English village?

Perhaps if he had family locally, or was in poor health, or was working on his sabbatical—but none of that seemed to be true.

Granted, she was utterly biased against the man; still, Grace felt certain that Sartyn was up to no good. There were too many coincidences: the fact that he had been doing fieldwork in Turkey, that he had been acquainted with Kayaci, that they both turned up at the same time in the same small English village. But most conclusive was his enmity toward her. Something about her bothered him to such extent that he went around bad-mouthing her—even trying to turn police suspicion her way. He *had* to be up to something.

Something that somehow involved Grace. But what?

Peter had not been serious when he suggested that Grace simply ask Sartyn what the problem was, but that approach did have the merit of a surprise attack. Caught off guard, he might actually reveal something.

Or he might not, but it wasn't like he didn't already know that she was suspicious of him.

Maybe he was wary of her fearsome skills as an amateur sleuth. Grace smiled at this notion and made her way to the front desk.

She waited till Sartyn was free, then leaned across the front desk, saying softly, "I'd like a word in private."

Sartyn whipped around. The flat colorless hair and huge glasses gave his face the appearance of a large benign insect. "I'm working, Ms. Hollister."

"This will only take a minute or two."

"I don't think so."

Despite her best intentions, Grace felt her temper rise. "You don't think so?"

"Please keep your voice down."

"My voice is down," Grace hissed. "What are you afraid of?"

"People have a habit of dying around you, Ms. Hollister!" And suddenly it was Sartyn's voice attracting the interest of the library staff.

So much for that plan. Well, it had been more of an impulse than a plan.

"Very well," Grace whispered. "But I'm warning you. You're not fooling me. I know you're up to something. And if you continue following me, we *will* have this conversation—in front of the police."

"Don't threaten me," he said angrily, and several heads rose out of books.

She turned on heel and marched out.

Roy Blade met her on the sidewalk outside. He flicked his cigarette butt to the pavement.

"That went well, don't you think?" she said brightly.

"You do have a knack with people," Blade agreed.

"He's up to something."

"No kidding." He looked uncharacteristically gloomy, grinding the butt with the heel of his leather boot.

"You don't have any idea what it might be?"

Blade was silent. "I can tell you one thing I haven't mentioned to the plods. I saw him with the bloke who was offed. The Turk. Thick as thieves."

"Seriously?"

"Straight up."

"When? Where?"

He thought it over. "I think it was last Tuesday. Behind the pub."

"*Behind* the pub?"

"The Boy Wonder doesn't drink."

"I *knew* he was evil," Grace muttered.

Blade sniggered. "Didn't want anyone to see them together, is my guess."

Grace decided not to ask what Blade had been

doing lurking behind the pub. "Do you have any idea what they talked about?"

He shook his head. "It didn't occur to me to get close enough to listen in."

Grace made a commiserating face, then realized she was sympathizing with his failure to sneak up and spy on another person.

"I admit I never thought he'd last this long. What a nutter. You should have seen him last week—accused me of pinching his bloody fountain pen."

"Why would he suspect you?"

Blade smiled a wolfish smile. "Sussed I'd enjoy watching him go into convulsions."

Grace shook her head.

A silver sedan pulled up alongside the curb. The driver rolled down his window, and Grace recognized DI Drummond.

"Get in," he said. He did not say "please."

"Mr. Scott Sartyn has lodged a complaint against you, Ms. Hollister."

"Are you serious?"

"Never more so. He says you have been harassing him at his workplace. And where do I find you? Outside the library with Roy Blade."

"Has he also filed a complaint against Roy Blade?"

"Not at this time."

Grace thought this over. "So you're arresting me?"

"I thought perhaps we should have a little chat."

"An official little chat?" They were pulling into the car park next to the police station.

Drummond parked, turned off the ignition, and turned toward her. "I don't want there to be any hint of impropriety in this investigation."

"What investigation? I admit I went to see Sartyn. I didn't harass him, however—unless you consider it harassment to tell him I would file a police complaint if he continued to stalk me."

Exasperated, Drummond said, "In case it has slipped your mind, I'm still investigating a homicide. You'll remember Hayri Kayaci, the Turkish national whose body you found in Cherry Lane Park?"

"And you believe these two things are related?"

"I've no doubt whatsoever."

The halfway pleasant and attractive Brian Drummond of the Curwen Fair was nowhere in sight that afternoon. They got out of the car—Drummond showing a fine disregard for such chauvinistic practices as opening doors for the female of the species—and went into the police station.

He led Grace to a small spartan office down the hall from Chief Constable Heron. There was a silver-framed photo on the desk, but it was turned away from Grace's chair. For the first time she wondered if there was a Mrs. Drummond. There were books on criminal law, art, and legal procedure on a small bookcase.

Drummond leaned back in his chair and fixed Grace with that steady gray gaze.

"You originally came to the United Kingdom to do research on your doctorate thesis, correct?"

"Sort of. You'd call it a busman's holiday."

His smile seemed too small for his face.

"And with the help of Mr. Fox's underworld connections, you were able to recover a valuable national treasure."

"Aren't all national treasures valuable?" Grace inquired tartly. "And furthermore, Mr. Fox's underworld connections were nowhere to be seen. We recovered the cameos through our own efforts."

"That remains to be seen."

"No, it doesn't. It's a fact."

"And in part, because of your recovery of these items, you were able to obtain a temporary visa."

Warily, Grace replied, "I'm here on a four-year Ancestry Visa, which is based on the fact that my great-grandparents were born in the UK before March 1922. It's a perfectly legitimate visa."

"Which you applied for, and which was granted, following your part in the recovery of the cameos."

"Correct."

"I think we would both agree that were you to find yourself in difficulties with the law—were you, for example, to be named as defendant in a murder trial . . ."

Grace's stomach knotted. She had to give Sartyn credit; his retaliation had been swift and well aimed. "Are you threatening to revoke my visa?"

"I'm merely pointing out the obvious: It is to your benefit to cooperate with the police."

"I *have* cooperated. I've told you everything I know—which is nothing."

He shook his head regretfully. "How well do you know Peter Fox?"

"Well enough to know he didn't commit murder."

"Are you so sure? From what I've read of the conditions of the prison where Fox was held—and from what we've learned of Kayaci—one could hardly blame him for wanting revenge."

"In that case, perhaps you should look at others within the Turkish community."

"What Turkish community? There is no Turkish community in Innisdale, or the Lake District, for that matter."

Grace suspected she had already said more than Peter would have wished, and held her tongue.

"Are you willing to bet your life on that?"

She thought about it. "Yes. I am, actually."

Nothing moved in the stony face across from her.

"What did you have for supper the night of the concert?"

What now? Had they violated some obscure food ordinance?

"That seems like a pretty weird question. How is that relevant to your investigation?"

"Just answer the question, Ms. Hollister."

"Turkey sandwiches."

He pounced. "And?"

"And *what?* Chocolates and fruit and wine."

"I'd like the entire meal from start to finish."

In the tone of one humoring a lunatic, Grace recited the menu.

"Who prepared the meal, yourself or Mr. Fox?"

"Peter. Do you now suspect Kayaci was poisoned?"

He ignored this, taking another tack. "What has Peter Fox promised you?"

"I have no idea what you're talking about."

"Has he promised to marry you?"

"Excuse me?"

Drummond's smile was knowing. "And he won't. You're one of many. He's using you as he uses all women. The man's an invidious womanizer."

Invidious? Surely he meant inveterate. Or possibly insidious. Grace told herself to focus, saying firmly, "Even if that were true, it doesn't make him a murderer."

"What did you see on the hillside that night?" he yelled, and Grace jumped in her seat.

"I. Saw. Nothing."

"You're lying, Ms. Hollister."

"I'm not lying!"

"Then you're hiding something. Someone believes you saw something. Someone wants to shut your mouth permanently. Peter Fox does not have an alibi for the evening that your car went into Swirlbeck, Ms. Hollister. He's claiming he was on the road to Yorkshire, but who's to say he wasn't on the road behind you?"

She opened her mouth, then closed it. Why waste her breath? Nothing she said to the jerk would change his mind about Peter and her. Or perhaps there was something else behind the sudden refocus on Grace. After all, he must have known before that day that Peter did not have an alibi for the night she had been attacked. And why had he waited so long to question her about what had been in the picnic basket?

Was it coincidence that Scott Sartyn seemed to have a hot line to DI Drummond's office?

She said coldly, "If you've only Scott Sartyn's word that I'm harassing him, it's hearsay. You've no witnesses because it never happened. Have you bothered to question him?"

"About?"

"The murder!"

"Naturally."

"Were you aware that he was acquainted with Hayri Kayaci?"

Drummond answered promptly, as though he had been waiting for her to bring up this point. "Yes. He was approached by Kayaci when he was a student doing fieldwork in Turkey. Kayaci tried to recruit Sartyn into his antiquities smuggling operation. Apparently Kayaci never knew it was Sartyn who turned him in to the authorities."

It was a jolt, but Grace rallied. "And you checked his story out, I hope?"

"Certainly. Sartyn had no reason to kill Kayaci."

"So that leaves Peter."

"And yourself."

"Me?"

"If you're willing to lie for Fox, to cover up a murder, who's to say you wouldn't commit that murder yourself?"

"I'm to say. That's the craziest thing I've ever heard."

He shrugged. "If it wasn't Fox, it was you. I should give it careful thought, Ms. Hollister. Just how far are you willing to go to protect that man?"

19

"*T*hough Lord Byron had been willing to honor his proposal to Leigh Hunt regarding *The Liberal*, patently he had lost all enthusiasm for the project. That it was within Lord B's means to rescue Hunt, and that he declined to do so, appalled Shelley, himself generous to a fault. Yet Byron had loaned Shelley fifty quid as though it were of no more consequence than a pinch of snuff. The man was a conundrum."

Grace forced her wandering thoughts back to the dais where Professor Fenwick Archibald was reading from *Blithe Spirit: The Life of Shelley*.

The reigning local Shelley expert was small, plump, and pink-cheeked like an elderly baby. He had an improbable circle of yellow curls around his ton-sured head, reminiscent of a Cabbage Patch doll. But he knew his stuff. For the last hour and forty-five minutes, an audience of ninety scholars and educators had listened enrapt to the all-too-brief tale of Percy Bysshe Shelley's life.

A few rows ahead, Grace could see the sleek,

almost identical dark heads of Mr. Matsukado and Miss Musashi. Mr. Matsukado had not spoken to Grace since two nights earlier, when he had, to all intents and purposes, shown her the door. Though it was maddening to be denied access to John Mallow's journal and the sketchbook she had barely had a chance to examine, Grace was by no means ready to concede defeat in the quest for the Shelley sonnet.

"Going to try to catch up with the old boy at lunch?"

Grace nodded in response to Roy Blade's question and checked her watch. Ten minutes till blastoff. Roy Blade jotted a note in the margin of his own copy of *Blithe Spirit: The Life of Shelley,* and gave her a crooked smile.

When the lecture finished, Grace watched Kameko clear a way to the dais with quiet efficiency. Mr. Matsukado followed in her wake, but Grace could see it was a wasted effort. Professor Archibald had already disappeared, and Grace and Roy changed direction midstep and filed out with the others toward the Rock Garden.

It was hot and humid in the garden. Lowering clouds gave an oppressive feel to the afternoon.

"Target sighted," Blade said out of the corner of his mouth. Grace, following the line of his gaze, caught a glimpse of Professor Archibald, surrounded by acolytes, making a beeline for the buffet table.

"Got 'em," she murmured.

"And here comes trouble."

She glanced around and saw Mr. Matsukado bearing down on Professor Archibald from the opposite direction.

"Want me to run interference?" Blade was eyeing Kameko with a certain gleam in his eye.

"You are enjoying yourself *way* too much."

Blade laughed, following Grace as she weaved her way through the crush of people—most of them intent on getting to the food line. Spying her, Kameko moved to intercept.

Blade stepped in front of her, and Grace darted forward in time to hear Mr. Matsukado exclaim, "Professor Archibald, old chap, I wanted to speak to you on a most confidential matter."

"Hey? What's that?" Professor Archibald blinked at Matsukado as though the daylight were too bright.

"A confidential matter. A matter of great literary and historical importance." Mr. Matsukado looked over his shoulder as though he felt the dragnet closing in. Spotting Grace, he babbled, "I wanted to ask you about John Mallow. I must speak to you about John Mallow. It is urgent that I speak to you about—"

Professor Archibald scowled. "You'll have to speak to Elsie Weeks. She's our registrar. I really cannot be bothered with such details." He nodded curtly. "Good morning."

Mr. Matsukado snatched at the old man's robe. "But wait!"

Professor Archibald waved his robed arms like a plump bird trying unsuccessfully for takeoff, and scuttled away.

Mr. Matsukado turned to Grace, the need to

express himself overriding their broken alliance. "He's lying! He must be!"

"Not necessarily. It was a long time ago." Grace moved past Mr. Matsukado, running the last few steps to catch up with him.

"Dr. Archibald, I'm Grace Hollister." She offered a hand and a smile.

Dr. Archibald responded to the smile, taking her hand and saying, "I didn't catch your name, my dear."

"Grace Hollister."

Dr. Archibald squinted, then his eyes widened. "The Byron cameos. My dear, my dear. It is *such* a pleasure." He patted Grace's hands. "What do you think of our little conference?"

"Wonderful," Grace said. "And your lecture was so moving. I'd never read Trelawney's account of the cremation of Shelley's body on the beach at Viareggio. I've seen Fournier's painting, naturally." The painting was one of those wonderfully romantic and totally inaccurate depictions so popular in the 1800s.

"A marvelous bit of stage management on Trelawney's part," Archibald said. "The construction of the funeral pyre, the anointment of the body with oil and frankincense, the libations of wine."

"You made it come alive. That moment when Byron is overcome and turns to the sea to swim out to the *Bolivar* . . ." Grace had been both fascinated and appalled at Trelawney's grisly and detailed account of the exhumation and cremation of Shelley's and Williams's bodies.

"The heart that would not burn," the professor

pronounced dramatically, referring to the macabre bit of lore that had Mary Shelley carrying her dead husband's unburnt heart in a silk hanky for the rest of her years.

"Most symbolic," Grace said, just as though she would have done the same.

Professor Archibald shook his fuzzy curls for a melancholy moment.

"And *I'm* looking forward with great anticipation to your talk tomorrow." He was beaming at her. "What an adventure!"

"It's funny you should say that. I'm sort of on another adventure now."

"Indeed?" Professor Archibald practically rubbed his hands with anticipation.

"Do you remember a friend of yours from many years ago by the name of John Mallow?"

Professor Archibald looked blank, then something flickered in his marble-bright eyes.

"Johnny Mallow?"

"He brought you a sonnet that he believed was written by Percy Shelley."

The old man moistened his lips. " 'Sate the Sphinx.' Or 'Sat the Sphinx,' in all likelihood." He caught himself. "Then you've found it?"

Grace shook her head. "No."

She studied his face, but the professor looked as guileless as a baby. Of course, he'd had an entire lifetime to perfect that look. "We were hoping you might have the vital clue. That is, were you able to authenticate the poem? Was it by Shelley?"

Professor Archibald cast an uneasy look over his shoulder and spotted Mr. Matsukado hovering hopefully in the background. He looked alarmed.

"We can't talk about this here. Too damned many foreigners lurking about. Come inside."

Grace cast a look back for Blade, but he seemed to be in deep conversation with Kameko. At least she hoped they were conversing and not squaring off. It was not easy to tell from their expressions.

She allowed herself to be hurried across the green and up the stairs that led inside the beautiful main building of Amberent Hall.

The professor led her down a long hallway of shining parquet floors and glossy paneling. The halls seemed to echo with the ghostly footfalls of generations of students, the shades of voices and laughter. With something like homesickness, she smelled the peculiar and somehow unique school scent possessed by every academic institution from Hogwarts to St. Anne's Academy.

Archibald opened a door in the paneling and ushered Grace into a cubbyhole of an office graced by an unexpectedly grand arched window. Years of books and papers and stacks of teacups were accumulated on the shelves.

Archibald removed an empty birdcage from a chair, dusted the faded velvet, and beckoned Grace to sit. He found a way through the pillars of books to his own seat behind the desk and lit a meerschaum pipe. The smell of tobacco and old books filled the room.

"Now, start at the beginning and leave out nothing."

But of course Grace could hardly start at the beginning, and there was a great deal she had to leave out, so it didn't take her long to bring the professor up to speed.

He heard her out in silence, blowing smoke rings into the dusty light from the window behind him.

"I see, I see. And you want to know whether the sonnet was genuine?"

"Right." Grace was clasping her hands so tightly together they hurt.

Another smoke ring drifted into the stream of dust motes above the professor's bald head. "Of course we hadn't the technological resources, and it was wartime. We weren't able to test the ink and paper for validity."

"But?"

"But as close as I could tell . . ." His voice dropped to a whisper. "It was genuine."

In the sudden silence that fell between them, the first few pinpricks of rain hit the giant window.

Grace whispered, "Did you copy it?"

The old man smiled a sad smile. "I did, you know. But I was living in Plymouth in August of 1943, and the house where I stayed was hit by a buzz bomb. Everything I owned was lost."

"How awful!" Grace was very fond of her material possessions.

"Wartime." The old man raised his shoulders dismissively.

"Do you remember any of it? What was it like? Was it dated? Could you tell when it had been written?"

Professor Archibald was unfazed by the barrage of questions. "It was not dated, but I believe it was written shortly before Shelley's death. It had the melancholy mysticism of those final months. Perhaps it was the last thing he attempted."

She was silent, listening to the lullaby of rain.

"Strange that you should come now," he said quietly.

Grace glanced at him. "What do you think happened to John Mallow?"

"After he ran off with Bella Monkton? I've always imagined they emigrated to the States. Bella was wild for Americans. Got into trouble with one of the young fliers stationed over at—" He cleared his throat. "Ah well, water under the bridge."

"So you have no doubt that he did run off with Arabella Monkton?"

"Doubts? No."

"But she was only sixteen."

Professor Archibald gave her a worldly look. "I imagine Eve wasn't much older when she persuaded Adam to bite from the apple."

"But Eden—"

"Eden was a grand girl, but Bella was a force of nature. There was no resisting her."

The faraway glint in his eyes gave Grace the impression he was speaking from personal experience.

"When did you return the sonnet to John?"

"My dear, my dear." He shook his round head admonishingly. "You're asking me to remember something that happened half a century ago."

"According to a letter we found, you still had the sonnet in early October."

The pink forehead wrinkled. "October? I suppose that's right. I must have returned it not long after that letter was written—reluctantly, I must confess." He smiled wryly.

But he had returned the sonnet. Grace had not missed that telltale *"You've found it?"*

"If you could narrow it down at all."

"Hmm. Well, the doodlebug hit us October 14."

"Doodlebug?"

"V1 rocket, my dear. So I suppose it would have been between whenever your letter was written and October 14."

"When did John Mallow disappear?"

"The exact date?" The old man laughed. "After I returned the sonnet." He shook his head. "I'm sorry, my dear, but it all happened a long time ago. A lifetime ago."

Mr. Matsukado was waiting for Grace outside the hall entrance. Kameko held a shiny black umbrella over him. Rain bounced off it like glass beads. Roy Blade stood beneath the eaves, watching them sardonically.

"What did he tell you?" Mr. Matsukado demanded.

She ignored him but could not contain her excitement at what she had learned. Pointedly to Blade, she said, "The sonnet is genuine. At least as far as Professor Archibald could tell."

But Mr. Matsukado would not be so easily dismissed.

"Where is it?"

"He doesn't know. He returned it to John."

"He's lying!"

Grace didn't bother to hide her exasperation. "Would you knock it off? Why would he lie?"

Matsukado laughed harshly. "Why? He wants the glory, the credit for finding it all to himself."

"Then why hasn't he presented the sonnet to the world as his discovery? He's had fifty years. There was no one to contradict him."

"Perhaps he was afraid John Mallow would come forward. Perhaps he feared someone like me would come forward. And I have!"

Blade growled something that didn't carry through the rain. Kameko shot him a dangerous look.

Grace, struggling for patience, said, "That doesn't make sense. If Archibald had stolen it from John Mallow, John would certainly have come forward."

"That's what I mean!"

Grace put her hands to her head. It was going to be a long weekend.

❧ 20 ❧

Grace turned out the light and fell back in the soft pillows of her own bed. It felt wonderful to stretch out after the cramped cot of the dormitory accommodations at Amberent Hall. The sweet, cool scents of the garden drifted in the open window.

She was exhausted but content. The conference had gone well; in particular, her talk about her part in recovering the Byron cameos had been well received. She had made the acquaintance of several respected scholars in her field, and there had been much enthusiasm generated for the release of her book. She had received two invitations to speak at other conferences.

And while Professor Archibald had not been able to hand over the lost sonnet, Grace had not really expected that. At least Archibald had been able to confirm that the sonnet was genuine, as far as he knew. And he had been able to narrow the window of when John Mallow and the sonnet had both gone missing.

Sometime in 1943, between October 8 and October 14, John Mallow had disappeared, taking the sonnet with him.

Grace's eyes widened in the darkness. And Arabella Monkton had disappeared, as well.

Maybe they needed to turn their investigation toward tracking Arabella. Surely if anyone knew what had become of John, it was she? True, she had only been sixteen—and a wild sixteen at that—so it wasn't likely that she had stayed with John, but even so, she had to know what had happened to him immediately following their flight from Innisdale. She would surely know whether John Mallow had the sonnet when he pulled his runner.

It was a pity Brian Drummond was such a pigheaded jerk. He would be very useful in trying to track down a missing person. Sleepily, Grace tried to come up with an argument that might convince him to use his resources to help her. She was still arguing with him when she fell asleep.

A small but distinct sound woke her.

Grace opened her eyes and stared into the darkness. She was wide awake, her heart beating fast.

Uneasily, she tried to classify the sound that had disturbed her much-needed slumber.

The window.

Someone had closed the window. She processed this swiftly.

She sat up, eyes probing the darkness. Nothing moved. Chair, trunk, secretary, all stood motionless in the moonlight.

No one was in the cottage. So . . . someone had reached in and closed the window. Why?

Pushing back the sheet, she crossed to the window, trying it. It didn't budge.

She turned. The cottage had a strange stuffy odor. She sniffed experimentally. Something about that scent was vaguely familiar. Ominously familiar.

She headed toward the kitchen. She could see her purse sitting wide open on the kitchen table. But no one was after her purse, for it appeared as though the kitchen window, too, was closed.

Tentatively she tried it. Then she pulled hard. The window resisted as though someone had fastened it from the outside.

But that wasn't possible.

Still more puzzled than alarmed, Grace tried to angle her head so that she could peer down over the sill. She was flabbergasted at the gleam of metal. Someone had wired the window closed.

A whoosh of sound from the other room caught her attention, then flames spiked up from the pool of darkness next to the front door. In fearful animation they danced in a ring of yellow and red, and then seemed to leap toward the overstuffed chair near the secretary.

Grace scrabbled to pull the sheet from the bed and toss it over the flames, but the sheet crackled away like paper.

By now the cottage was thick with smoke. It was almost impossible to see.

Coughing, Grace raced back to the kitchen, soaked

a tea towel, and held it against her face, breathing through the damp cloth. She had to get out. But how? The door was blocked by flames, the windows were fastened shut.

The heat was intense. The living room was a wall of fire. The cottage was going up like a tinderbox.

Grace grabbed the milking stool she kept in the corner and smashed it through the diamond pane window. Wood and glass went everywhere as she jabbed the stool one-handed.

The sash stayed in place. She reached through, groping for the wire. It felt thin; that was good, surely. She tried to wiggle it loose. A shard of glass cut her hand, but she barely felt it.

Blindly, she followed the length of wire until the ends pricked her fingers. She felt feverishly back along the loop till she found the twist. She worked it, yanking it back and forth, trying to free it. The blood from her sliced hand made the wire slippery.

Every nerve in her body shrieked for speed, but she made herself slow down and make each motion count.

At last the wire slipped loose and fell away.

Grace swung open the empty frames, stepped up on the milking stool, and reached back for her purse. She tossed it out and crawled awkwardly through the window.

She dropped to the grass in her bare feet then stumbled away from the cottage.

In the distance she could hear sirens.

"Grace! Dear God, Grace!" Her landlady, Sally

Smithwick, was running down the garden flagstones. The curlers in her hair fell as she ran.

Curlers, Grace thought stupidly. I didn't know anyone still slept in curlers.

She turned back and the flames were poking fingers through the roof of the cottage. Yellow smoke billowed behind the cottage windows. For one crazy moment, she wondered how she could see the smoke so clearly with no lights on.

Sally joined her but Grace did not hear anything she said. She was absorbing the fact that everything she owned here was going up in smoke.

She watched the carved wooden heart on the front door of the cottage turn black. The door had not been blocked or locked to prevent her escape, but it hadn't been necessary. After petrol was poured through the mail slot and a match was lit, there had been no chance of Grace's escaping out the front.

"Oh, Grace," Sally kept repeating. "You might have been killed."

Embers drifted to the grass at Grace's feet, and she began to tremble with reaction. Someone had done their level best to murder her.

Her car was gone. Her home was gone. Her books, clothes, photos—decades in the future, no one would sift through the detritus of Grace Hollister's life, because there would be nothing but ashes to sift through.

The fire brigade arrived at last, aiming hoses of water at the cottage over the wilting hydrangeas and rhododendrons. Sally put her bathrobe around Grace and led her back up the flagstone path to Renfrew Hall. Grace spotted pink curlers lying in the grass every few feet.

As they reached the house they were joined by Chief Constable Heron and Detective Inspector Drummond.

"Thank heavens you're all right," Heron said gruffly. "We weren't sure what we'd find here."

"How did it happen?" That was Brian Drummond, dark hair on end. He was wearing jeans and what looked like a pajama shirt sticking out from under his jacket.

Sally shooed them all inside, settling Grace in one of the comfortable oversized chairs in the sitting room. Outside, they could hear the commotion of the fire brigade. DI Drummond stood at the window watching. No one seemed to have much to say.

Sally bandaged Grace's hand, scoffing at the idea that paramedics would do a better job.

"Tea, that's what we all need," she said briskly, and bustled off to the kitchen.

"You're in shock, and that's no wonder," Heron muttered, draping an afghan around Grace's shoulders.

Drummond left the window and dropped down on the flowered ottoman across from her. "Tell us what happened," he urged. His pajamas, she noticed, were a dignified blue-and-gray stripe.

"What is there to tell? Someone locked me in and set the cottage on fire."

The doorbell rang, and Grace started.

"That will be the press," Heron said somberly. "Sally will sort them out."

Drummond leaned forward, pressing, "What did you see? Did you see who started the fire?"

But Grace recognized the deep tones answering Sally's voice. She turned toward the doorway as a tall, familiar figure entered the room.

"Peter." She could have cried with relief. Cool and groomed and civilized, not a fair hair out of place, he might have stepped out of an expensive whiskey advertisement. Even his Levi's and green flannel shirt looked like wonderful product placement rather than mere clothes.

He stared at Grace across the room for a long moment, then the tension seemed to leave his frame.

"What are you doing here?" Drummond stood up.

Peter barely glanced at the younger man. "I thought you were supposed to be a detective."

The chief constable turned his shrewd and appraising gaze from Peter to Drummond, as Drummond demanded, "And exactly how did you learn of the fire so quickly?"

"I've news for you, mate," Peter said. "Half the village is down by the vicarage gates."

The DI did not look convinced. Heron said, "I believe Mr. Fox keeps a telescope in his front room."

"Very observant of you, Chief Constable."

"And he just happened to be gazing out at the village at three o'clock in the morning?"

"It happens I don't require much sleep." Peter moved over to Grace, dropping to one knee with utter lack of self-consciousness. He found her undamaged hand in the folds of blanket, his long strong fingers caressing Grace's chilled ones.

"No woman ever looked lovelier without eyebrows," he said.

Grace's laugh was half sob. She felt her forehead. Her eyebrows were still there . . . sort of.

"I still don't see—" started Drummond.

Peter said wearily, "And you never will. With or without a telescope." His eyes were still on Grace's face. "I think you should stay at Craddock House for a time."

She nodded.

Drummond objected and looked to the chief constable, but Heron shrugged. His black-button eyes still studied Peter. "I think that's an excellent notion," Sally said, setting the tea tray down on the table near them. "Now let's have our tea, and Grace can answer your questions. And then she needs sleep. I've no doubt she's in shock. I am myself."

So they drank their very hot, very sweet tea, and Grace answered Heron's and Drummond's questions, although she felt as little emotion as though she were under hypnosis. When at last the questions were done, Peter led her out into the night that smelled of smoke, tucked her into the Land Rover, and drove her to Craddock House.

She did not speak on the drive. She was beyond speech. She was relieved that she was with Peter; she felt safe with Peter. He was so competent. So utterly and unfussily competent. How much better it was to concentrate on Peter's hands moving with smooth surety on the steering wheel than to think about the fact that someone had tried to kill her, not once, but twice—and would probably try again.

Her eyebrows were still there, though singed. Her hair was frizzed about her face, although she did not recall being that close to the flames. There were smudges on her cheekbones and forehead, but those washed off. Her hand was down to a manageable throb, thanks to the two painkillers Peter had offered. She was incredibly lucky that all the damage seemed to be washable or repairable with scissors.

"This should fit," Peter said, when she stepped out of the washroom. He handed over a pale green silk shirt.

"It should?" Doubtfully she studied the shirt. Peter was tall and lean, and the shirt looked tailored. Grace was a grown-up woman with a grown-up woman's curves. "Because that's all I need tonight—to feel fat."

It was not the fear that she looked fat that put the waver in her voice; it was the knowledge that she hadn't so much as a T-shirt to her name.

"Bed for you, Esmerelda." He pulled back the comforter on the guest room bed. She had slept in that room, in that very bed, when she had stayed with Peter during their first adventure.

She couldn't imagine sleeping; she was afraid of what her dreams would bring. Besides, her brain seemed to be going a million miles an hour, flooded with worry and anxiety that no amount of sleep could stem.

"Call me, and I'll tuck you in." He turned toward the door.

Grace sat down on the bed. "I don't want to be alone tonight."

"Er—I'll sit up with you, if you like."

"Do you mind?" She held out her hand. The bedsprings squeaked as he settled beside her, easing an arm around her shoulders. He gathered her closer.

"You're safe, love." His voice was husky.

"I know. But for a few moments there . . ."

"Better not to look back on that."

She thought of the photos of family and friends turning brown and curling into flames, of her books charred black.

The awful shadow of some unseen Power floats through unseen among us—visiting.

"Thank God I remembered my purse."

"Yes. Thank God." His arms tightened briefly.

For some reason, the huskiness in his voice closed her throat and brought tears to her eyes. "I know it's silly to cry over material objects . . ."

"Go on, if you'll feel better." He kissed the top of her head.

She nestled into him, put her arm around him.

Peter made a strange un-Peter-like sound.

"I know it's a cliché," Grace agreed, shakily. "But circumstances are such . . ." She wiped another tear away. She was not crying, but every so often, a tear seemed to leak down her cheek.

He gave her a light, tender kiss, and stroked her back as one comforts a child.

But Grace was obeying an instinct as old as time itself, and her response turned the gentle pressure of Peter's mouth into something else.

She lay back into the bedclothes, pulling Peter down with her. Breathless moments passed, then Grace murmured, "You can turn the light out."

Peter rolled on elbow. "At the risk of being mistaken for a gentleman . . . are you sure?"

She nodded.

Still he hesitated. "I—er—fear I'm taking advantage."

She made a shaky effort to mimic his usual drawl, "I fear you're . . . not."

His blue eyes held hers for a long moment. He reached for the lamp.

❧ 21 ❧

"*I*'ll tell you what's really weird," Grace said.

"I'm bracing myself." Peter sat on the edge of the bed, fully dressed and looking utterly unruffled, as though they had not spent the last hours before the dawn making what Shelley had referred to as *delicious moan upon the midnight hour.*

Awaking to find herself alone in the bedroom, Grace was not sure if she was disappointed or relieved; she did not regret the instinct that had driven her to seek comfort in lovemaking—exactly. But she told herself she could no longer distract herself from the reality of this latest disaster forever. She must face up to her plight—to her danger—and the sooner, the better.

And so she had been lying in bed, staring at the dark wood ceiling beams, and "facing up" in an uncharacteristically apathetic way when Peter had walked in on her.

Feminine curiosity slipped through the apathy as she studied him. Peter smiled wryly, meeting her eyes, and it seemed to Grace that there was a hint of curiosity in his gaze, also.

"For all the wisecracks about my being a Miss Marple, I haven't made one single effort to find out who murdered Harry Kayaci. So why would anyone be trying to get rid of me?"

"Maybe the two things aren't connected."

"But according to Brian Drummond, someone is trying to kill me because of what he or she thinks I know about Kayaci's murder."

"Brian?" Peter repeated.

"DI Drummond."

Peter was silent for a long moment. She turned her head to meet his quizzical gaze. "Are you sure this is what you want to talk about?"

"Yes, of course," she said a little quickly.

He raised one eyebrow but said only, "I expect it's occurred to you that possibly DI Drummond is talking through his hat."

She smiled faintly. "True. But why would someone try twice to kill me?"

"At a guess, it's something to do with the Shelley sonnet. That's where you've spent your time and energy these past weeks. You've made no secret that you're looking for it."

"Mary Shelley's original manuscript for *Frankenstein* sold for about 5.2 million dollars, but that's an unusual case. If we were to discover an original poem by Shelley, it would certainly be valuable, but probably not worth millions. The greatest worth of these original works or first drafts or notes lies in their ability to help scholars figure out the poet's original intentions."

Peter was shaking his head. "That may have been true once, Grace, but cultural properties, including literary works, have appreciated at astronomical rates over the past few decades. In fact, art and antiquities theft is right there next to smuggling and drug trafficking. Partly because there's not an infinite supply of these items, and partly because a legitimate market does exist."

"Even if it's the finest thing Shelley wrote, it's not worth *killing* over. Trying to kill me? Destroying everything I own?" Unexpectedly, her eyes filled with angry tears. "Everything I own in the world—"

Silence.

"Not actually," Peter said. "You've got a blue jumper, three hair combs, and a pair of earrings downstairs."

The prosaic tone was like cold water, and for an instant it startled Grace speechless. But she could not stop inventorying her losses. "The earrings you gave me for the Hunt Ball," she wailed. "They were antiques." She was sick at the loss of those delicate pearl-and-filigree earrings, and all the other lovely things he had given her over the past months—including the book of poems by Ella Wheeler Wilcox.

"They're just things, Grace." His voice was quiet. "The only irreplaceable item at the Gardener's Cottage was you."

And he meant it. She had noticed before that for all his love of the beautiful, the rare, the old, Peter was essentially pragmatic. He had carefully constructed a controlled and civilized environment for himself, but somehow she knew that if he had to, he could walk away from it all without a backward glance.

Grace was not like that. She treasured the mementos of her childhood, the souvenirs of her adolescence. She took good care of all her belongings and fretted over every chip and crack.

He said suddenly, "That hat you shipped back to the States—"

"Hat?" She wiped away the tears with the back of her good hand.

"The one you bought when you first came over. Black felt trimmed with violets and white roses, I believe you said."

"Fancy you remembering that," Grace said shakily. "I'd all but forgotten that hat. You're right. I had it shipped home."

Home.

"Well, you know what they say," Peter said lightly. "Home is where the hat lies."

"I'll pay you back, of course," Grace said, receiving the stack of parcels Peter had purchased for her in the village.

"My dear girl," he murmured, as though she had said something truly shocking.

It was late in the afternoon. Grace had showered, tried to eat some breakfast, and waited impatiently for Peter's return. She carried the parcels into the bedroom and began opening boxes.

She supposed it was not exactly a good sign that he was so obviously experienced and comfortable at buying women's clothing. But he had taken time and trouble, and apparently spared no expense; the tightness in her throat seemed to grow to the size of the apple wedge that had choked Snow White. There were lovely wisps of delicate lace-edged satin and silk, probably supposed to be bras and panties, but in Grace's opinion about as useful as meringue. They would have to do until she could get into town and buy something more practical, something . . . cotton.

She moved on to shopping bags, lifting aside tissue to find Levi's and leggings—and she was touched again, because she knew Peter abhorred women in leggings and Levi's.

She moved on to discover two dresses, a sweater, and a number of T-shirts and blouses. She had asked for a change of clothing and he had purchased a week's wardrobe right down to the shoes. And with the exception of the undergarments, all the kinds of things she liked. He had had her measurements, of course, but the fact that he had picked the colors and styles that suited her, that she would have picked for herself, was surprising and immensely flattering.

Grace dressed in the Levi's and a jewel-necked knit top in olive green, slipped on her new sneakers and the one pair of earrings she had left, and set out to examine the ruins of her home.

She was glad that she had Peter with her as she poked around the debris of the Gardener's Cottage; it was the sort of chore that required the presence of a staunch friend. Sally Smithwick was also there with an insurance adjuster. She and Grace hugged in what had once been Grace's living room.

DI Drummond appeared while Grace was sifting through the rubble.

"It was arson, all right," he said shortly, his gray eyes resting on Peter, who stood a few feet away.

"The perpetrator poured petrol through the letter box slot in your door, then threw a match in. Quite simple. The only two windows were wired shut. It's a miracle you got out in time." Drummond scowled at the blackened steps that had once led to Grace's front door.

"Yes." She remembered the heat and panic of those moments when she had feared the worst. The cut on her hand seemed to pulse in sympathy.

"Out of curiosity," Peter said suddenly, approaching them, "where were you the night Kayaci bought it in the park?"

"Where was *I?*" Drummond's face paled with anger. His eyes were diamond-bright. He looked from Peter to Grace. "What's that supposed to mean?"

"Is it an awkward question?"

"It's none of your damn business. *You're* the suspect here. *You're* the criminal."

"You seem angry," Peter remarked mildly. "Any reason?"

Drummond's hard gaze moved to Grace.

"She's not interested; I am," Peter said. "The thought hasn't occurred to her yet."

Understanding flooded Grace, and with it came an instant horrified rejection that she didn't understand.

Whatever he read in her expression changed Drummond's mind. He cleared his throat, and said gruffly, "I was . . . performing."

"You were performing?" Clearly whatever Peter had expected, it wasn't that.

"With the string quartet. In the gazebo that evening." Drummond directed his words to Grace. "I play the violin."

Grace turned to Peter.

"I need a drink," said Peter.

"Very Holmesian," Peter said, putting two beer mugs on the table and sitting down across from Grace. "A violin-playing detective."

"You have to admit, it's a pretty good alibi."

"It puts him in the park at the right time. We'd have to know the exact time of Harry's death, alongside the exact time that Drummond quit the stage."

"You can't really think—"

Peter said grandly, "I suspect no one. And everyone," and Grace surprised herself by laughing. There had been little enough to laugh about that morning.

"Do you have some reason to suspect Drummond, or is this based on mutual dislike?"

His eyes flicked to hers, then his lashes lowered, veiling his thoughts. "A bit of both, perhaps."

She made an exasperated sound.

"Sorry?"

"Do you have any idea how annoying that is? That secretive streak in you. Mine is the life in danger here. If you've found something . . ."

"Something, yes. I'm not sure where it leads us, but I made a few phone calls this morning, and I've got some intel on your boy Sartyn."

"What kind of intel?"

"It appears that young doctor Sartyn was booted out of Turkey on suspicion of smuggling antiquities."

"Now, that is interesting. The official version is that Sartyn turned Kayaci in to the authorities. But if that were the case, surely Kayaci would know, so why would he and Sartyn be in partnership together? This makes more sense to me."

"What makes you think they were in partnership?"

Grace related Roy Blade's story.

"You think they were partners in the smuggling business, as well?"

"Why not?"

"I thought Drummond investigated Sartyn's story."

"Who knows what that means? For all we know, he got his information from Sartyn. How reliable is your source?"

Peter grimaced. "Let's say he's in a position to know."

"He has no ax to grind and nothing to gain by implicating Sartyn?"

"As you say."

"Then Sartyn must be after the Serpent's Egg."

Peter's expression seemed odd. "It's possible," he said vaguely.

"Can you think of another explanation for an ambitious archaeologist to bury himself in a quiet country village like Innisdale?"

"Maybe he was hiding from someone."

"Kayaci?"

Peter gave that sidelong smile. "It would be quite a coincidence if Sartyn chose to hide in the very village where Kayaci came looking for me."

"Coincidence happens." It was a long shot, though, and it didn't jibe with Sartyn and Kayaci being in cahoots. Grace thought hard. "The first morning I went to see Miss Webb, she said Sartyn had been asking about Sir Vincent Monkton."

"And who's this Sir Vincent when he's at home?"

"I told you about him. The Egyptologist. A contemporary of Howard Carter. He's credited with discovering something called the Tomb of the Sorceress. He wrote a book called *Kingdom of the Dead*, describing how he found the tomb and what it meant. Or at least, what he thought it meant. He was kind of a loony."

"The chap whose collection was conveniently lost in the Blitz?"

"Right." She smiled wanly. "What a suspicious mind you have. But remnants of recognizable pieces were identified in the rubble of his London home, so at least a portion of his collection was truly destroyed."

"And why was this Monkton more of a loony than any of the other tomb raiders?"

"Well, from what I've read so far—the book was burned last night, by the way—Monkton really delved into the whole Egyptian thing. He taught himself to play the reed flute and write in hieroglyphics. He tried his hand at mummifying small animals. He kept about twenty cats—live ones, I think. And he lined his eyes with kohl."

"*That's* going too far," said Peter.

She smiled, but said austerely, "I'm sure it's Sartyn."

"Trying to kill you, you mean? You don't know it, Grace, and mistakes at this point could be fatal."

"Well, who else? The Yakuza?"

Peter's eyes narrowed. "I shouldn't shout that about."

"I'm not shouting. I'm asking. Who else would have reason besides maybe Mr. Matsukado? Miss Webb? Professor Archibald? Professor Plum? Seriously."

"All right. Seriously, I don't think the Yakuza waste time on subtleties like running cars off the road or setting cottages on fire. They'd yank you out of your bed one night and put a bullet in your brain."

Grace swallowed hard. "Thanks. That's an image I needed."

"You can't make the mistake of trusting anyone, Grace. You like this cop, Drummond, but—"

"No, I don't!" What an annoying idea. She said shortly, "Anyway, he has an alibi."

"He's new to homicide. He used to be with the Yard."

"I know that."

"The Art and Antiquities Squad."

❧ 22 ❧

"The original draft of my book manuscript."

Peter tucked a strand of hair behind Grace's ear. His thumb lightly traced the outline of her ear.

"The gown I wore to the Hunt Ball. I loved that dress."

He smoothed the frown line between her eyebrows. The room was dark, so unless he had eyes like a cat, he couldn't see her frowning. It seemed he knew her well.

His muscles tightened as Grace restlessly shifted position once more.

"Sorry. Did I jab you?"

"Uh, think nothing of it."

It had been a long and depressing day for Grace. She had spent most of it talking to police, firemen, and insurance people. Even these last few hours spent in Peter's arms had not fully distracted her. The shock of finding herself homeless and possessionless was not nearly as great as the strangeness of realizing that someone wanted her dead.

The instinct that had guided her decision to bring a minimum of her possessions from home had been a good one. "Maybe my parents are right. It would be easier to sort through my stuff and decide what to bring back, if I went home."

"Is there so much to sort through?" His fingers lazily, gently combed through the waves of her hair.

Only her entire life. Her entire life before coming to England and meeting him.

"I haven't been home to visit in nearly two years. I'm not sure . . ." She let it trail, wondering if they were talking about her furniture and clothes, or something less tangible and much more important. She waited for him to say something, but he didn't speak. His fingers continued to stroke her hair in that absent, gentling way.

She wondered whether it really mattered to him if she stayed or left. He cared for her in his way, she was sure, and he had clearly enjoyed sharing this physical union; but as he had said, he wasn't much for commitment.

No one could have been more supportive, more generous, more kind than Peter had been that day, but somehow she knew he would have been there for any friend. Surely if he wanted their relationship to be more than friendship, it was the time to speak up? When she was cut adrift, wouldn't that be the time to suggest that they try and make a go of it— assuming he had ever believed such a time might come?

She remembered Brian Drummond's saying that

Peter would never ask her to marry him. Maybe he knew something she didn't. Well, given his time with the Art and Antiquities Squad, he almost certainly knew something she didn't.

Was anyone what he or she seemed? Sadly, Peter seemed to know what he was talking about when he said there was no one she could trust. She closed her eyes, breathing in his warmth and scent, and told herself that the moment was enough.

When she opened her eyes, the room was full of moonlight and shadows, and the bed beside her was empty. Grace felt the sheet, and it was cool. She lay there for a few moments feeling alone and lonely, then it occurred to her that she was in Peter's bedroom. It made no sense for Peter to abandon his quarters to her.

She rose and went into the front room, pausing at the silhouette of Peter looking out the telescope at the night sky, then going toward him.

Although she had been walking softly, he turned, quick and ready—ready for what?

"Sorry. I just . . . wasn't sure where you went."

"I should have warned you. I don't sleep much."

The thin silk of his pajama bottoms outlined lean muscle in a way that somehow exposed more than nudity. He wore no shirt. She touched his back lightly and was surprised at the rigidity of his muscles, the dampness of his skin.

"Bad dreams?"

She felt rather than heard the breath of his laugh. "Not really. I've never needed much sleep."

Gently, she pressed. "Bad dreams tonight?"

"Memories." He moved, adjusting the telescope so that Grace could peer through to the milky spread of stars. She fit her eye to the eyepiece and gazed up. She swung the long tube and could see the purple shadow of the nearest mountain.

How quiet it was. Just the sound of their breathing.

She straightened at last. "Well, I've got nothing to do for the next six hours."

He took her place at the telescope, adjusting the eyepiece.

"There were six of us," he said at last, as though commenting on what he saw in the zoom. "We planned the job for a year. It was the biggest thing we'd tried to pull off, but we thought we had an inside track."

Grace was afraid to speak or even move, lest she break the spell.

He straightened, one hand resting lightly on the telescope, still facing the window. "They said that the summer came early that year. I remember it was hot, and crowded with tourists. People and cars everywhere. But you still felt the magic of the place."

"I've seen pictures," she murmured.

"Pictures can't do it justice. It's ancient, fantastic. Like something out of the *Arabian Nights*. It's green, too. Greener than you would think. Almost as green as home. I used to dream about those green hills surrounding the city. The sun. The breeze off the Bosporus."

That would have been later, she thought. After it all went wrong.

"The air's electric with the shopkeepers shouting their wares and the smell of the food stalls in the Flower Bazaar. You can buy anything in that bazaar except flowers." He smiled faintly at some memory

Had he tried to buy someone flowers? "I've heard it's amazing."

"It is that. A mix of old and new, of Europe and Asia. The streets are narrow and labyrinthine, there are tea gardens and coffee bars, and then you turn a corner and there's some ugly modern blight on the landscape. The sun sets and you hear the muezzin chanting from the mosques, and then it's night and the city comes alive. The nightclubs and bars and discos are all packed. Music pours out of the shops; it's a regular street scene."

She could see the fleeting smile in the moonlight, an enigmatic smile like those of courtiers in Renaissance paintings. "We stayed at the Hilton Istanbul, like all the other tourists. Picturesque view of the Bosporus. Twenty-four kilometers from Ataturk International Airport and ten minutes from the palace."

She didn't need to ask which palace. Topkapi.

He was silent for so long, she thought he had regretted his decision to open up. Then he said flatly, "We were sold out. They were waiting for us. Cat and I were cornered in the main treasury room. I gave her the stone and a head start."

Grace knew from the newspaper account that he had been captured in the main treasury. She could imagine the desperate confusion and panic of those minutes when they had realized they were trapped. What had passed between Peter and his former lover in the final moments of their partnership?

"What happened?"

She did not expect him to answer at all, so she was not surprised when she got the abridged version. "She handed off the stone to Roget."

"Roget?"

"Gordon Roget. He was our fence. We'd worked with him before. A gray little man. The kind of chap you never took notice of." He smiled faintly. "The last person in the world you'd expect to have the nerve for a double cross."

"She was in it with this Roget?" She could well believe that and worse of Catriona Ruthven.

"Cat? No." Peter sounded startled. "No, she gave the stone to Roget as arranged. Roget contacted us, you see. In a sense, he hired us. Anyway, the job went south. The others scattered one step ahead of the Turkish cops and the army. That was the agreement. But Cat stayed on and tried to use the rest of the haul to bribe—" He broke off.

"And that," he finished lightly, "was the last any of us saw of the Serpent's Egg."

"Gordon Roget stole the stone?"

"One must assume."

Apparently that had been the last anyone had seen of Gordon Roget, as well. "And Hayri Kayaci?"

"Ah yes, Harry. The trouble with Harry," Peter said, "was that his greed outweighed his common sense.

He wanted to believe I knew where the stone was, so it wasn't hard to convince him I did." He said softly, "We made a deal, Harry and I. A devil's bargain."

"But you escaped," Grace said. "You got away from him."

"Oh yes. His greed was like a ring through his nose. I led him like a dancing bear."

She thought of the things she had read, the stories of beatings and starvation, of torture and humiliation. The bitterness in Peter's voice revealed the cost of that fourteen-month balancing act. There were clues to what he had undergone: his dread of confined spaces, the pale marks of scars on his back and ribs, the revealing dreams of food and fresh air. She wanted to know it all, every moment, every detail, and at the same time felt that she had already heard too much. It had taken him eighteen months to share that much with her—longer than he had been in prison.

"Where is the Serpent's Egg now?"

"I don't know." He expelled a long, weary sigh. "And I don't bloody care."

"You never found out what happened to Roget?"

"I never tried."

She put her arms around his waist, resting her cheek against his back. His skin was warm and smooth against her own. She could hear the beat of his heart, strong and steady. More than anything, she felt grief for him. She could never begin to understand what he had suffered. That kind of thing changed a person forever.

She was sure that he had killed Kayaci. She didn't know if it was justified; she knew only that she couldn't begin to judge.

And she knew that despite everything, Peter was a good man. A man worth loving.

It was one time she didn't want to know the truth.

❧ 23 ❧

Scott Sartyn locked the front door of the library and walked briskly down the street, his figure moving in and out of stripes of lamplight. He got into a black sedan parked a few shops down. After a moment or two, the car headlights came on and the sedan drew away from the sidewalk. Grace gave him a good head start before putting the Citroën in gear. She winced at the accompanying combustion and hoped that Sartyn had his radio cranked loud.

Well, as they used to say back home, the best defense was a good offense. She knew what most people would think about such a stunt—she knew what *she* would ordinarily think—but she still believed she was justified in investigating Sartyn. Her house and car had been casualties in a secret war against her. The police believed she was involved in Kayaci's murder. She must go on the offensive, not only to clear her name but to protect herself.

Scott Sartyn had to be behind the attacks. He had made no secret of his unprovoked dislike of her; he had deliberately tried to throw suspicion on her. He had known Kayaci; he had been in Turkey. He had been in the park the night Kayaci was murdered—only a few yards away when Grace had discovered the body.

Well, perhaps that was circumstantial; and besides, Grace believed that it was most likely Peter who had been driven to kill Kayaci, but Sartyn was involved somehow. It was Sartyn who posed a threat to her, of that she was sure. And that was why, while Peter believed she was visiting Sally Smithwick, Grace had been sitting in her car half the night watching Scott Sartyn. She had been watching him every spare minute since the fire at the Gardener's Cottage, but so far there had not been much to see. Aside from spending—according to local gossip—as much as a Yank on hygiene products, he seemed to lead a blameless life.

Following as far back as she safely could without losing sight of the taillights ahead, the Citroën sputtered along behind the sedan as it wound through the narrow side streets. Grace kept her headlights off. It was risky, but she knew the roads well, and at that time of night they were deserted except for her and her quarry.

Within a minute or two, she suspected she knew where Sartyn was headed. She was unsurprised when he turned in and parked before the tall iron gates of the Monkton Estate.

Grace pulled beneath the spreading trees and killed her engine.

She watched Sartyn get out, unlock the gates, and slip through them. He made his way across the overgrown lawn and disappeared behind the back of the house.

She gave him several long minutes, started the car, and, lights still out, drove past the tall gates, rolling to a stop, tires crunching on gravel a few yards down from the house.

She got out, closing the car door stealthily, and tiptoed up to the gates. They squeaked rustily as she opened them wide enough to squeeze through, and for a moment she froze, eyes pinned on the silent house.

Nothing moved.

Grace darted across the lawn, keeping to the shadows of the ancient trees. The night air was warm and humid. The breeze that stirred the branches felt like a hot breath on the back of her neck.

There was no sign of Sartyn.

Reaching the house, Grace skirted along the terrace till she came to an elegant swirl of brick steps. At the far end of the terrace, past the empty stone urns and gently banging shutters, she could see an open window.

Softly, softly she ran on the balls of her feet across the bricks and cautiously peered through the open window.

A leaf skittered behind her on the terrace and she turned, startled, but saw nothing but moonlight and shadows. Her nerves were getting the best of her.

A sound from inside the house caught her attention, and once more she peered inside.

She was looking into a small downstairs bedroom, probably in the servant's quarters. The room was empty except for a narrow brass bed without a mattress. She could barely make out an open door and a dark hallway beyond.

She could hear footsteps moving off down the hallway. Brisk, confident footsteps.

Sartyn had been there before, that was evident. Often enough that he was not concerned with concealing his activities.

Grace sat on the sill and dropped down into the room. Crouching, she waited a moment or two.

She rose, went into the hall, and switched on her flashlight. Nothing happened. She shook it. A set of stairs appeared in the wan light, running upstairs from the left. To the right, the hall turned a corner and disappeared who knew where.

Which way?

She listened intently. The footsteps seemed to be coming from the left.

Sneaking along the hall, she tiptoed up the stairs. This was the kitchen. Grace made her way through the cutting tables and old-fashioned appliances.

Ahead of her, the footsteps had stopped.

She snapped out the light and held her breath, listening.

A floorboard creaked. The sound seemed to come from the hallway behind her. Whirling, she stared, but she could see nothing.

The old house settling, she told herself.

From somewhere above, she could hear a muffled tapping. It sounded like bad plumbing. The sound seemed to travel down the length of the room.

Now, what was that about?

She turned the flashlight back on and crept softly down the next hallway. At the far end she could see a light shining.

Sticking to the wall, she edged along toward the light. When she reached the doorframe, she paused, gathered herself, then peeked around the corner.

The long, narrow dining room was empty of furniture. An elegant fireplace dominated one wall. A huge chandelier sparkled overhead. Even with the heavy draperies drawn, this seemed brazen to Grace.

She could still hear the rapping coming from the room beyond the dining room. What was he doing? Hammering something?

Grace steeled herself to cross the brightly lit room.

As she reached the doorway, the knocking ceased. Grace stopped short. A long, dark shadow slid across the polished floor.

She heard a queer sound, like a strangled cough. A moment later, the light went out in the room ahead of her.

Grace hesitated. The light from the chandelier cast flickers of blue and green and yellow against the rich wood paneling.

Beyond was silence. Dark.

A strange, unreasoning terror swept over her. Stepping back against the wall, she flicked off the light switch. The room plunged into darkness. Grace stood motionless, trying to control her breathing.

Her flashlight formed a small spotlight on the floor beside her and she turned it off, too.

She could not identify the sounds in the room ahead of her, but atavistic instinct warned her that something horrible had happened.

She began to edge backward the way she had come.

The floor squeaked loudly a few feet ahead of her.

Grace switched on the flashlight.

Caught in the circle of light was a nightmarish figure—black and bulky, and advancing with one arm poised to strike. A ski mask covered the face and hair, something sharp glittered in the light.

Grace squealed and threw her flashlight at her attacker.

The light cast macabre shadows as it tumbled through the air, missing its target. Something brushed past her face, and bright pain lanced down Grace's shoulder and back.

She turned to run and smacked into a wall.

Half-dazed, she crouched. The beam of her fallen flashlight illuminated a pair of stout black walking shoes. The shoes did not move.

Grace held perfectly still, not daring to breathe, not daring to swallow. Her eyes never wavered from the pair of black brogues in the spotlight.

Black brogues and charcoal trouser cuffs above them, still as a statue.

And then the flashlight moved. The beam swung up and across the opposite wall. He had picked up the flashlight. What could she do? If she moved, he would hear—and see—her. If she stayed where she was, he would find her in a moment.

The flashlight dimmed and went out.

She heard him shake it. The light flickered on the chandelier, then nothing. There was a bang across from her, and Grace nearly screamed. He must have thrown the flashlight.

She bit her lip to keep hysterical laughter from bubbling out. She didn't dare so much as exhale.

He was listening for her. Listening for which way she had run. Could he sense her presence? Feel the heat and panic emanating from her tense body?

After what felt like a lifetime, the floorboards creaked.

The soundless, careful tread raised the hair on Grace's scalp. She pressed her hands tight against her mouth to muffle the sound of her own breathing. Her shoulder twinged, and blood trickled down her back, itching as it went.

There was another creak by the doorway. He was leaving, retreating.

She stayed statue still. Seconds passed. She couldn't trust her senses. Was the whisper of sound from down the hall or in her imagination?

She tried to think. He must have followed her in. He could still be waiting for her, in the servant's room or outside on the terrace . . . or in the backseat of her car.

She trembled.

She was afraid to move, but she had to get out of that house.

And she needed to know for sure what had happened to Scott Sartyn.

Or was Sartyn the man who had tried—no, no. Sartyn had been wearing khakis and a dark shirt.

Her shoulder and arm throbbed. She felt with her good hand. Her shirt was torn; she could feel the long gash down her upper arm. It was bleeding a lot, although any blood seemed like a lot when it was your own.

Still she waited, ears alert for any sound. Her legs began to cramp. She couldn't stay there all night. Sartyn's car was parked outside the gates; it might draw attention. The police might show up—not that she wouldn't prefer the police to whatever might be waiting for her in the maze of hallways and staircases beyond.

She could hear her wristwatch ticking.

At last, cautiously, she crawled across to where she thought she had heard her flashlight fall. Her hand closed around its smooth barrel with relief. As weapons went, it wasn't much, but it was all she had.

She shook it hard, flicked it off and on. Watery light pinpointed the entrance to the next room.

Her heart pounding in sickening thuds, she crossed the long room and stepped through the doorway.

The fading light picked out the figure crumpled on the floor before the immense fireplace.

Blood pooled on the polished floor behind Scott Sartyn's head. His eyes were fixed in terror.

❧ 24 ❧

"What the hell were you thinking?"

"I just wanted to know what he was up to."

"*Jesus.*"

"Ouch!" She flinched as Peter, taping her shoulder up with remarkable efficiency, pressed too tightly on the puncture through the meaty part of her upper arm.

Grace was so exhausted she could barely think straight. Her panicked escape from the house and the seemingly endless drive back to Peter's was a blur. The whole evening was a blur.

"I could bloody well murder you myself." He finished bandaging her shoulder and stepped back, running both hands through his hair as though he had to do something with his hands or throttle her.

The bright light bouncing off the gleaming porcelain and brass fixtures was not kind to him: pale hair ruffled, blue smudges beneath his eyes, and lines carved from his mouth to his nose that she didn't remember seeing before. He looked as though he had been walking the floor half the night; and though his insomnia could hardly be laid at her door, she still felt guilty for dragging him into her problems when his position was already vulnerable.

"I'm sorry," she said. Not least because her shoulder hurt like blazes, adding to the list of aches and pains she'd picked up over the past weeks. She moved it cautiously and winced.

"I suppose you left fingerprints everywhere?"

She nodded guiltily.

"Footprints? And tire tracks?"

She protested, "I didn't expect him to be murdered. I was merely . . . observing him. As we theorized, he's searching for something. Or rather, he was."

Peter put a hand to his head as though he felt a headache coming on. Or possibly a stroke.

"I know what you're thinking."

His eyes opened wide like those of a cat dumped in a tub of ice water. "No," he said. "You don't. I'm not sure what I'm thinking."

"Could you tell what he stabbed me with?"

"Do I look like a forensics expert to you?"

"I don't think it was any kind of knife. It felt like a screwdriver."

"Had a lot of experience being stabbed by screwdrivers?" He raked a hand through his hair. "Are you positive Sartyn is dead?"

She closed her eyes for a moment against the memory of that sight. She nodded.

"And you couldn't see who the other was?"

"No."

"Man or woman?"

"Man. I think."

"Could you judge the size of his feet?"

She was tempted to retort, "Do I look like a podiatrist to you?" but managed a docile, "Big for a woman, small for a man. They looked like men's shoes. And men's trousers. They looked old-fashioned."

"How tall was he?"

She closed her eyes, trying to see the murderer in her flashlight beam. "Medium. Stocky, I think."

"How did he move?"

"Like he intended to kill me."

"Did he move fast and loose like a kid? Did he seem to know what he was doing?"

"I don't know."

He stared at her for a long hard moment.

"I didn't think it would go this way," she said feebly.

"You didn't *think.*" But he said it absently, his eyes narrowed, focused on some inner vision. Then he shook his head as though clearing it.

"Hell. We've got to go back."

"What? *Why?*" Nothing on earth would induce her to go back there. The thought of the creepy house and what waited within . . . "I can't," she told him. "Sartyn left his car out front. Someone may have seen it by now. The police may already have discovered the body. It's too dangerous."

"We've got to risk it. You've admitted you left your fingerprints everywhere."

"My fingerprints aren't on file—not in a police database."

"You've no notion where they're on file. Do you

think the police won't try to match fresh, unidentified prints to their prime suspects? We've no choice."

The good news was that he kept saying "we." The bad news was that he kept insisting they had to go back. "What if the murderer comes back? What if he's waiting for us?"

But Peter was already out of the bathroom. She could hear him opening drawers, closing them, footsteps moving swiftly back and forth. Grace rose and splashed cold water on her face.

He was back in a moment, and Grace was startled to see that he had changed into black jeans, black turtleneck, and black canvas shoes.

He tossed her a pair of black gloves.

They made the drive back to the Monkton Estate in record time, Peter cruising slowly past the front of the house where Sartyn's car still stood outside the gates.

"It doesn't look like anyone has been here," Grace said uneasily.

"Where did you park?"

She pointed out the spot as he drove on down the lane. They bumped over the small stone bridge, then turned off the road to cut through the woods. At last Peter brought them up on the back of the estate, pulling to a halt behind the tall iron fence.

Grace got out of the Land Rover, staring doubtfully at the tangled garden beyond the tall fence—and farther on, the black windows of the house.

"I've got a bad feeling about this," she murmured.

"It's called fear. You'll get over it." He beckoned to Grace, who shinnied with more haste than grace up a tree whose fallen limbs made a rough ladder over the fence. Her injured arm hurt like blazes. Her hand, injured in the fire, throbbed. All in all, she was not having a good night.

Perched in the tree, she stared down at the spear-points of the iron fence, so perfect for impaling one-self.

Peter swung up beside her. "All right?"

She nodded jerkily.

He lowered himself lightly to the grass and gestured to Grace to jump down. She took a deep breath and dropped down in the grass. As a result her shins *and* her shoulder hurt. She really needed to work out more if she was going to make a habit of this kind of thing.

She started forward, but Peter caught her arm, scanning the neat rows of windows for any sign of life.

"Do you see anything?"

He shook his head, gesturing for her to follow him.

They made their way through the garden, narrow paths covered in dead leaves, wildflowers and weeds springing through the dead vines and scummy ponds. They passed a reflective pool with a bronze statue of an ibis standing at the murky water's edge.

At last they came to the terrace.

Peter said, undervoiced, "We're going to retrace your footsteps exactly. Point out to me any place where you think you touched."

She nodded. He motioned for her to take the lead.

She went up the stairs, pointing to where she had

touched the balustrade. Or at least where she thought she had touched it.

Peter wiped down every place she motioned to. They crossed the terrace and slipped inside the house through the still-open window, Grace trying to repeat every motion she had made before. Peter wiped each place she touched, sill, doorframe, wall.

They made their way through the passages leading from the servants' quarters, up through the kitchen, and into the other hallway. She glanced over her shoulder. Peter was so quiet, his motions so economical, she would not have been surprised to find herself alone in the echoing emptiness of the corridor.

If he had not been with her, nothing on earth would have persuaded Grace to return to that creepy mausoleum of a house. As it was, she hoped they were not walking into some kind of a trap.

They crossed the dining room and entered the main hall. Grace shuddered. She could see the black outline of Sartyn sprawled on the floor where he had fallen.

Peter's flashlight beam moved over the body.

"It sounded like he was tapping the walls," Grace whispered. "Probably trying to sound out a hidden room or hidey-hole."

Busily going through Sartyn's pockets, Peter didn't seem to hear her.

"What are you doing?"

"Looking for spare change." He cast her a quick exasperated look. Finding Sartyn's keys, he tossed them once and caught them, an unexpectedly jaunty action.

Oh, the cleverness of you, she thought wryly. Though he would never admit it, she suspected that Peter was almost enjoying himself. Was there a bit of Peter Pan in Peter?

"The police will expect to find those on the body."

"And so they shall." He rose, lithe as a dancer. "Did you go into any of the other rooms or touch anything else?"

"No."

"Sure?"

"Yes."

"Positive?"

"*Yes.*"

They retraced their steps back to the terrace.

"The gate," Grace murmured. "I touched it when I followed Sartyn in."

Peter nodded.

She watched him cross the lawn. Or rather she watched for where she was sure he must be, but he moved fast and stayed to the deep shadows of the fence and trees. She had a glimpse of him when the gate moved. A few moments later, the headlights on Sartyn's car blinked on. The car reversed and she watched it move along to where Grace had parked earlier.

Nervously she paced up and down the end of the terrace. Through the trees she could see the car rolling forward and back. Peter pulled across the road and circled back around, attempting, she realized, to obscure her tire tracks. The headlights on Sartyn's car went dark again.

For what seemed like forever, she waited. She tried to read her watch in the dim light. Only about four minutes had passed. She raised her eyes in time to spot Peter sprinting back across the drive. He vanished almost immediately from her sight, sticking to the shadows and the stone and cement.

She was startled when he seemed to step out of the ground in front of her.

He came up the stairs fast, but still had wind enough to speak to her in passing.

"Start back for the car."

He kept going. Grace turned, bewildered, as he disappeared back through the open window. Then she remembered: the keys.

Uncertainly, with many looks over her shoulder, she started back across the gardens.

He caught her up before she had reached the ornamental pond, still breathing fast but evenly.

She thought of the old joke, "Friends help you move, real friends help you move the body."

They retraced their way through the overgrown garden. Peter gave her a boost, and she scrambled back up the tree and over the dangerous fence.

"Thank you," she said, when they were in the Land Rover and speeding back toward Craddock House.

"All part of the service."

"I'm sorry to have dragged you into it."

"That's my line, isn't it?" He looked away from the road, offering a wry smile, the first since she had shown up bleeding and panicked on his doorstep. "You used to be such a quiet, restrained girl. What happened?"

"You."

"LIBRARIAN FOUND SLAIN. POLICE SUSPECT HOMICIDE," read Grace over breakfast the next morning. She glanced at Peter as he poured more tea into the oak leaf china cup at her elbow. "Do you think *The Clarion* is being ironic?"

"Sadly, no."

"They found him so fast." She browsed the article. Sartyn's body had been discovered when a gardener at the neighboring estate had noticed the dead man's car parked outside the deserted house. The police were conducting an inquiry.

"They're being awfully close-mouthed about this." She thumbed through the rest of the paper.

"Don't read anything into it."

"No pun intended?"

He smiled faintly, but he seemed preoccupied.

She was rearranging an assortment of small clocks when DI Drummond showed up at Rogue's Gallery to request Grace's presence at the station.

While Grace stood there silently warning herself not to panic, it turned noontime, and the clocks began to chime the hour in a range of silvery tones. By the time the last note died away, Peter had appeared from the stockroom.

He leaned against the doorframe, drawled, "Ah, could this be that much-anticipated invitation to the Policeman's Ball?"

Drummond's gaze was chilly. "Hardly."

"Are you arresting her?" Peter inquired.

"We can do," Drummond said flatly.

"Merely curious," Peter answered. "Are you sure you wouldn't prefer to ask me a few questions? That's what this is really all about, isn't it?"

"You're not helping her, Fox."

Peter's lip curled. "Does she really need help? Surely you're not that stupid."

This was so blunt, so out of character for Peter, that for a moment Grace thought she must have misheard. Drummond's flushed and angry face indicated she had not.

"Uh . . ." she interjected quickly, looking from one man to the other. "I don't mind helping the police. I have nothing to hide."

For a long dangerous moment Drummond held Peter's gaze. Peter raised one eyebrow in that deliberate—and maddening—way.

"Let's go," Drummond said, curtly taking Grace by the arm and marching her outside to the waiting car. She tried not to show his grip was painful on her cut arm. It would be difficult to explain away that injury.

"He's on thin ice," he said under his breath, glancing back at the tranquil facade of Craddock House.

Aren't we all, thought Grace.

𝕖 25 𝕖

*I*t went through Grace's mind that the police might
be using her to get to Peter. Peter believed that
Drummond's sole reason for coming to Innisdale was
to try and nail him. It made sense, given Drummond's
history with the Art and Antiquities Squad.

But if that were the case, he was doomed to disappointment. Grace was quite certain Peter would not
sacrifice his freedom for anyone or any reason.

"What is it you think I've done now?" she asked, as
Craddock House disappeared behind the trees.

"We'll discuss it at the station," Drummond said
curtly. He was certainly a stickler for the rules.

So Grace forced herself to sit quietly, exuding inno-
cence and moderately expensive floral fragrance, and
hoping both were doing their job.

Once they were settled in Drummond's tiny office
he wasted no time in getting down to business. "Where
were you Tuesday night between the hours of nine and
one o'clock?"

Technically one o'clock would make it Wednesday

morning, Grace reflected, then wondered what in her psyche led her to focus on such trivial details rather than deal with looming threats.

"I'm staying at Craddock House, as you know." The chief constable would have pegged her response as prevarication, and he'd have been right.

"Were you alone?"

"No. Peter and I spent the evening together."

His upper lip curled, indicating what he thought of her alibi.

He stabbed a finger into what was apparently her file. He had nice hands, Grace thought. Well shaped and well cared for. Musician hands. No wedding ring.

"I want to ask you again about your argument at the library with Sartyn. You need to think carefully before you answer. A lie at this juncture could be most damaging."

"I've already told you the truth. I wanted to know why he was saying all those terrible things about me, why he was trying to implicate me in Kayaci's murder."

"And?"

"Nothing. He refused to talk to me in private."

"Why?"

"He pretended to be afraid of me."

"Pretended?"

Grace glared.

"Why should you think Sartyn was pretending? Patently his life was in danger."

"Not from me," Grace said.

"Did you see Sartyn after your altercation in the library?"

"No. And it wasn't an altercation."

"You didn't arrange to meet at another time? Did you go to the library again?"

"No. I haven't had time. My house burned down, if you'll recall. And before that I was at a three-day conference."

"The literary conference at Amberent Hall. Yes, I'm aware that you were in attendance."

She hoped he wasn't tracking her movements too closely. It would be difficult to explain away the previous night.

She said, "Anyway, it's my belief Sartyn himself killed Kayaci."

Drummond's brows rose in exaggerated surprise. "Really? And then I suppose he committed suicide?"

"No, I think one of their confederates killed him."

"Whose confederates?"

"Sartyn and Kayaci's. I believe they were involved in something together."

"Such as?"

The last thing she wanted to do was introduce the subject of the Serpent's Egg or Peter's imprisonment. "I don't know."

He rolled his eyes, which in Grace's opinion was a very unpoliceman-like thing to do.

"Your relationship with Mr. Fox has given you a warped view of how the world operates."

"Say what you like," Grace said. "Sartyn was up to something."

"Whereas you, Miss Marple, have no agenda?"

She was getting rather tired of the Miss Marple

comments—had no one in that wretched country ever heard of Nancy Drew? However, if Drummond was likening her to spinster sleuths, he couldn't be too serious about holding her as a murder suspect. Perhaps he thought he could intimidate her into giving away information on Peter.

Tentatively, she asked, "Can I ask you about the murder weapon?"

"No."

"For heaven's sake! If I'm the killer, you're not telling me anything I don't know. If I'm not the killer, then I have a better chance of defending myself against my homicidal maniac boyfriend, right?"

Drummond looked skeptical, but at last said, "We believe both victims were killed with a long, narrow metal implement such as a meat skewer."

Death by shish kebab, Grace thought, suddenly queasy.

When Grace returned to Craddock House she found Peter going over the books. He was a meticulous bookkeeper, she had noticed. It always took her by surprise, although attention to detail was apparent in every aspect of his life. Perhaps it was because he never seemed to think much about money.

"All clear?"

"The police definitely believe I had something to do with Harry's death," she told him.

"Did you?"

"Very funny," she snapped.

His blue eyes narrowed. "You're losing your sense of humor."

"I'm just struggling to see the lighter side of being suspected of murder. Maybe once I'm in prison and have time to reflect . . ."

He laughed, and reluctantly Grace joined in.

"It's that DI Drummond," she muttered. "Heron as good as told me he suspects me. Drummond, I mean."

"Then he truly is an idiot." Peter eyed her quizzically. "You rather like that idiot, though, don't you?"

"No."

He laughed, but it had a hardness to it.

Before Grace could say anything, assuming she knew what to say to that, the bell on the front door jangled and the next wave of customers entered. Peter locked the ledger in his desk drawer and came to help her in the fray.

A handsome older man with a thick shock of gray hair and a vaguely familiar smile approached her while she was ringing up a German couple's purchases.

"Grace Hollister?" And when Grace nodded, "Jack Monkton."

"How do you do?" She offered her hand, amazed and delighted.

"I've had quite a time locating you. Old Fen gave me your name."

"Professor Archibald?"

"That's right. He said you were looking for the sonnet."

"You know about the sonnet?" There was no reason he shouldn't, now that she thought of it. In fact, if his mother had shared anything at all of his parentage, she had probably mentioned the sonnet.

"Oh yes. It's a bit of a family legend."

Grace wondered if the quest was going to end there and then. Perhaps Jack would say that he had the sonnet, had always had it. She found the idea disappointing.

"Do you have the sonnet?"

"Me?" Jack looked surprised. "No. As far as any of us know, the sonnet disappeared with my father. For obvious reasons, I feel I have a stake in your hunt." His smile was regretful. "Unfortunately, my mother rarely spoke of my natural father. She spoke of the Shelley sonnet even more rarely, and I confess I wasn't interested—not then. I wish now I'd paid closer attention."

Grace shared that wish.

"The thing I thought you'd be interested to know, the thing I thought might help you in your quest, is that before my mother died, she donated my father's journals and letters and her own personal papers to the Innisdale Historical Society.

"You're kidding!"

"No. I assure you I'm not."

Grace couldn't understand why Miss Webb would have feigned knowing nothing about the Monktons or what had become of Eden Monkton or the Shelley sonnet, when she had in her possession John Mallow's journals and letters and Eden Monkton's private papers. It didn't make sense.

"Do you live locally?"

"I live in London, but I had to come down here in any case. They discovered a body in the home I own here. I meant to get in touch with you sooner, but I was out of the country on business."

Jack Mallow checked his watch, and added, "As a boy, as far as I was concerned, Aubrey Mason was my father. I hated the very thought of John Mallow. But I'm older. Mellower, perhaps. I've made my own share of mistakes. I realize it's unlikely Mallow is still alive, but if he is, I'd like to see him. And if he's dead, I'd like to know what happened to him."

"I'm not really investigating what became of John Mallow."

"It's my belief—it was my mother's belief, as well— that when the sonnet turned up we would learn what became of my father."

She suggested delicately, "You never heard from your aunt?"

He shook his head. "You've been listening to local gossip. My mother never believed that her sister ran off with my father. She was sixteen, after all. A kid."

"But then what happened to your Aunt Arabella?"

"I don't know. By all accounts she was a wild one. They weren't close, Mother and my aunt. My mother believed the girl ran away and that the timing was coincidence. She once said that she thought it was possible that my grandfather knew where my aunt had gone to earth; however, he managed to get himself killed in Turkey not long after the war ended, so who knows?"

"That reminds me. The Egyptian girl," Grace inquired. "Your grandfather's second wife? What became of her?"

"No one knows. After Grandfather died in Egypt, she disappeared. From what I understand, she was not happy in England."

Grace thought this over.

"If your mother didn't believe Mallow ran off with her sister, what did she think happened to him?"

Monkton shook his head and glanced at his watch again.

"She never expressed any theory at all?"

"Mother thought it might have had something to do with the war. He was with the SAS, you know. A hush-hush mission, something along those lines. Something even the War Office might not be privy to"

Grace had learned quite a bit about the Special Air Service while researching John Mallow. Formed in 1941 to conduct desert raids deep behind German lines in North Africa, the SAS had proved a fearless and relentless enemy—living up to their motto, Who Dares Wins. It remained Britain's main Special Ops force and one of the world's toughest fighting units.

Grace could more easily believe Mallow had been lost on a covert special mission than that he had deserted. Apparently the woman who, at least in theory, should have known him best agreed.

Peter, who had carried out a large white porcelain elephant for a customer, returned with Cordelia in tow. He was saying, "I should have another think. She eats a frightful lot, you know."

Cordelia, gurgling with laughter, spotted Grace. "Hiya! I've had the most super idea." She noticed Jack Monkton and became instantly self-conscious as she set her course for where Grace stood. Peter followed, steadying the vases and figurines she set rocking in her wake.

"Hul*lo*."

Jack nodded, glanced away. Glanced back again.

"Grace, why don't you come and stay with us for a while? Till your cottage can be rebuilt. It'll be a sort of holiday."

"Um, I don't know that there's any plan to rebuild the Gardener's Cottage," Grace hedged.

"All the better. Stay the summer. We could have lots of fun, you know." As she spoke Cordelia fixed Jack with that bold, dark gaze that was so at odds with her gawky movements.

Grace made introductions, observing them ruefully.

Eden Monkton might have dismissed the idea that her sixteen-year-old sister could have waltzed off with her fiancé, but years of riding herd on disconcertingly worldly adolescent females had given Grace a more jaded view.

Jack Monkton had to be in his sixties, but he was a handsome man, a man of substance; and Cordelia was a girl bent on broadening her experiences. There were not many weapons in her arsenal beyond baby-smooth skin, lovely eyes, and an appealing coltishness—but her aim was true. Jack Monkton seemed mostly amused by her interest, but Grace noticed that he stayed around chatting for longer than he had intended.

Somehow, without noticing, Grace seemed to have been drafted into the Big Sister program. Cordelia showed up uninvited the next morning as Grace was setting out for the Innisdale Historical Society.

She tried gently to discourage her, but Cordelia insisted that she found the idea of gaining access to Eden Monkton's letters and journals utterly thrilling. Grace accepted the inevitable, and they set out for the village and Landon House.

Miss Webb heard them out in bewildered silence.

"It's my belief your Mr. Monkton is mistaken," she said finally, uncertainly. "I'm sure I would know if any such exhibit had existed." Proof of her emotional upset, she had dropped her usual crisp telegraphic speech pattern. She seemed elderly and slightly confused.

"Maybe there was no exhibit," Cordelia said. "It was pretty racy stuff. Maybe it was all simply packed away. Kept under lock and key." She wriggled her dark brows suggestively.

"I would know if such articles existed."

"Perhaps the donation was made before you took charge," Grace offered, remembering Miss Webb had told her that she was relatively new to Innisdale. "I think this was back in the sixties."

"The sixties." Miss Webb frowned—possibly at the memory of frost white lipstick and go-go boots. "Well, I suppose it's possible." She brightened. "Attic is bung full of boxes and trunks. Suppose it could be up there. Haven't had a chance to sort through everything."

"Would it be possible for us to have a look?" Grace asked eagerly.

"Er . . ." Miss Webb looked uneasy again. "Not really practical. Place is a hazard zone. Spiders, mice, dust layers thick. Not in good repair. Not at all."

"That's all right," Cordelia said buoyantly. "We don't mind a bit of dust."

"But it's not all right. Not really. Not safe, you see."

"We'll be very careful," Grace said in her most responsible manner. "I realize there must be many items of historical and cultural value up there."

"Well, there are, you know, and I can't really risk—" Miss Webb seemed to rethink that, saying more diplomatically, "You're not authorized, my dear. If something were to happen, it could mean my position."

Grace sighed. "Whom do I need to talk to?"

Miss Webb looked taken aback. "Don't really know. Village Council, I suppose."

"All right. Thank you." Grace glanced at Cordelia, who looked ready to argue. "Come on."

Reluctantly, Cordelia followed her out. "You gave up easily."

"I haven't given up." She was momentarily distracted as a bright blue sports car zipped past, winding through the narrow village streets with ruthless disregard for the tourists dawdling across the road.

"What's wrong?" Cordelia inquired

"I thought I recognized the driver."

Cordelia did not seem to find anything amazing in this, and perhaps there wasn't, but Grace was still surprised to see Professor Fenwick Archibald speeding through the village.

"Perhaps he had a hot date." Like Cordelia, Peter did not seem to see anything puzzling in her Archibald sighting.

Grace made a face at this unlikelihood—the un-English phrase sounding more unlikely in Peter's public school accent. "He doesn't live locally, that's all. There are bigger villages closer to Amberent Hall, and we're not really on the way to anywhere."

"Perhaps he was visiting Matsukado-san."

That made sense, although she didn't much like the idea. She was confident that she was miles ahead of Mr. Matsukado in the quest for the lost Shelley, but if Professor Archibald revealed the substance of their conversation, her rival could come up to speed in short order.

"Or perhaps he was visiting Lady Vee," Peter offered.

"Perhaps Lady Vee was his hot date," Grace retorted.

"It's possible. The Cumbrian Circle did seem to emulate the spicier elements in the lives of their Romantic idols."

Grace was back to considering the potential threat of Mr. Matsukado. "How do I get in contact with the Village Council?"

"Tell them you're building a monster in the laboratory, and they'll be here shortly, torches in hand."

"Seriously."

Peter told her whom to contact without much interest. He had spent the last hour trying to evaluate a painting of Mount Scafell recently discovered in a local woman's attic. The sooty clouds and jagged black peaks seemed to form one glum blob to Grace's untrained eye.

"The frame is nice," she offered.

Peter grunted acknowledgment.

For a moment Grace watched him, chin propped on elbow. "One thing I want to do before I leave here is hike up one of the mountains."

"That sounds rather final." He didn't glance her way, continuing to thumb through a dog-eared copy of the current *Hislop's Art Sales Index*.

"You're not getting rid of me that easily. I simply mean since I've booked my flight home, there are a few things I want to do, and I've been meaning to climb at least one mountain since I arrived here. You can't really have a Lake District vacation and not climb a mountain."

"What does the local constabulary think about that? Your trip to the States, I mean." Peter glanced her way, but there was nothing to read in his voice or expression. Was he so sure she was coming back? Would he miss her at all if she didn't? "When's your flight?"

"Not till the nineteenth. Hopefully they'll have— well, I mean, they can't keep me prisoner here."

"Not yet."

She gave a weak laugh.

In the end, it turned out that Grace did not need permission from the Village Council to investigate the attic at Landon House. That same evening Miss Webb called, sounding much more like her normal hearty self, and told Grace that after a jolly visit with Jack Monkton, she had decided to allow Grace access.

No sooner had Grace got off the phone with Miss Webb than the phone rang again. It was Professor Archibald.

"My dear, *how* is the adventure progressing? Have you discovered anything?"

"I've got permission to view Eden Monkton's private papers, which were donated to Landon House back in the sixties. I'm hoping to turn up a clue." It sounded lame; she hoped the professor would not be disappointed with her lack of initiative.

"But that's why I've phoned, my dear. *I* have a clue. I don't know what use it may be, if any, but last night I suddenly remembered when it was that Johnny Mallow retrieved the sonnet."

"Oh? When was it?"

"The evening of the thirteenth. The night before the buzz bomb hit us."

Grace absorbed this slowly. "Do you know if he returned immediately to Innisdale or did he stay in Plymouth?"

"I suppose he must have spent the night in Plymouth. I can't recall now what his plans were. He was on leave, I do recall that. Looked very well in his uniform, I remember, but he always cut rather a dashing figure. Always popular with the ladies, eh?" He laughed heartily.

Rusted hinges shrieked as Grace raised the lid on the brass-bound trunk. The smell of mothballs and mildewed clothes walloped her.

"Pew. Smells like old ladies," Cordelia remarked from behind her.

"Or maybe a mummy."

"Or maybe an old lady's mummy."

"I wouldn't be surprised. There seems to be everything else in here."

Grace went to the attic window of Landon House and tried to push it open. The window was stiff with years of grime and disuse. With Cordelia's help, and using all her strength, she at last managed to shove it open.

As the window scraped open the last foot, hot air gusted in. The rotten clothes on the dressmaker's dummy next to the wall moved with a semblance of life. Empty picture frames knocked back and forth.

Grace stared out of the window. A black Audi was

parked in the weed-choked drive below. Miss Web appeared to be entertaining.

She returned to the trunk, found a relatively clean patch of floor, and began to sift cautiously through the contents. Linens edged with lace, now brown and stained, embroidered pillowcases, crocheted doilies and antimacassars. Miss Haversham's hope chest, she thought.

For some time they searched in companionable silence.

Cordelia, going through a box marked "personal papers," sneezed.

"Bless you. It's a shame these things have been left to rot," Grace muttered.

"These are the wrong date."

"Are you sure other dates haven't been mixed in?" She replaced the linens carefully. "This has all been left in a terrible state."

"Maybe that's what Miss Webb didn't want us to discover."

Grace smiled absently and closed the lid on the trunk. Stepping onto a rickety stool, she lifted down another box marked "letters," which she handed to Cordelia.

Cordelia promptly screamed and dropped the box. "Spider!"

"Oh, for—!" Grace jumped down and squashed the, in all fairness, science-fiction-sized spider that appeared to be pursuing Cordelia around the crowded attic.

"I think it went mad with the heat," Cordelia panted.

Grace grinned. "It's not the only one."

They both jumped as the attic door banged shut behind them, the sound as loud as a shot in the silence and heat.

"The wind," Grace said quickly in answer to Cordelia's horrified look. She went to open the door, but it didn't budge.

"Is it locked?"

Grace shook her head, testing the knob. "Jammed, I think." She wiggled it and shouted, "Miss Webb!"

They listened. The old house creaked. From down below, they could hear a radio playing.

"Miss Webb, can you hear me?"

"Why do people always ask that?" Cordelia inquired. "If she could hear us, she'd answer. If she can't—"

"Not right now, please." Grace banged on the door. "Miss Webb!"

"Maybe she's gone."

"Gone where?"

Cordelia had wandered over to the window. "Her car is gone."

Grace joined her at the window. The driveway below was empty. "What makes you think that was her car?"

"I don't know. It's her garden, isn't it?"

Duh, as the young ladies of St. Anne's were wont to say.

"I don't understand. Why would she leave without telling us?"

Cordelia did not seem particularly troubled. "Maybe she forgot we were up here. She's pretty old. Or maybe she plans on coming right back." She wandered back to the scattered letters that had fallen from the box she dropped.

"Maybe." It couldn't hurt to wait a few minutes, and they still had stacks of boxes to sort. Reluctantly Grace joined Cordelia on the floor and began dividing up the letters. The job was not made more pleasant by the quantity of dust and mouse droppings.

When they had gone through the spilled contents without result, Grace lifted down another large hat box tied shut with string. It was unexpectedly heavy.

Setting it on the floor, Grace worked the strings loose. Inside were neat stacks of yellowed letters bound in blue ribbon. Grace picked up the stack and her heart leaped at the address. *Eden Monkton.*

"I think I've found something," she said, and Cordelia came over and joined her.

For another hour or so, they were lost in the world of a young woman long dead.

Cordelia grew restless and began to circle the room. "How long are we supposed to wait?"

Grace resurfaced from the near dream state she had been in. Rising, she tried the door once more, knowing it was a waste of time.

"This doesn't make sense," she muttered. "Miss Webb should have been back before now."

"Maybe the car wasn't hers. Maybe someone knocked her over the head and robbed her."

"What does she have that anyone would want?"

"Information?"

"Well, then—never mind." Grace thought it over, frowning.

"Maybe she fell down the stairs or had a stroke or something."

"You're just full of cheery thoughts."

"Don't you have a mobile phone?"

"It was ruined when my car went off the road. Let's think about this for a moment."

"I don't have time to think. I have to use the loo."

Swell.

Grace tried banging on the door a couple of times. She looked around to try and find something to take the hinges off the door but could find nothing.

"The situation is becoming desperate," Cordelia said plaintively.

"I'm working on it."

"Perhaps you could try and climb down the drainpipe. You've done stuff like that before, haven't you?"

"*Me?*"

Cordelia shrugged. "That's what Auntie says. You've written a book all about it, haven't you? All about your adventures."

"It wasn't like this. It was . . ." Whatever it had been, it wasn't as though she had courted death and danger.

Grace studied the drop from the window over the alley. They were about twenty feet above the ground, so it was doable, inasmuch as the fall probably wouldn't kill her. The drainpipe, conveniently positioned near the window, looked reasonably sturdy, and what, after all, was a broken leg or two in the grand scheme of things?

"Whatever you're going to do, you'd better do it fast," Cordelia said ominously.

"I must be out of my mind," Grace said under her breath, but she sat down on the window ledge and swung her legs out over the driveway. It was a good thing she wasn't afraid of heights, because all at once the cracked pavement and weeds looked a very long way away.

Don't look down. Grace tore her gaze away from the dizzy drop, and reached out for the drainpipe. It was exactly like grabbing onto a fireman's pole, she assured herself. A really old and battered fireman's pole.

There were rungs on the pipe on every foot or so. Grace stretched her sneakered foot till her toe rested on the nearest rung; she let go of the window frame and wrapped both arms around the pipe.

With a terrible groaning sound, the pipe broke away from the side of the house, and swung brokenly out over the drive.

Grace squealed, half-sliding, half-falling, her arms and legs wrapped monkey style around the pipe.

Above her, she could hear Cordelia giggling maniacally.

"Don't look down!" she shouted.

Grace cast a quick look down. She was about nine feet about the pavement.

Cordelia, still in stitches, called, "One day they'll make a movie about you. Grace Hollister, Attic Raider!"

That brought a reluctant laugh from Grace, which immediately turned into a strangled gasp as the drainpipe did another bend.

She landed safely, if not gracefully, brushed her hands, and tried the side door. It opened soundlessly on well-oiled hinges.

Calling for Miss Webb, Grace stepped inside.

Her footsteps sounded hollowly down the corridor. A cursory glance into the museum showed that it was open to the public but empty.

Grace ran upstairs, pausing only to peek inside Miss Webb's living quarters. She glimpsed the over-size black cat on the table drinking out of a teacup. An old-fashioned table fan with deadly metal blades rotated back and forth, a ribbon trailing in the breeze. One of the table chairs was overturned.

"Miss Webb?" she called in a hushed voice.

The cat looked up and meowed at her.

Grace continued up to the attic. The door was closed, the old-fashioned key sticking out of the lock. Funny that the wind hadn't knocked the key out when the door slammed shut.

She turned the key and pulled open the door.

Cordelia hurtled past, flew down the staircase, barged into Miss Webb's flat, and vanished. Following more cautiously down the narrow staircase, Grace went into the flat and looked around.

Other than the overturned chair, there was no sign of violence. Then again, perhaps the thug of a cat had knocked the chair over. Perhaps the cat had done away with Miss Webb. It was as disreputable-looking an animal as Grace had ever seen.

She checked quickly through the rest of the rooms. All seemed tidy and in order.

Cordelia exited the bathroom. "No sign of her?"

Grace shook her head.

Not speaking, they went downstairs and looked through the museum. There was no sign of foul play, but there was no sign of Miss Webb, either.

"I think we should call the police," Grace said slowly.

Cordelia, examining her face in the oval mirror, said, "In that case, I think you should put whatever you want of that rubbish upstairs in your car."

Grace met her eyes in the mirror.

Guiltily—but speedily—Grace and Cordelia loaded Eden's journals and letters into her car. Then, a little out of breath, Grace phoned the police.

DI Drummond showed up a few minutes later. He listened to Grace's story—punctuated at intervals by Cordelia's opinions and stray thoughts—skeptically.

"She's a grown woman, Ms. Hollister. And it is broad daylight. You don't feel you're overreacting?" He poked his head into Miss Webb's bedroom and withdrew it hastily, apparently put off by the sight of her voluminous flowered nightdress.

"No. I don't. There have been two murders already. Miss Webb was very uneasy about letting us go through the attic, yet she suddenly takes off without a word, leaving us loose upstairs? You don't find that odd?"

"I do find *that* odd," Drummond said sourly. "But I find it odd that she let you in at all."

"Ha-ha," said Grace. "What about the chair? Doesn't that look suspicious to you?"

"Perhaps she was in a hurry. Perhaps she remembered she was late for an appointment She's only been missing for a matter of hours."

"You're making a terrible mistake," Grace said. "If something has happened to Miss Webb, every moment could mean the difference to her survival. I'm absolutely positive her disappearance is linked with the Kayaci and Sartyn murders."

"Of course you are, Ms. Hollister. But as you know, I already have a suspect in those crimes."

"Do you believe that Sartyn and Kayaci were killed by the same person?"

He said noncommittally, "They appear to have been killed by the same weapon."

Exasperatedly, she said, "Well, doesn't that mean anything? Or are you suggesting that a second murderer stole the first murderer's still-unidentified weapon?"

He gave her a long, unfriendly look. "That doesn't let Fox off the hook."

But it did, although Drummond did not know it yet. If Sartyn had been killed by the man who killed Kayaci, then Peter was in the clear. He had not killed Sartyn, she was sure of that. The person who had attacked her was shorter, broader, and had moved quite differently. Had smelled quite different.

Peter was innocent of murder.

Despite the fact that she had never fully believed it, that she had tried not to judge, and that it had only slightly altered her feeling for him, the relief was incredible.

She opened her mouth to tell the detective inspector what she knew of Sartyn's death. But as she met Drummond's bright and curious gaze, some niggling doubt stopped her.

If Peter was correct, and Drummond's real purpose in coming to Innisdale was to capture and convict the "Ice Fox," she might be handing Drummond the very excuse for arrest he needed. She might end up getting herself arrested as well.

"And?" Drummond said, seeing her hesitation.

"Was there a question?"

He said smoothly, "In fact, I do have a question for you, Ms. Hollister. I'd like to know why you've attempted to book a flight back to the States when you are currently part of a homicide investigation."

"Are you saying you plan to prevent my traveling indefinitely?"

"Indefinitely? I understood you had a four-year visa. Why the sudden hurry to return home?"

"I haven't seen my family in almost two years, and during those two years some fairly . . ." She groped for the word. "Momentous things have happened. I feel like . . . I guess I'm homesick."

"I see. So this would be just a quick visit, is that correct?"

Grace nodded. She didn't quite understand his tone.

Drummond said smoothly, "In that case, Ms. Hollister, perhaps you can explain why you have not purchased a return-trip ticket?"

"*T*here's nothing about Miss Webb in here."

It was the next morning, and Grace was breakfasting in the garden while she browsed *The Clarion*.

"Most likely she's returned home safe and sound." Peter replaced his teacup in the saucer, tilting his head up toward the bright sun.

Grace gave him a brief, disapproving look over the top of the paper. However, it was difficult to disapprove of someone who looked so undeniably sexy. He wore only Levi's; chest and feet were bare. He was all lean muscle and elegant bones.

She said primly, "Maybe the killer has claimed his next victim."

Peter smiled faintly without raising his head. "Maybe she is the killer."

Grace made a tsking sound, continuing to read. A butterfly flitted down and landed on the sugar bowl. Folding up the newspaper and setting it aside carefully, so as not to disturb the gentle folding and unfolding of delicate wings, Grace reflected that because of years of living in apartments, she had never really appreciated how glorious a real garden was. She knew they were beautiful to look at it, but she had never appreciated how soothing it was to watch birds and butterflies, listen to the lazy buzz of bees, or smell the truly gorgeous scents of massed flowers. Especially soothing when you were suspected of being an accomplice to murder.

With effort, she put aside the memory of her latest encounter with DI Drummond. The fact that he could even suggest that she might have deliberately taken part in a crime—well, in a murder—was offensive.

She ignored the whisper that pointed out that she had withheld evidence and engaged in breaking and entering; Drummond didn't *know* that.

"Anything useful turn up in Eden's letters?" Peter asked, sitting up and raking the hair out of his eyes.

"Not really. They're fascinating, though; they give such a picture of what life was like in Britain during the war years, especially for the literary set. I'm going to go back when I have time and really read them through. And it's so interesting to read about Sir Vincent. Someone should write a book on him."

"Uh-oh."

"Not me. I don't like him enough. The more I read, the more I can believe that he probably pocketed a few artifacts here and there along the way. But one intriguing thing cropped up. Eden had no idea why her father and John's fell out. When she asked Sir Vincent about it, he brushed her off with some story about John being the son of farmers and not a suitable match."

"Are you sure it was a story? Sir Vincent sounds like a candidate for class prejudice, especially if he was enamored of Egyptian society and culture."

"Well, Eden didn't buy it. The Mallows were gentlemen farmers. It's not like John and his brothers were out milking the cows and picking the apples themselves."

"She must have asked John about it."

"The antipathy seems to have been on Sir Vincent's side. John apparently didn't know what the problem was."

"Or he wasn't telling his girlfriend."

"Possibly." She watched the butterfly take wing. "There are no letters from John after the end of September. He was coming home on leave. The letter we found was probably the last he wrote to her. It must not have been mailed."

"Obviously he reached home safely."

"Yes. It's clear from Eden's diary, and cards and notes from different people, that she saw John a few times after he returned home. She had a journal, but she didn't keep it up. She mostly wrote in it when John was away and she had too much time to think."

The garden gate clanged behind them. Peter glanced around. Grace saw Jack Monkton walking their way on the flagstone path. He waved cheerily.

Grace waved back.

"Don't encourage him," Peter murmured.

Jack reached the patio. "Sorry to burst in on you!" He was carrying a brown-wrapped parcel.

"Can we get you something?" Grace offered.

"I could do with a cuppa."

"Allow me," Peter said, before Grace could rise.

"I spoke to the old girl at the Historical Society. You should have no trouble seeing Mother's papers."

"Actually, I was there yesterday," Grace said.

"What did you think?"

"I've only started looking through everything. It's difficult to say."

Monkton nodded, not really listening. "I've been thinking things over. Thought I'd like you to see this." He shoved the parcel across the table to Grace. She looked her inquiry.

"It's John Mallow's journal. His final journal."

Grace's breath caught. She picked the parcel up as tenderly as she would have a baby.

"I don't know what you'll make of it. I read some of it once, years ago. I was never able to make much of it. But as you're researching this stuff, maybe something in here will make sense to you."

Grace nodded. She laid the package on the iron table, pulling at the strings. The paper fell away. She touched the leather cover gently, then opened the journal, flipping through to the end.

The last entry was for October 11, 1943.

A kind of shadow seemed to touch her heart, and yet she felt a strange relief. Surely this was the closest to a happy ending. Better that it ended as it apparently had—even with the loss of the sonnet.

"Jack, I think I know what happened to your father. And the sonnet."

He sat up very straight. "And that is?"

"I think he may have been killed in Plymouth during an air raid. He had gone there to pick up the sonnet from an old friend, a Shelley scholar who was evaluating it. He picked up the sonnet on the thirteenth. It seems likely that he spent the night; he must have decided for some reason to stay on another day. There was an air raid on the fourteenth, and Plymouth was badly hit. Many people were killed, many buildings destroyed."

"But surely his body would have been identified?"

"It would depend. Not all bodies were identifiable."

His eyes held hers for a long moment, then he nodded curtly.

"Your father's last entry in his journal is for October 11. Your mother's journal entries are less regular, but I can't find anything in her letters and other papers to prove that she ever saw or spoke to him again after that date."

John started to speak, but Grace went on. "In '45, she mentions in her journal that Tip was getting feeble. I'm pretty sure Tip was your father's dog. If John had lived, if he had run off with your aunt, even if he had returned to his regiment, he would have taken Tip with him. He was crazy about that little dog. He had him in Egypt. I don't believe that he would have left him—any more than I believe he abandoned your mother and you."

Monkton was silent for a long time. At last he cleared his throat and nodded. His eyes, meeting hers for a brief moment, glistened.

"Can any of this be proved?"

"I don't know. It would take a lot of research, checking and rechecking old records."

"But you believe that's what happened?"

"I do, yes."

He nodded again and rose from the table. "Thank you."

Grace placed a hand on the journal. "Would it be all right if I kept this for a day or two? I've come to feel I know John. I'd like to read the last chapter."

"Of course. Of course. If anyone has the right . . ."

He awkwardly patted Grace's shoulder and walked swiftly down the path. The gate clanged shut behind him.

She was reading through the journal when Peter came out with the tea tray a few moments later. He glanced around as though he expected to find Jack hiding behind the shrubbery.

"That was quick."

"I'm afraid I blindsided him."

"It's one of your more charming talents."

She barely heard him, turning over another page in the journal. "How very odd: the last entry is written in hieroglyphics."

🐾 29 🐾

Your shadow in deceiving moonlight
Your voice in the whisper of sand
I drink from the waterskin, not water, but your memory
And at night wine cannot dull the ache

Grace recognized that line about the waterskin. Unless she was mistaken, John Mallow must have reworked some ancient Egyptian poetry. Ezra Pound had done something similar in the 1960s.

John had written a lot of pleasantly innocuous poetry, and he had done some really clever sketches. He had written movingly of the war and the world around him. She thought he would make wonderful material for a book.

If she wasn't going to return to teaching, she would have to earn a living somehow. Or perhaps she could return to teaching and still write.

"This is the kind of detective work I like," she remarked, when Peter looked in on her later that afternoon. "No danger, no dead bodies, just figuring out an intriguing historical puzzle."

"Fancy a visitor?" he inquired.

"Who?"

"Your trusty sidekick, the fair Cordelia."

"Oh." She slipped her specs up. "You don't mind, do you?"

"Not really. I trust we're not planning to adopt?"

Grace shook her head. Peter ducked out but was back a few seconds later with Cordelia in his wake. That day's ensemble consisted of hip-hugging pink jeans and a white tube top. Cordelia was about as thin as a girl could get, but she didn't look any better with her belly exposed than the chubby girls who favored that fashion statement. And why any flat-chested adolescent insisted on wearing tops designed to emphasize endowment was beyond Grace. She itched to give Cordelia a makeover.

"I hope it's not as boring here as it is at home," Cordelia announced.

"Boredom is the sign of a tiny mind," Grace informed her, reaching for the pencil she had dropped.

Cordelia groaned. "Did they make you memorize this stuff, or was it your own idea?"

Grace nudged a box of letters toward her. "Here. Sort these by date."

They spent a couple of productive hours while Cordelia sorted and Grace continued to read through John Mallow's final journal.

It appeared that Eden's instinct regarding her sister was correct. The only direct mention of Arabella was when John wrote in passing that she was "making rather a nuisance of herself."

It continued to puzzle Grace that there was nothing to explain why John and Sir Vincent Monkton had fallen out. Could it have been something as simple as class prejudice? Grace had grown far too fond of John to believe that he could be at fault for any bad blood. It was easier to believe that the eccentric Sir Vincent had taken an unreasonable dislike to his daughter's suitor. But it seemed strange to her that John had no comment on the subject. Surely Sir Vincent's attitude must have rankled?

Peter joined them—to Cordelia's obvious delight—for tea.

She was going to miss this, Grace reflected, reaching for a lemon tart. Miss the easy graciousness of afternoon tea and the pleasure of sharing her thoughts with Peter.

"Super!" Cordelia exclaimed through a mouthful of praline biscuit. She reached across the tray for another.

Make that sharing her thoughts with Peter . . . and Cordelia.

"So how did Shelley drown?" Cordelia interrupted, as Peter and Grace discussed the probable fate of the sonnet in the Plymouth bombing.

Grace replied, "There are three theories. One is that it was an accident. Shelley and his friend Edward Williams weren't very experienced sailors, and a squall came up suddenly."

"What are the other theories?" Cordelia popped another biscuit in her mouth and wiped her fingers on her jeans. Observing, Peter arched his eyebrow.

"Well, Shelley had been depressed for months. He was in poor health, and he'd suffered a number of recent tragedies. He believed that he would die young, and he'd had dreams that seemed, after the fact, to foretell his death. So some scholars believe that he might have done something deliberately to cause an accident."

"You mean suicide?"

"Yes. The thing is, Shelley could have committed suicide any number of ways. He had asked a friend to provide him with laudanum for that very reason."

"But he believed that he would die of drowning, didn't he?" Peter put in.

"Yes. But Shelley was very kind, very sweet-natured. It's hard to believe that he would have acted in a way that harmed Williams or Charles Vivian."

"Who was Charles Vivian?"

"A sailor boy Shelley and Williams hired to help with the boat. He was about your age," Grace told Cordelia, knowing the adolescent love of the gruesome.

Cordelia, however, looked unimpressed. "And what's the third theory?"

"The third theory is that the *Ariel* was deliberately rammed and sunk by an Italian fishing boat because Shelley and Williams were mistakenly believed to have a lot of money on board."

Cordelia's eyes brightened. "Murder?"

"A child after your own heart," Peter drawled.

Grace ignored this. "Sort of. There's supposed to be a deathbed confession from one of the sailors."

The phone rang. Peter rose, returning a few moments later.

"Jack Monkton."

Grace took the call in the kitchen, listening absently while she watched Peter and Cordelia. As Cordelia talked, she threw looks at Peter from under her lashes. He was watching her with an indulgent smile, one hand idly working a small cloisonné *Baoding* ball with nimble fingers. Keeping his hand in—literally?

Monkton said, "It skipped my mind when we spoke earlier—and I don't suppose it matters now, in any case, but after my mother's death I found a record of payments my grandfather made to a post office box in Scotland. The payments stopped after my grandfather's death. The arrangement was made without the knowledge of the family solicitors, so they were unable to shed any light. I was never able to find out who had cashed the checks or what they were for."

Grace thanked him and hung up thoughtfully.

"Do you know anything about hieroglyphics?" Grace asked Peter later that evening. Cordelia had left a few hours earlier, and Grace had reached the end of John's journal.

There was nothing of a revelatory nature because John, of course, had not known it was the end of his journal. He mentioned his prospective trip to see "old Fen" and the fact that his leave was almost up; but as usual, most of the page space was devoted to Eden.

Having read Eden's letters and journals, Grace

couldn't understand the attraction. Eden might have been a terrific girl, but she was utterly devoid of humor. And, in Grace's opinion, she took herself way too seriously. But in fairness, life during a world war had not exactly been a laugh fest.

"Such as?" Peter inquired.

"I'm not sure. There are several . . . I guess I would describe them as sidebars, and they're all in hieroglyphics. I don't know if John wrote them down because he thought they were beautiful and interesting, or whether he was really recording some information."

Peter studied the page over her shoulder. "I know that hieroglyphics are written in rows or columns and can be read left to right, right to left, or top to bottom."

"Hmmm."

"The key is supposed to be in the way the animals or humans are facing. They always face in the direction the line should be read."

"So if all the animals are facing right, you'd read from right to left. If all the animals are facing left, you'd read left to right."

"Correct. I have a book that might help you decipher them."

He left the flat and was back in short order with a copy of *Egyptian Grammar: Being an Introduction to the Study of Hieroglyphs.*

Grace spent the next few hours comparing John's tiny drawings with the list of hieroglyphic signs in Alan Gardiner's book.

Late that evening, she showed Peter her results.

"You see, this symbol seems to refer to a room. But with this over it, it seems to indicate a hidden room." She handed him the translation book.

Peter studied the page.

"And *this* would seem to indicate that it was a room belonging to a king."

"Possibly," he said. He glanced back at the open book.

"Or maybe a king is in the room. It's hard to tell, since I'm less fluent in ancient Egyptian than John. But what if he's talking about the Monkton Estate?"

"Why would you think he's talking about the Monkton Estate?"

"I know it's a stretch, but hear me out. First off, although it's documented that there was bad blood between John and Sir Vincent, no one knows what the reason was, and John never said a word against Sir Vincent. When John first showed interest in Eden, Sir Vincent seemed to be entirely in favor of the match. That means that something changed along the way. And since Sir Vincent lied about the reason for the split, it seems to me that Sir Vincent was the one with something to hide."

"Maybe he didn't realize originally that Mallow and Eden were serious."

Grace ignored this. "I think it's in John's character to protect the father of the girl he loved—or at least not speak out against him. Or at least not speak out against him until he had given him a chance to set things right."

"In other words, you have no idea."

She pulled her glasses off. "You have to grant that the psychology is correct."

Peter laughed. "I do?"

"I'm serious. Now, the thing that Monkton and John had in common, besides Eden, was Egyptology. John was stationed in Egypt, and it seems likely he would have heard the stories about Monkton's making off with ancient treasures. And from everything I've learned about John Mallow, he would *not* approve of that."

Peter set the translation book aside. "Your theory is that Monkton amassed a collection of Egyptian artifacts and antiquities during the 1920s, which he later claimed was conveniently lost in the London Blitz?"

"Yes. Besides the numerous complaints about him from other archaeologists, he had been declared persona non grata in Egypt by the government. In fact, proceedings had begun to retrieve some of the smuggled artifacts, when the collection was lost in the Blitz."

Peter raised a skeptical eyebrow.

"Suppose Monkton had the foresight to remove part of the collection before his London home was bombed? Museums were stashing artworks with the gentry all over the country for that very reason."

Peter's eyes narrowed. "You believe he hid the collection in his country home?"

"Despite the fact that destroyed pieces of the collection were identified in the rubble of his home, the rumors still persist that he had hidden his collection."

Dryly, he said, "And where there's smoke . . ."

Grace shivered at that particular analogy.

"True, those rumors could be wishful thinking. It's awful to consider that Monkton carried off irreplaceable artifacts, only to get them blown to bits in England."

Peter studied John Mallow's meticulous hieroglyphics. "It would make sense on one score. It would explain what Scott Sartyn was up to."

"Exactly! He wasn't hiding out here; he was trying to discover where Sir Vincent might have hidden his collection. But then Kayaci showed up and jeopardized the whole show."

"Or, more likely, wanted a piece of the action."

"So while Kayaci was stalking you, Sartyn was stalking him. Sartyn killed Kayaci and . . ."

"I'm interested in this next bit."

Grace wrinkled her nose. "Okay, that's a problem. Who killed Sartyn? But the rest of it makes sense, don't you think?"

Peter didn't reply, flipping back through the pages of Mallow's journal and beginning to read from the beginning once more.

"So what I want to know is," Grace said, "would it be possible to get blueprints of the Monkton house?"

❧ 30 ❧

"The other reason I like the idea of a secret treasure room," Grace was saying, as she rapped on the walls of the room where Scott Sartyn had died, "is that Monkton was fascinated by the secret doors in the Great Pyramid and the idea that there might be a hidden chamber beneath the Sphinx."

"Popularized by Edgar Cayce and his Atlantean Hall of Records." Peter spoke absently, his fingers probing knowledgeably at the underlip of the fireplace mantel.

"Yes, although I don't think Monkton needed Cayce to set him off. He was plenty eccentric all on his own. Lots of modern scholars also believe in the idea of a subterranean hall beneath the Great Sphinx. The passages are there; they just don't seem to lead anywhere."

"Odds are, you're right," said Peter. "This house was designed by the same architect who planned Craddock House. A secret passage or a hidden room is not out of the question."

"The same architect might have used some of the same tricks twice," Grace pointed out hopefully. And who better than Peter, who had uncovered so many of Craddock House's secrets, to figure out the mysteries of the Monkton Estate? "Otherwise, we'd have to start pulling up floorboards and cutting up walls and . . ." She was kidding. At least she hoped she was kidding.

Peter did not respond to this.

"The irony would be if there really is a room full of hidden treasure somewhere in this house, and Catriona and her band of cohorts were sitting on it the entire time and never knew."

"That would certainly be ironic," he murmured.

It was very irksome to her that she could never get him to say anything sufficiently critical of Catriona.

Peter stepped back from the fireplace. The furniture beneath dustcovers looked like a host of politely seated ghosts. Above the mantel hung a macabre Romantic portrait by John Fuseli of a sleeping woman with an incubus sitting on her belly, clearly a souvenir from the Ruthvens' sojourn. Monkton had never been interested in any decor that was not straight from the Middle Kingdom.

Before the fireplace was a chalk outline of where Sartyn's body had lain. A dark and ghastly stain marked the floorboards. Grace tore her gaze away from this and concentrated on Peter.

They had focused on that particular room because Sartyn had seemed to concentrate his efforts there on that fatal night—whether because he had already searched the other rooms, or because the room seemed the most likely locale. After several minutes, Peter had centered in on the fireplace. He knocked on panels, pressed different places along the molding, tugged on fixtures.

Watching him in action, Grace wondered who had introduced whom to a life of crime. She preferred to think Catriona had seduced Peter into it, but he wasn't the type to be led into anything he didn't want to do.

"So where did you meet her?"

"Who?" His voice was muffled as he was now inside the fireplace, pressing along the brick interior.

"Catriona."

That disembodied voice replied, "We were both modeling in Paris."

"Modeling?"

He spared her a glance. "That's right."

"You were a male model?"

He withdrew from the fire-scarred but otherwise immaculate mouth of the fireplace and gave her an exasperated look. "And bloody hard work it was."

"I—" She couldn't believe it. Of all the possible occupations she had dreamed up for him— Not that his elegant bone structure and striking features wouldn't photograph like a charm, and he certainly wasn't above capitalizing on his attractiveness. She'd seen that often enough.

"Drop it. There's a good girl." He went back to pressing bricks.

"How do these things usually work?" She tried

tugging on a tall, ornate sphinx-shaped andiron. It was very heavy. Then she realized that it was fixed to the stone floor. Was that normal? "Not exactly a practical place to put a doorway."

"It depends on how often you plan on using it and how desperately you need to hide the room—and whatever's in it." He ran his hands lightly down the wall as though he were brailling the stone, learning it by heart. "It's here," he murmured. "I can feel that."

She watched him commune with the stone for a few moments, then examined the andiron more closely. She tried pulling it to the left. Nothing. She tried pulling it to the right. Nothing. She tried turning one sphinx head. It didn't budge. She tried the next one. Nothing. Perhaps they were fastened to the floor to prevent anyone from making off with them. They were quite impressive.

She tried pulling it with both hands as though it were a joystick. She rotated; the andiron stayed stuck.

"What *are* you doing?"

Grace was bearing down on the left andiron, shoving it toward the floor. To her shocked delight, the floor seemed to give. There was a heavy grating sound, and the back of the fireplace wall scraped a few feet open.

"Oh *my* . . ." she gasped.

Peter looked taken aback as he stared at the cavernous black opening beyond the parting in the wall.

"Beginner's luck," he said, but a smiled tugged at the corner of his mouth as he met Grace's wide eyes.

The light from their lantern shone into the dark

room beyond, and they could see the dull gleam of metal fixtures, tall braziers.

"It's real . . ." Her voice gave out. She whispered, "We found it!"

He nodded and turned on his flashlight, slipping into the dark opening. Grace followed on trembling legs.

A strange mixture of scents greeted her, a musty mixture of bitumen and spices and—cheese and onions.

Her flashlight beam played over the floor and ceiling, then froze on what appeared to be a golden face staring back at her.

A funeral mask of gilded cartonnage, she realized after a dry-mouthed moment. "I thought it was alive." She gulped.

Peter did something to one of the braziers. There was a hissing sound, and a tiny flame sprang into life. Weird shadows danced across the room, but Grace only had eyes for the tumble of treasure dominating the center of the chamber. Stacked from floor to ceiling was every kind of imaginable item, from delicate painted chests to rough-hewn stone carvings.

"It looks like Tutankhamen's burial chamber," she said faintly.

"Or his rummage sale."

She laughed unsteadily. This was so much more than the few stolen trinkets and artifacts she had expected to find. There were even several mummy cases. It was . . . outrageous.

"The rumors were true. It was all true."

The brazier flame sputtered, and for a moment the room went dark.

"Tut tut," said Peter. The light flared once more.

Grace laughed nervously at the bad joke. "I suppose we can't complain. It's amazing they work at all."

In silence, they prowled around the room.

"We should call the police," Grace said at last.

Peter said nothing, fingering a fabulous necklace of gold and blue beads adorning the stone bust of an elegant bronze woman.

In the far corner of the room, a mummy case lay on a bier surrounded with mason jars. The jars were coated in dust, concealing their contents. Grace stared at the incongruously modern jars and felt a little light-headed.

"Peter," she called feebly.

She didn't hear him moving through the aisles of priceless junk, but all at once he was beside her.

Grace pointed at the jars. Her hand shook, her shadow wavering against the wall.

"Jesus," he said very quietly.

Trust Peter to understand instantly. His eyes met hers; they looked black in the pallid light.

"It's not possible, surely." Her voice was tight with tears. She wasn't sure why she was so near tears; she refused to define the suspicion lurking on the outskirts of her conscious thoughts.

Peter's face was stern.

He went to the mummy case and levered the enormous carved lid off. He gazed down at the contents, his face expressionless.

Grace stared at his face, then moved toward the case.

"Grace," he said in a strained voice.

She ignored him, gazing down at the wrapped corpse within the box. Between the bandaged hands was a thin roll of paper.

Her eyes met Peter's.

Gingerly she reached out and slipped the browned paper from its resting place. Cautiously she unrolled a bit of the paper.

The writing was faded and spidery.

This lament of soft sky and sunny wind . . .

"It's the sonnet," she said in an unfamiliar voice. "Sate the Sphinx."

The brazier light gave another jump and went out.

Peter swore softly and switched on his flashlight, moving toward the brazier.

Grace turned her flashlight back to the sonnet.

There was a small sound, like a cat-sized yawn. Grace directed her flashlight toward the sound.

The mummy case against the wall was opening, and as she stared, a shapeless form seemed to slip out of the case.

"Peter!"

He turned, but the figure had melted into the crowd of statues and furniture.

"Someone's in here with us," she hissed. She shined her flashlight in the direction where she had seen the other. Here and there a painted eye or ancient smile on a funerary stela caught the light, a gleam of gold or the sparkle of a jewel was briefly illuminated in the electric beam.

"Don't say anything else," he warned. "Turn off your torch."

Grace snapped out the flashlight, understanding the danger. In the tomblike darkness they were at the disadvantage of this other, who clearly was on familiar ground.

Replacing the sonnet in the case, she ducked, hands outstretched to guide her. She moved softly, carefully away from where she had seen the other. What did Peter want her to do? Should she try and make her way toward him, or should she try and get out of the room, or should she find a corner to hide in? Their best bet was probably to try and close in on their quarry from both sides, but Grace wasn't any too keen on trying to corner a murderer, especially with her bare hands.

She caught the whisper of footsteps coming toward her. Her heart began to thud so loudly in her ears she could hardly hear over it. It wasn't Peter, because Peter's flashlight was still on—she could see his silhouette magnified against the far wall, his shadow within devouring range of the shadow of jackal-headed Anubis.

Her groping fingers knocked against a small vase or statue. She heard it rocking and grabbed blindly, surprised when her fingers closed about it, keeping it from pitching off a carved table.

The nearly soundless scuff was drawing near. She felt blindly ahead of herself, then scooted through an

opening between a crate and a wooden pillar. She
was in a maze of artifacts and statues piled in the center of the room.

Peter's beam slowly traversed the room, briefly
illuminating a golden death mask, a cat statue, a
painted throne. Something flickered on the outer
edge of the spotlight and was gone.

Grace swallowed hard and huddled closer to the
feet of a six-foot statue of a woman with the surprisingly graceful head of a cow.

Peter's beam held steady. He was deliberately setting himself up as the target, and Grace didn't think
her nerves could take the suspense.

There was a ghastly shriek and a figure crossed
Peter's flashlight beam, something long and silver
glittering in the upraised hand. Grace cried out in
warning.

The flashlight rolled and fell from the deck of the
funeral boat where Peter had propped it.

As it hit the floor, Grace heard sounds of a struggle.
She stood up, shining her flashlight in the direction of
the fighting, and saw Peter struggling with a shorter,
bulkier figure.

She tried to place the beam of her flashlight in the
intruder's eyes, and hoped she wasn't hindering
Peter. The shorter figure slashed and stabbed wildly at
Peter's agile form.

Peter's arm went back, and he punched the other
squarely in the face.

The bulky figure crashed down, taking a small
table and several faience figurines with it.

Peter stood for a moment staring down, his ches
rising and falling. He looked up as Grace crawled ou
from under the cow woman's throne and clambere
toward him over furniture and statuary.

"Speaking of overlooking the obvious."

She reached his side and turned her flashlight o
their unconscious attacker. A ski mask covered th
face. A darning needle lay a few inches from the la
fingers. Grace processed this in silence, then looked t
Peter.

"You've got to be kidding me!"

"It does explain—"

"You're telling me *Miss Webb* faked her own disap
pearance? *Miss Webb* tried to kill me? *Miss Webb* kille
Scott Sartyn and Hayri Kayaci?"

"Yes. And no." He knelt and pulled the ski masl
from Miss Webb's head. She murmured a protest; he
eyes fluttered and opened.

Peter said dryly, "Introducing—"

"Oh, don't tell me," interrupted Grace disgustedly
"I've already figured it out."

"Arabella Monkton," concluded Peter.

Miss Webb groaned.

❧ 31 ❧

"What I don't understand is why Miss Webb staged that mock abduction?"

It was the afternoon after Miss Webb had tried to kill them in the hidden treasure room. As they were sitting down to tea, Detective Inspector Drummond had stopped by Craddock House to bring Grace and Peter up to speed on the latest developments in the case.

"*That's* the bit you don't understand?" Peter raised his brows.

Drummond said, "It doesn't sound like she had thought it out properly. Monkton came to see her about his mother's letters and journals, and apparently said something to the effect that she looked familiar. At the same time, you were pestering her about the journals. The body count was climbing, and it looks like she decided to do a bunk."

"But she only ran as far as the Monkton Estate."

"It's not as though she's, well, quite right in the head," Drummond said. He was looking around

Peter's elegant living room with barely veiled curiosity.

Peter said evenly, "It was home, wasn't it? Where it all began so many years ago. And she was too old for life on the run. Things have changed now. You can't turn up someplace without any ID and build a new life, no questions asked."

Drummond's gray gaze moved to Peter, and he shrugged. "I suppose that was part of it."

Grace poured tea into the ivy china cups.

"The one good thing that's come out of this is that Jack Monkton knows now what happened to his father. That mystery is solved. It's too bad that Eden couldn't have lived long enough to learn the truth." But perhaps she had always known the most important thing—that John Mallow had not deliberately abandoned her and her unborn child. Grace wanted to believe so, anyway.

"There's more good things than that to come from this," Drummond said cheerfully. He was in terrific spirits that afternoon. "There's a bloody treasure trove in that hidden room. More than one museum is going to have cause for rejoicing."

"Certainly the Egyptian government will be interested," Peter murmured.

"True." Drummond reached for a cream-filled bun.

Grace said, "The sonnet will go to the Bodleian; that's what Jack said this morning when I spoke to him."

"And you will get the credit." Drummond smiled at her. Peter directed a level look his way.

"John will get the credit. He's the one who deserves it."

They were silent for a moment, recalling John Mallow's gruesome fate.

"Personally," Grace said at last, "my money was on Sir Vincent Monkton. It's difficult to think of a sixteen-year-old girl committing murder."

"Really? After all those horror stories about the belles of St. Mary . . ." That was Peter. Grace shot him a dark look.

"St. Anne's," she said.

Drummond said, "Miss Webb is clear enough about her recent crimes, but she's vague about what happened sixty-odd years ago. Partly, I suppose, because of the time lapse, and partly because it seems to have been a crime of impulse."

"I can guess some of what happened," Grace said. "John must have gone that night to confront Monkton. I can't imagine he would have wanted to expose him, because of Eden, but Monkton's own attitude would have made it difficult. They must have argued."

"That jibes with what Miss Webb told us. Mallow seems to have somehow discovered Monkton's secret. They rowed that night, then Mallow left. Unfortunately, he ran into Arabella, who had just learned that Mallow and her sister were making plans to run off to Gretna Green. Whether she was acting out of her own frustration at being rebuffed or to protect her father, she struck him over the head with a poker as he came out of the secret room."

"And then there was no going back," Peter said.

Drummond said curtly, "Not for her, apparently. Even now she doesn't seem to feel a flicker of remorse. Monkton, perhaps to protect his daughter, or more likely to preserve his precious collection, dragged Mallow back into the treasure room."

"And . . . mummified him," Grace said, not quite steadily.

"Apparently so. Eventually."

Grace asked, "Whose idea was it that Arabella should leave that night? Did she really leave a note saying that she and John were running off together?"

"That seems to have been her father's idea. He had her write the letter, then sent her off for safekeeping to friends in Scotland."

"But he died suddenly in Egypt not long after the war," Peter said thoughtfully. "The lolly would have stopped then, and the girl would have had to make her own way in the world."

"Which she seems to have managed ably enough. Doesn't appear that she ever looked back until she returned here."

Grace, the product of a close-knit and loving family, protested, "How could Monkton let his own daughter believe her fiancé had abandoned her?"

Drummond shrugged. "I think that was the least of his concerns. Monkton hated Mallow, and I'm sure he managed to self-justify his actions. After all, he allowed Eden to keep the child, which wasn't typical of those days. He supported her and the baby until she finally married."

"So the money to the post office box in Scotland was Monkton paying off Arabella?" Grace guessed.

"Or supporting her. Unfortunately he didn't appear to make provision for her in the event of his death, and Arabella was left to fend for herself. Eventually she came back to Innisdale with a new name and a new identity."

"But why did she come back here? Especially since she could never admit who she was or claim her share of her inheritance. It was such a dangerous choice."

Drummond said, "No one can answer for sure. Until Sartyn started nosing around, she seems to have been content to live out the role she chose for herself."

"And you say that she confessed to killing Kayaci?" she asked innocently.

"Yes," Drummond said, not meeting her eyes. "It seems pretty clear that Sartyn had done his homework and came to Innisdale hunting Monkton's lost collection. Once here, he discovered Peter Fox was living locally"—his eyes flicked toward Peter—"and contacted his former partner, Kayaci. It doesn't sound like he had ever heard of John Mallow or had any idea there was anything to his disappearance, but Miss Webb couldn't have him digging around. She knew what he would find if he discovered the hidden room."

Grace shivered, thinking of the terrible secret of the mummy case.

"From what we can make out, she was stalking Sartyn."

"And she just happened to be carrying a darning needle?"

"Apparently she used to carry one all the time for protection when she was out walking. It's the sort of thing old ladies do, isn't it? I'd an auntie who used to carry a railroad tie nail. Anyway, she overheard Kayaci and Sartyn discussing Mr. Fox, and must have seen a way to narrow the field. She assumed Sartyn would be blamed for the death. If the police didn't nab him, she could always take care of him herself."

"The best-laid plans," Peter said dryly.

Drummond shot him a cool look. "Yes. Naturally we suspected you. That wouldn't have troubled Miss Webb any, but then Ms. Hollister poked her nose in."

Grace made a face.

Drummond told her, "Miss Webb began to follow you. It was she who caused your car to go off the road into Lake Swirlbeck. She says she was only trying to warn you off."

"Rather a stern warning," said Peter.

"She claims Grace's going into the water was an accident." He held his cup out for a refill. "But there's no mistake about her setting your cottage on fire. She believed you were getting too close to her secret and had to be stopped."

When the tea cakes had been eaten and the last of their questions answered, DI Drummond rose, and Grace saw him downstairs.

He hesitated outside the front door.

"Grace, oddly enough, it turns out I'll be in Los Angeles around the same time as you," he said very casually.

"Really? That's a coincidence." Then she realized he had never called her by her Christian name before. "I hope," she added, suddenly wary.

His smile was rueful. "It is a coincidence. Every other year or so, Interpol organizes an international training conference on cultural property trafficking. This year it's going to be held at your Convention Center."

"Er . . . really?" She kept saying that.

"Maybe we could have dinner one night?"

Grace stared. "Oh! I—well, yes, I suppose so." At his expression, she said honestly, "I'm surprised. I was under the impression you were only interested in me as a means of getting to Peter."

He looked uncomfortable. "I used to notice you in church long before I knew who you were. I thought . . . well, I thought you looked like someone I'd like to get to know. Then I found out about your connection to Peter Fox."

"Oh."

"Yes. Well." He was awkward. "So when you come back, are you and Fox . . . is this an exclusive arrangement?"

"I . . . well, we never actually discussed it."

"But you want it to be?"

"Yes, if—"

If what? If she knew for sure that Peter loved her? If she knew for sure that they could be happy together?

If she didn't feel compelled to make a pilgrimage back home?

"As I said, we've never discussed it."

He laughed.

He had a nice laugh, she realized for the first time.

❧ epilogue ❧

A sparrow hawk circled high, high above,
crying out in the blue emptiness of the sky.

"Why do hawks do that, do you think?" Grace asked, a little breathless from the climb. She placed a cautious hand on a boulder that jutted out from the mountainside and leaned forward, gazing down at the checkerboard of green fields and golden meadows. The lakes and streams gleamed like silver. From their vantage point she could see the entire valley. Innisdale Wood, the village, a tiny white dollhouse that was surely Craddock House; they looked like illustrations in a child's story.

Peter shaded his eyes, searching the sky. "Hunting, perhaps."

"Maybe he's warning us off." She dropped to the ground, tired but exhilarated from the hike that had taken the best part of the morning. "Or maybe he's just happy."

His thin mouth curved; he still gazed upward.

"Maybe." He lowered his hand and found a place on the ground beside Grace.

"Thank you for bringing me here."

The cold, clean wind off the top of the mountain stirred the tendrils from her damp temples and ruffled Peter's pale hair.

He said, "I used to hike here often when I first moved to Lakeland. Not so much now."

She could understand the desire, after what he had been through in Turkey, to climb as far as humanly possible from the noise and dirt of cities and the men who built them. This was as close as you could get to God. Nothing but sun and sky—and the echoing cries of wild things.

"It's beautiful. Beautiful beyond words."

His lean cheek creased. "Praise indeed."

She chuckled.

They were silent for a few minutes.

"Your plane leaves Monday?"

She nodded.

"And there's no talking you out of it?"

She laughed and shook her head.

"But you're coming back." It was a statement, yet there was something very . . . neutral . . . in his tone.

She studied his profile. "Yes."

"But you don't know when."

"As soon as—well, as soon as is reasonable."

"Ah, sweet reason," he murmured.

She smiled, but she wished she were better at reading his thoughts.

Your shadow in deceiving moonlight
Your voice in the whisper of sand
I drink from the waterskin, not water, but your memory
And at night wine cannot dull the ache

She thought of the Egyptian poem John Mallow had rewritten for Eden. A work of heart rather than art, perhaps, but the sentiment was timeless and universal. Already she could feel the emptiness of separation.

"When you do get back," Peter said very casually, "you might consider moving in with me."

"I might?"

He lifted a shoulder. "If you like."

She teased, "This is so sudden, Mr. Fox. You must be confident I'm not coming back."

"Oh, you're coming back," he said. "Even if I have to fetch you."

Startled, Grace met his gaze. He was smiling a mocking smile, but his eyes held her own.

"Thou art my long lost peace," he quoted.

Unexpected tears filled her eyes, and she wiped at them hastily. He caught her hand and kissed her wet fingertips.

High overhead, the sparrow hawk had his answer.